A GRAVE GIFT

ELECTRA POOLE
MYSTERIES

CHRISTY CARLYLE

OLIVERHEBERBOOKS

Cover Design by Kim Killion

Published by Oliver-Heber Books

0 9 8 7 6 5 4 3 2 1

Chapter One

F og muffled sounds and storm clouds darkened the evening sky as Electra Poole stepped down from a hansom cab onto the quiet streets of Mayfair. A fierce breeze whipped at her cloak, and she pulled up her hood to keep out the cold. Stopping near one of the golden-haloed gas lamps that lit her path along the wet pavement, she consulted the letter which had summoned her to this fashionable part of town.

As she confirmed the address, she impulsively removed one black glove. Wearing gloves, even when indoors, had become a habit, as they tended to dim her abilities. She folded her bare fingers over the fine vellum but sensed no feelings or sensations emanating from the letter. She had when it had been delivered to her friend's home—the address she listed on her business cards. It wasn't entirely surprising that nothing came through now. Her abilities worked best when touching a living person or an object they'd recently touched.

Whatever the rules of her odd talents, Electra was still discovering them herself. She'd suppressed her abilities almost as soon as they'd begun plaguing her as a child. When they'd broken through occasionally, she'd willed them away, not wanting to be labeled mad, as her mother had been.

Only in the past few months had Electra willingly opened herself to exploring her strange gifts, and they sometimes failed her entirely. As a novice, she was not fully in control of her powers. Sometimes she doubted she ever would be.

Images came to her unbidden when she touched someone. At other times, without touch or even effort, the feelings of others pulsed toward her, often in shimmering colors her eyes and no one else's could perceive. When a person's thoughts played in her mind, they were sometimes as sharp as her own. Other times, they were shadowy and faded quickly. And just as often, she failed to feel or see anything at all. Some individuals seemed inaccessible. She wasn't certain if her abilities failed her at those times, or whether some were simply resistant to *second sight*, as her mother had called it.

One thing she knew for certain: when she'd first touched Lady Becknell's letter, she'd felt fear. Now, nearly at the noblewoman's door, Electra felt an odd sense of portent, as if fate were playing a hand in this encounter. She felt an urgency to meet this troubled lady and help if she could. Though when she'd first received her letter, Electra had almost refused the request.

A summons from a noblewoman was not entirely out of the ordinary. The more seances she conducted, the more her name was passed from drawing rooms to tea houses to salons. Yet Lady Becknell invited her to conduct a *private* consultation, and that had given Electra pause. In the last few months, she'd only conducted small, intimate group sittings, often in the homes of wealthy ladies like Lady Becknell.

It had been her dearest friend from finishing school, Lady Cordelia Redmayne, who'd encouraged her to offer sessions for paying guests. Cordelia knew of Electra's meager finances and how deeply she longed for independence. She also understood Electra's interest in exploring her abilities, claiming them, as her mother had been unable to do. Now, her psychical sessions were her main means of paying rent at the boarding house she'd recently moved into.

Yet she wasn't at ease calling herself a true medium. She didn't attempt to see ghosts or speak to the dead, at least not directly. At times, she sensed answers she sought during seances and wondered if her rare visions of future events were passed to her from those beyond the veil, but she didn't hear voices as some mediums claimed to do. No spirit spoke through her, nor rapped on tables, during her sittings.

But Electra was learning how to read the crescendo of emotions from others in a room. The gathering of several people, intent on seeking answers, seemed to spark her psychic energy. But would it be so in a private meeting?

In the end, the fear she'd sensed from Lady Becknell's letter had been too intriguing to ignore. Now, she stood before the impressive Becknell townhouse situated between a line of others in Hanover Square. The house stood tall and grand, its windows dark but for one on the upper floor and one on the lower, both of which glowed orange in the fog-thickened dark. She tucked the letter into her coat pocket, then paused before the front door.

She lifted a hand and knocked.

Moments later, a brunette young maid in a crisp black and white uniform opened the door. She held her shoulders straight, but her brown eyes looked tired. Electra sensed an echo of what she'd felt from the letter—fear and sadness. And perhaps something more.

"You must be Miss Poole." The young woman kept her voice low, almost conspiratorial.

"I am she," Electra replied.

"Please come in, miss. Lady Becknell is expecting you." The girl glanced nervously over her shoulder and then gestured for Electra to follow her inside.

The entryway was dark and narrow, the walls lined with deep purple wallpaper that echoed the colors in Electra's violet-hued gown. The shadows seemed to swallow the light from a single ornate gaslight atop the staircase's bottom newel post. Though the marble floors, potted palms, and gilt-framed art inside Becknell House were as elegant as the white-washed columns on its exterior, the air in the house felt dense, as if its inhabitants were filled with worries.

"This way," the young servant urged. She maintained a quiet tone, as if she didn't wish to disturb anyone. Though from the utter, stifling silence of the place, Electra would have guessed no one else was at home.

After depositing her in a teal-papered drawing room, the young woman hesitated. "She's upstairs, but you'll not be disturbed. I'll tell her ladyship you've arrived."

"Thank you."

Only a few ticks of the clock later, a lady stepped into the room. She was younger than Electra expected, perhaps a decade older than her own twenty-six years. Her auburn hair had been styled in a loose chignon and dark rings shadowed the skin below her pale blue eyes. Though her lips curved slightly, her mouth seemed tight, the smile forced. She wore a dress of mauve silk that might have been elegant if not for how loosely it hung on her frame.

"How do you do, Miss Poole. I am Helen Becknell. Thank you for responding to my letter." She glanced at the threshold Electra had just walked through. "I was so grateful when Grace suggested I speak with you."

"Grace?"

"Grace Dobbs. Our maid. She would have admitted you. Are you not acquainted?"

"I don't believe so, my lady." Electra was certain she'd never met the girl in her life.

"Well, perhaps it was a long while ago. No matter. I am grateful you're here now."

"I'm eager to help however I am able." Electra noted how the noblewoman twisted something nervously in her hands.

Lady Becknell gestured toward a polished mahogany table arranged between damask armchairs.

"Shall we begin?" There was a nervous eagerness in the lady's voice.

Her letter had given little away, and Electra had arrived filled with questions, but it seemed those would need to be asked during their sitting.

"I'll only need a moment to prepare."

Her ladyship watched as Electra opened the satchel she'd brought and laid out a black velvet cloth upon the tabletop. She'd found it kept her from reading anything from the table itself, which many may have touched. Then she extracted a teacup saucer, placing a single white candle atop it. Somehow, the light helped her focus her mind. She did so now as she lit the candle and then she pulled a polished, palm-sized moonstone from her pocket.

It had been her mother's. Electra didn't know if it had any effect on her psychic abilities, but it had become a protective talisman of sorts. Much like her mother's cross that she wore on a chain around her neck. She never sought answers without both. During formal readings, she kept the stone in her hand or somewhere on her person. Sometimes, she feared it was nothing more than a pretty bauble—but she clung to it anyway.

Once everything was in place, she nodded at Lady Becknell, who took the chair on the right. Electra sat in the one on the left.

The noblewoman immediately laid the object she held on to the tabletop. "I thought this might help you."

The gold locket was burnished at its center, and Electra immediately suspected the shine was from the someone's fingers persistently rubbing at the metal, as if it was their own sort of talisman.

After removing both black gloves, Electra took up the locket carefully, as if the object on a delicate gold chain was as precious to her as it seemed to be to Lady Becknell.

"May I?" she asked, her fingernail at the locket's edge, ready to spring it open.

"Yes, of course."

Inside, Electra found a snippet of hair curled inside to fill the locket's interior. The strands were thin and delicate and the same striking shade of auburn as Lady Becknell's hair.

"My...brother. Can you contact him?"

Snapping the locket shut, Electra closed her fingers around it, silently seeking whatever it might tell her of Lady Becknell's relation.

I loved him then. I love him now. The thought came from Lady Becknell. She directed it at the locket clutched in Electra's hand.

"He knows you loved him," Electra told her gently, her voice catching, turning rough. She understood that kind of love—aching and unfinished. She felt Lady Becknell's yearnings, not just in her mind but in her own chest.

"You may be at ease on that score," she told the noble-woman, wanting to give reassurance, to lift her burdens a bit. It was the one of the reasons Electra had decided to use the abilities she'd denied for so long—the possibility of giving people answers. Those who attended her gatherings were always searching, either out of a sense of love, or guilt, or grief.

"You've contacted him?" Lady Becknell's blue eyes widened. "On the...other side? Are you certain?"

"I sense your love for him," Electra offered noncommittally.

"I need to know if he comes through. There's doubt in my heart. I don't wish to be duped."

Electra nodded. No one wished to be duped, and she strove to never feign any facts during her seances. She told participants only what she felt, saw, and sensed as she touched each of them, or objects they offered up to her as Lady Becknell had. Though sometimes when she sought answers for those in a gathering, her abilities failed her. Or the visions that did fill her mind were not helpful at all.

"He has not come through."

Lady Becknell settled against the back of her chair. "I see."

She was distant from this person in her mind, uncertain of the life he'd led or even where he might be. To Electra's surprise, she couldn't even fix on an image of the boy as she attempted to sift Lady Becknell's thoughts. Presumably, he had auburn hair if the treasure in the locket was cut from his head.

"You are not close anymore." Electra felt the lady's worry and curiosity. "Do you doubt that he's passed on?"

"I doubt everything these days, Miss Poole. And everyone. But I only want the truth now. Though I may not deserve it."

Guilt hung over the lady at that moment, almost like a fog obscuring Electra's view of her. But whatever the cause of her guilt, the lady kept those details hidden away. No matter how Electra focused her efforts, she felt resistance now when she attempted to read Lady Becknell. As if someone held a door shut to keep her out.

The noblewoman blinked and notched up her chin. "Let us go on, Miss Poole."

"Very well." Electra laid the locket on the table and reached out her hand, palm up. "May I take your hand?"

"What will you know if I do?"

The question told Electra, without the aid of any other-worldly gifts, that the lady kept many secrets she did not wish to have exposed.

"I can sometimes sense a person's thoughts and feelings. Memories occasionally. Other times, I get glimpses of events yet to come. Though I promise no certainty in my prognostications. The future is not set. We make choices each day which can alter our paths."

The viscountess gave a tight smile. "I should like to believe that." After another moment's hesitation, Lady Becknell reached out and laid her palm atop Electra's.

Like a curtain pulled across her vision, Electra saw as if through Lady Becknell's eyes. A garden, rain dappling the grass and overgrown flowers. As the images shifted, she saw a small wooden cross and an etched stone set at the edge of a rounded heap of newly dug earth. The resting place of a child, she knew. Lady Becknell held these memories in her mind, Electra sensed, and they were from a time long past.

Then the noble lady's feelings rushed in—a storm of grief, fear, anxiety. *Is he lying to me? Is she? I need to know the truth. Why would they lie to me?* Those thoughts rang in Electra's head as if Lady Becknell were repeating them over and over.

"I sense a great deal of anxiety, my lady."

"Can you find the truth I seek or not?" Lady Becknell shivered and Electra felt the ripple of it where their hands touched. "My mother? Perhaps you could reach her. She might speak to you from...beyond. She would know the truth, I think."

Her mother had died. Electra saw a memory Lady Becknell held in her mind's eye. A middle-aged woman, her face creased in pain, eyes fluttering until they stilled forever.

Then the noblewoman's thoughts turned immediately back to the question of trust. She feared someone was deceiving her.

A man's face appeared. Dark hair, dark eyes, a charming smile. She felt as much heartache as anger toward the man.

Electra willed some vision of future events to fill her mind, but nothing did. Even her reading of Lady Becknell's thoughts began to fade.

"I do not speak directly to the dead," Electra admitted. "But I sense your fear of duplicity on a gentleman's part."

"Yes." Lady Becknell reached out and grasped Electra's arm just above the wrist. "Can you divine the answer? The truth. I'm desperate to know."

Electra closed her eyes and steadied her breathing, attempting to open herself to the answer the noblewoman sought.

She willed her mind to once again evoke whatever gentleman the lady feared, and to her shock, images of multiple men flashed in Electra's mind. A blond-haired man, then another. The dark-haired man filled her vision again. Then an auburn-haired child in a tiny miniature painting—the child whose hair lay in the locket. The images came like a flood. Little snippets of memories. Some romantic. Others fraught with anger and accusations. Yet others fogged over with regret.

Overwhelmed, Electra gripped her moonstone with her free hand as if it might anchor her back to the here and now. She forced her eyes open, then released the breath that had gotten pent up in her throat.

Lady Becknell stared at her, mouth agape, eyes expectant and unblinking. "You saw something," she whispered.

"I did," Electra admitted, "but I'm afraid the visions came in a rush."

It was an experience unlike any she'd had before, and it chipped at her usual composure. There'd been no chance to hold one image in her mind, to truly study it. She'd had no control to sift and select that which she needed to know.

Would she never learn to control her abilities?

"What did they reveal?"

Electra hesitated to answer. The images indicated that there were many gentlemen in Lady Becknell's life. She'd mentioned a brother. One had been her husband, Electra sensed, but she couldn't divine which one. Others she loved, though in varying degrees—affection, passion, adoration.

"Is it your brother you fear deception from? Your husband? Or another man?" Electra pressed, needing some clarity.

Lady Becknell frowned, her pale eyes shuttering. "Shouldn't you be offering me revelations rather than quizzing me, Miss Poole?"

For a few ticks of the longcase clock, they merely observed each other.

"I didn't find an answer to your query, my lady. I cannot discern if you are being deceived." Electra hated disappointing anyone. And she felt empathy for this noblewoman, whose desperation and fear were as palpable as when she'd first touched her letter.

Lady Becknell's shoulders dropped, then her chin, until it was almost pressed to her chest.

Never in her life had she seen a woman who appeared so defeated.

Not since the last time she'd seen her own mother.

"I could try again," Electra said quietly.

Lady Becknell lifted her haunted gaze, and her delicate features softened into a smile. "Would you? Please do."

"Certainly." Electra reached out her other hand. "May I have both your hands?"

With a squaring of her shoulders and a glimmer of hope in her eyes, Lady Becknell laid the palm of her free hand on Electra's. Her wedding ring's clustered diamonds glinted in the candlelight.

Electra closed her eyes and waited for that familiar shift in her body, a subtle jolt that served as the harbinger of a future vision. That's what she needed. Reading Lady Becknell's thoughts and feelings would not give her the answers her lady-ship sought. Though she suspected if she could touch the man in question, she might know in short order whether he was a deceiver or truthful.

As the frisson of a deeper awareness made her spine stiffen, a knock came at the townhouse's front door. Lady Becknell immediately withdrew her hands.

"Oh, heavens." She grimaced as another insistent knock echoed through the townhouse. "No one is expected. I wished to be sure we'd have privacy." The noblewoman stood. "Even the staff is off for their half day."

"But not Grace." Out in the hallway, Electra heard the young maid's voice directing the visitor.

"Yes." She smiled and it seemed genuine. "Thank goodness for Grace. If you'll excuse me a moment, Miss Poole." Lady Becknell stood and quickly slipped from the room.

Electra settled back in her chair, her heart racing, though she'd seen nothing of Lady Becknell's future yet. Still, she'd sensed images forming, as if a revelation, a knowing, hovered just out of reach.

"Miss Poole." Grace appeared on the drawing room thresh-old. "Lady Becknell says she must have you return on another day. She asked me to see you off."

"Then I'll just collect my things." Electra held her hand cupped around the candle's flame and blew it out, though during group sittings, it was usually done with much more cere-mony, serving as a closing of the circle. Once the light was doused, she pulled herself fully back to the present and donned her gloves.

Often, she felt drained and craved quiet in the moments after a sitting.

Now, a strange restlessness made her movements clumsy. She nearly dropped her moonstone before resettling it in her pocket. Though she usually folded her black velvet cloth carefully, she merely folded it in half. A sudden urgency to depart had come over her that had nothing to do with Grace's presence.

After she'd secured her bag, Grace led her out into the hall, then toward the townhouse's entry hall. As they proceeded, Electra heard voices from a room on the right side of the hallway. Its door stood slightly ajar. She spied bookshelves and assumed it was the Becknells' library or perhaps his lordship's study.

As they passed, Electra glanced inside and saw Lady Becknell with a man. He snapped his gaze toward Electra.

His blond hair and square jaw were familiar because she'd just seen an image of him in Lady Becknell's thoughts. To her surprise, Lady Becknell stepped out of the room and drew Electra aside.

"Forgive me for ending our visit so abruptly, Miss Poole." She reached for one of Electra's black-gloved hands and held it between hers. "Promise you'll come back."

With her gloves on, Electra's ability to sense anything from the noble lady was muted. They protected her from being caught unawares by others' thoughts and feelings, but Lady Becknell's emotions rang in her tone—urgency, almost desperation.

"Of course I will, if you wish it." Though even as she agreed, Electra yearned to withdraw her hand.

Lady Becknell's eyes locked on hers. "I think you could be of great help to me." Then she threw her arms around Electra and drew her into an embrace. She held her for several moments, the coolness of her cheek brushing Electra's, as if she didn't wish to let go.

Electra's body stiffened as a familiar ripple rushed through her. Images and sounds whispered through her mind—Lady Becknell reaching out as her body shuddered, arms stiff and windmilling in front of her as she fell backwards. In the next flash, Electra saw the lady lying motionless, her eyes glassy and unseeing, her face distorted in a frightful grimace.

"I'll send a note to arrange our next meeting," Lady Becknell said as she released Electra. Then she turned, strode back into the room where the gentleman stood waiting, and closed the door behind her.

Electra reached for the door handle.

"No, Miss Poole," Grace called to her. "Her ladyship and her visitor won't wish to be disturbed."

"I must speak with her again. How long will they be?"

The maid gave her an odd look. "I can't say, miss, but you shouldn't wait." The young woman glanced toward the closed door. "No doubt, they'll want privacy."

The maid thought Lady Becknell and the gentleman were lovers. The thought was clear and vivid in the front of the young woman's mind.

Without waiting for Grace to lead her, Electra strode toward the Becknells' front door and rushed out to the pavement, striding quickly until she reached the square beyond. She stripped off one glove and laid her palm against the thick trunk of an oak tree, needing its solid, grounding energy to steady her. Pressing a hand to her middle, she struggled to catch her breath against the tight hold of her corset.

The vision had shaken her.

She'd never seen such a thing—a premonition of death for a lady who stood alive before her. The images had arisen when

Lady Becknell embraced her. Electra wondered if perhaps she wasn't seeing the lady's fate but her deepest fear.

Still, she shouldn't have rushed out. She had to tell her.

Making her way back across the street, she rapped on the door, expecting Grace to answer again. But no one did. She tried knocking with her fist, harder than was polite. Still, no one came.

Rain had begun to fall, and after trying for several minutes, she turned away from Becknell House and made her way down to the busy cross street to hail a hansom cab.

Rushing through the drizzle, Electra tried to push down a sense of dread. For the first time since opening herself to the strange gifts she possessed, she prayed her vision was wrong.

Chapter Two

The Becknell townhouse, like so many in Mayfair, wore its wealth for all to see—brass polished to a gleam, windows spotless, white-washed columns uncracked. But Detective Inspector Gideon Pierce didn't see its appeal. He saw only a house whose secrets it was now his task to uncover.

He straightened the cuffs of his coat and checked the knot of his neckcloth—small rituals to compose his thoughts. Presentation mattered, especially for a man such as him. He'd learned long ago that polish was a kind of armor, especially when a man had no pedigree or easy charm to smooth the way. After years of hard work and diligently pursuing promotion in the Metropolitan Police, he'd gained respect and learned control.

Control above all—over his demeanor, his appearance, his impulses.

An investigation required control, a focusing of his mind and senses.

In the Becknell case, the summons for a constable had come just before dawn. Gideon was sent for not long after. Now, as he stood outside the illustrious family's residence, he prepared for the day ahead, the onslaught of details to be pieced together, the lies to be uncovered.

As often happened at the outset of an investigation, Gideon thought of his mentor, Erasmus Poole. The man had found him, a mud-caked boy on the banks of the Thames, and given him something more than a warm meal and a roof over his head—he'd offered him a purpose.

Now, Poole's legacy was both a burden and a shield. A precedent to be lived up to, but also a bulwark of skills. The man had taught Gideon all he knew about the art of investigation.

Gideon gave Becknell House's brass knocker a sharp rap and waited.

The door opened to reveal a middle-aged woman with red-rimmed eyes and a grip on composure that looked close to breaking.

"Detective Inspector Pierce," he said, his voice even, manner polite but not warm. He rarely offered warmth. It made people too emotional in such situations and that tended to blur facts.

"Come in, Inspector. The coroner, Dr. Tate, is waiting for you."

"Tate himself?" Usually, a coroner's assistant would come. A jury's inquest, led by a coroner, was required in any suspicious or violent death. But it highlighted the importance of this case—or perhaps the influence of the Becknell family—that Dr. Alfred Tate had come himself. Even more extraordinary was that Tate would wait for Gideon's arrival to deliver his findings. Usually, the man sent his findings via a written report. Tate's decision to linger was either another indicator of the family's importance, or perhaps the coroner had something interesting to tell Gideon about what he'd found.

Gideon stepped inside Becknell House and immediately

noted the shrouded figure at the foot of the main stairs. The servant kept her gaze averted.

"Are you the housekeeper?"

"Yes, sir. Cora Evans."

"Mrs. Evans, I'd ask that you admit no visitors until Dr. Tate and I have finished."

"Of course, Inspector."

Rumors would be hard to contain with a Mayfair murder. By the afternoon, the Hanover Square townhouse's activities would no doubt be fodder for neighborly whispers and gossip column ink. A suspicious death brought the sort of scrutiny, and infamy, the upper classes feared more than poverty.

Gideon hoped to hold off journalists for a few more hours while he examined the scene and questioned the household's staff, but the case would draw reporters soon enough.

Constable Clegg, who served as foot patrol in the district, arrived in the wee hours of the morning, summoned by a maid named Grace Dobbs. She'd been beside herself, according to the report Gideon had read. It was clear from Clegg's notes that murder wasn't immediately suspected. When Lady Becknell was found at the bottom of the stairs, the maid insisted that she must have fallen.

Gideon had been dispatched with an admonition from his chief that discretion in this matter was of the utmost importance. The chief was acquainted with Lord Philip Becknell. So many in London society were. He was known as a gracious host, progressive in his views in the House of Lords, and had trained as a barrister before inheriting his title. Thus, the man was known by everyone from lawbreakers to law keepers to lawmakers.

Gideon had never met Becknell but knew of his reputation.

"The doctor is in the drawing room, second door on the left,

17

or perhaps you wish to examine..." Mrs. Evans pressed her lips together.

"Thank you. I'll speak to you and the rest of the staff before I depart."

"Of course, sir."

He approached the spot where Lady Becknell lay beneath a white sheet. The positioning seemed too neat, as if she'd been moved since tumbling down a dozen steps. He knelt, then carefully lifted the sheet. The housekeeper let out a soft gasp behind him.

"You needn't remain if it troubles you," he said quietly, gaze never leaving the body. His voice, though low, carried the quiet authority of someone used to being obeyed. The housekeeper scurried off.

Gideon had encountered death many times, but Lady Helen Becknell's expression was one he'd never seen. Jaws clenched around a grimace and her fists balled tight. She wore a low-necked night rail that revealed her neck and throat. Bruises and abrasions marred her skin. The muscles of her neck seemed taut, as if she'd been straining at the moment of her death, but the most significant wound was a gash at her temple. He couldn't imagine the neck wounds were caused by a fall. Especially since he'd seen similar marks on the throats of those who'd been throttled.

"Inspector Pierce." The bearded, gray-haired coroner approached from behind, and Gideon lowered the sheet and rose to face him.

"Dr. Tate."

Tate dipped his head and looked at Gideon above the rim of his spectacles. "It's a strange business, Inspector."

"Tell me more."

"The maid who sent for the constable was certain her mistress had fallen down the stairs." Tate cast an assessing glance up the length of the steps. "Apparently, Lady Becknell takes a tonic to aid her sleep, which makes her unsteady on her feet if she leaves her bed."

There was a skeptical note to Tate's voice that Gideon recognized from working with the man for years.

"But you've found something else," Gideon concluded.

"Quite a lot." Tate stepped close to the foot of the stairs and cast a look around as if to ascertain whether any servants were within hearing of their conversation.

He squatted down on his haunches, and Gideon did the same on the opposite side of where Lady Becknell lay.

The doctor pulled back the sheet to expose the lady's upper body, arms, and hands.

"What's caused this clenching of her jaws and fists?" Gideon asked Tate.

"I shan't speculate until we see results of the postmortem, but I did wish you to see these." With his little finger, the doctor gestured toward the abrasions Gideon had noted—a ring of marks around the ladies' throat and along her neck. Some were oblong—very like the shape of someone's fingers.

"Strangulation?"

Tate nodded. "Though some of these scratches and bruises seem older. Some show signs of healing and the yellow color there indicates that bruise is older."

"Then strangulation did not cause her death?"

"No, though the lady did sustain a significant blow to her head, presumably when she fell." He pointed out the wound Gideon had spotted on the noblewoman's temple. "But there's so little blood."

"What does that indicate?" Gideon asked.

Tate lifted his gaze and stared at a spot on the far wall. "Two hypotheses come to mind. Either the lady was injured and bled elsewhere, or she was near death when she fell."

"So throttled at some point, perhaps to the point of death, and then she fell?"

Tate arched a thick white brow. "Or was pushed."

"Can you determine the time of death?"

"My conclusion is an approximation."

"Of course." Gideon understood why Tate offered such warnings. Still, an estimation narrowed the window of opportunity, and that was vital information as he began investigating.

"Based on rigor and temperature, I would estimate no earlier than ten last evening and no later than two this morning."

"You said there was quite a lot found."

Dr. Tate pointed to Lady Becknell's left hand.

Gideon spotted blood under a few of her fingernails. "Her attacker's blood?" Gideon posited. "So she fought back."

"Very possibly."

"And might have left scratches." Gideon hoped she had. It would certainly aid him in identifying potential suspects.

"It is a reasonable supposition."

"Is there more?"

Tate worked his jaw. "A few other *confounding* pieces." The elderly doctor lifted a brow. "Accompany me to her ladyship's bedchamber." Tate resettled the sheet, then led Gideon up the staircase.

Along the way, he noted that one of the spindles was damaged, bowed out a bit, but he detected no blood on the polished wood. He mulled whether it could have caused the gash on her ladyship's head. Perhaps Tate would find other injuries during the postmortem.

"I only searched for the sleeping tonic and left the rest just how it was arranged for you to see."

Gideon scanned his gaze around the dimly lit room, spotting a piece of paper on a gilded writing desk next to a typewriter. It was a rather newfangled thing and he'd only ever seen another in a London doctor's office. It shocked him to see one atop a dainty desk in an otherwise lavishly decorated noblewoman's bedchamber.

He approached to read the typed words on the sheet of paper.

My darling Edward,

It's all too much. Too many lies. Too many regrets. I cannot bear another. But I need you to know that I have

Gideon frowned. "Seems she was interrupted."

"It does appear that way."

"Or became so drowsy, she left her letter unfinished and tumbled down the stairs." It sounded ludicrous to Gideon even as he voiced the thought. The letter appeared to have been written by someone overwrought. There was a confessional urgency to the words.

"Mmm. Though her sleeping tonic was tucked away in the drawer of her bedside table." Tate pointed to an open drawer. "The bottle is roughly half full."

"Is there any evidence the lady consumed the tonic last evening?"

"No." Tate shot him a dubious look. "I'll make a note for the police surgeon to seek such signs during his examination, but it may be difficult to know with certainty."

As coroner, Tate would oversee the inquest to determine the cause and manner of death, but his medical knowledge was key in moments like these. He noticed things a coroner without medical training might not.

Tate gestured toward the bottle and note. "Odd, it is not?"

Gideon couldn't disagree.

"When can the surgeon have the results of the postmortem to me?"

"Tomorrow, possibly, depending on when the body can be

transferred to the mortuary." The police surgeon, Farringdon, would be expected to move quickly in such a case.

"I say let us do so immediately," Gideon told him.

Tate nodded, then started toward the door. "I can send to Vine Street for a couple of constables to conduct the removal of the body. I'll remain here until they arrive."

"Would you ask them to collect the sleeping tonic and that typed page? I'll head down to begin questioning the servants."

"Certainly, Inspector."

"Thank you." Gideon was eager for the police surgeon's findings and even more so to divine what he could from the Becknells' staff before their master's arrival.

Lord Becknell was due back from a hunting party in Oxfordshire on Tuesday, but a telegram had been sent requesting that he return early. Gideon couldn't be certain when the man would arrive.

After parting from Tate, he found the servants gathered together in the townhouse's kitchen. The low chatter among them dimmed to silence when Gideon descended the stairs.

A slim, brown-haired young woman seemed to be the most affected by the shocking events in the household. She sat at a long table with tears streaming down her cheeks, and Mrs. Evans sat beside her, a hand on her shoulder.

Clearing his throat to get their attention, Gideon met each wary gaze with his usual cool one. "I'd like to speak to each of you in turn. Mrs. Evans, can you suggest a room where I may question the staff?"

"You're welcome to use my office or Mr. Paxton's."

At his name, a tall, balding man with white whiskers stood to attention. "I am the butler at Becknell House, Inspector, and you're welcome to whichever office you please." His brow furrowed—in worry or perhaps grief—and he glanced at the younger staff members. "We all wish to assist in whatever manner we're able."

"I'd like to start with Miss Grace Dobbs." Gideon was not at all surprised when the brown-haired young lady startled and then slowly stood.

"Would you lead the way to Mrs. Evans's office?" he said to her in as amiable a tone as he could manage when on the hunt for a killer.

"Must I go on my own?" The young lady cast a frightened look in Mrs. Evans's direction.

"May I accompany her, Inspector?"

Gideon understood the maid was young, scared, and most likely haunted by what she'd found. Though he much preferred a private conversation in which she'd feel at ease to speak freely, he was not an utter ogre.

He nodded at the older woman, who led the younger toward a narrow, tidy office at one end of the kitchen.

When both ladies were seated—Mrs. Evans in a chair against the wall and Grace Dobbs in front of a desk that took up much of the room—Gideon settled into the chair behind the desk and withdrew his notepad and pencil.

He sensed both ladies tracking his every movement, and he could hear the ragged, unsteady rush of the maid's breath, which seemed even louder than the steady ticking of a wall clock.

"Tell me about yesterday, Miss Dobbs. Start in the morning, please."

The girl drew in a shaky breath. "Much like any other to start, sir. Her ladyship took breakfast in her room. Said she wasn't feeling well."

Gideon lifted his head. "Was that not unusual?"

Grace shook her head. "No, sir. Her ladyship is often taken poorly."

The lack of concern in the maid's voice struck him as odd. A lady of Helen Becknell's wealth could see as many physicians as she pleased and need not suffer ongoing poor health, unless it was some lingering malady.

"Who usually attended her ladyship for her ailments?" he asked.

"Dr. Francis Henshaw," Mrs. Evans put in.

"What did her ladyship do in the afternoon?" Gideon prompted.

"She received or paid calls, sir, as she usually does."

"To whom?"

"I don't accompany her, sir." Grace turned a glance back towards Mrs. Evans. "But she visits Mrs. Ellsworth and Lady Ashcombe often, or one of them comes to call."

"But she left on calls, you said."

"Yes, sir."

"And when she returned from her visits?"

"Her ladyship asked me to stay longer than usual before departing for my half day. She promised me an extra half day the following weekend."

Gideon glanced up at Mrs. Evans.

"Lord and Lady Becknell allow staff a half day on Sundays," the housekeeper explained. "Off by noon. Curfew at midnight. A most generous concession from Lord and Lady Becknell."

"And who else was at Becknell House at that time?"

Grace Dobbs shook her head. "No one, sir. Lady Becknell said her sister had gone out and that she was to have a visitor that I must speak of to no one."

"Her sister lives with the Becknells?" Gideon did not recall mention of a sister in Clegg's report.

"Yes, sir. Miss Beatrice Linwood."

"But she was not at home?"

Grace hesitated. "So mistress told me."

"Has she returned?"

"She's upstairs and in quite a state, Inspector," Mrs. Evans told him.

"So all the staff were away last evening, Lord Becknell was in Oxfordshire, and you and Lady Becknell were at home alone. What time was this?"

The girl nodded. "Around six in the evening."

"And what visitor did Lady Becknell expect?"

Grace cast another glance at Mrs. Evans, then lifted frightened eyes to Gideon. "A fortune teller, sir. A psychic, or so her ladyship said. That's why no one could know. She said it was a delicate matter."

Mrs. Evans emitted a tsking sound. Grace lowered her head again.

Gideon's pencil stilled. "A fortune teller?"

"Did she leave a calling card, Grace?" Mrs. Evans asked the maid. "If so, you must give it to the inspector."

"I can fetch it, sir."

"Please do."

Once the maid departed, Mrs. Evans cast her gaze around the room, seemingly unable to meet Gideon's scrutiny.

"When did you return to Becknell House, Mrs. Evans?"

"Shortly after eleven in the evening, sir."

"And you heard nothing that night or in the early morning hours?"

"No, sir."

"Did you know this psychic lady visitor was expected last evening, Mrs. Evans?"

"I did not, Inspector. It dismays me to hear of it."

"Does it seem out of character for Lady Becknell to consult with such a person?"

Gideon expected a defense of her employer, but the housekeeper admitted, "In truth, no, sir."

Before she could say more, Miss Dobbs returned. She looked once at Mrs. Evans and then held out a plain ivory card to Gideon.

The name on the card stopped him cold. Time stalled. His muscles tensed. His breath tangled in his throat.

Electra Poole.

He hadn't seen her in three years. After the death of her father, she'd left everyone and everything she knew behind. There'd been no letters, no attempt to contact him at all. From the moment her father had taken him in and she'd become a part of Gideon's life, she'd been a maddening puzzle. And when she'd cut all connection between them, Gideon had tried, and failed, not to care.

Most days, he managed to put her from his mind entirely. Now, it seemed she was wrapped up in a noblewoman's murder. And she was a...fortune teller.

Gideon forced himself to unclench his jaw.

"What time did you admit Miss Poole?" His voice had sharpened with irritation.

"Shortly after six," Grace told him.

"And when did she depart?" Focusing on his notebook, he poised his pencil over the page.

"Not long after, sir."

"Estimate when, please."

"Around half past. Perhaps twenty minutes after her arrival."

Gideon studied the girl. "A very short visit then."

"Yes, sir." The maid bit her lip and looked again at the housekeeper. "Another visitor came."

Mrs. Evans titled her head as if surprised. Though Grace had provided the same information to Constable Clegg, perhaps out of Mrs. Evans's hearing. Still, Gideon wanted to hear it from the maid's own mouth and watch as she recounted the night's events.

"The name of that other visitor?"

"Lord Martin Ballinger, sir."

Gideon knew of Ballinger in relation to a public health bill he'd supported.

Mrs. Evans stiffened. Grace stared at him as if dreading his next question.

"Is he a frequent visitor?"

"Yes, sir."

"So he was expected?"

"No, sir. At least not that I know of. Lady Becknell spoke of only one visitor last evening and that was Miss Poole."

"Do you know anything of the meeting between your mistress and Lord Ballinger?"

Gideon could see that she did, though she'd given no such information to Constable Clegg. Perhaps the young constable hadn't asked.

"They had a disagreement of some sort." Grace pressed her lips together as if she longed to say more but wouldn't. Or couldn't.

"Did you overhear the disagreement?"

"No, sir." Her eyes widened.

Gideon would have bet a crown that she had. The young woman's expression was too open for her to be any good at prevarication.

"Then how could you know of a disagreement?"

"I heard raised voices." Grace looked down at her hands, which she clasped tightly in her lap. "I left soon after his arrival," she offered without Gideon asking.

"What did you say to Lady Becknell before you departed?"

"Oh, I..." The young woman drew in a breath. "I knocked at the library door and let her know I would be on my way."

"How did Lady Becknell appear?"

Grace Dobbs's forehead pleated. "Pardon?"

"Describe her appearance, please."

For a long moment, Miss Dobbs simply stared at him. Gideon resisted the urge to interrupt the silence or even blink.

"She held a hand to her neck and she looked..." The young maid shook her head.

"Go on, Miss Dobbs."

"Her hair was falling from its pins."

Mrs. Evans shifted in her chair and drew in a sharp breath.

"I asked if all was well," Miss Dobbs said as if confessing. Tears began to well in her eyes. "She told me to go. Assured me all was well." A tear fell, and she swiped it away. "Shouldn't have left her, should I?"

"She told you to." Mrs. Evans reached out a hand and patted the young maid's back.

"When did you return?" Gideon asked when Miss Dobbs had composed herself.

"A bit before midnight, sir."

"Did you see or notice anything amiss when you returned?"

"Not at all. Came through the back garden door and went straight up to my bed, sir."

"And when did you discover your mistress?"

"Not until near seven this morning, sir. I have duties in the kitchen, so I didn't go up to the family rooms until close to seven. I didn't find Lady Becknell in her chamber, so I came down the main stairs." The young woman had balled her hands into fists, and she lifted one to press against her mouth as if to hold in emotion.

"Had her ladyship's sister returned?"

"No, sir. I called for her, but Mr. Paxton heard me first. Then Mrs. Evans and the other staff came soon after."

Gideon closed his notebook and focused on the housekeeper. "Mrs. Evans, could you provide me with a list of all the staff members? I'm keen to speak to the chambermaid or whoever saw to Lady Becknell's bedchamber."

"I did, sir," Grace told him. "I'm the chambermaid as such."

"Tell me about the typewriter in her ladyship's bedchamber."

She looked surprised by the question. "Lady Becknell thought them clever and his lordship gifted it on her last birthday."

"Do you know how frequently she used it?"

Grace shrugged, and Gideon looked at the housekeeper.

"Quite frequently, Inspector," Mrs. Evans said. "She typed correspondence and even the day's menus."

"And what of her sleeping tonic?"

"She used it occasionally." Mrs. Evans's tone had grown tight, her shoulders stiff.

"Did she use it last night, Miss Dobbs?"

The maid shrugged. "I've no notion. I'd gone by then, sir."

A knock on Mrs. Evans's office door stopped the questioning, and they all turned as Mr. Paxton poked his head inside.

"Inspector, Dr. Tate asked me to inform you that he and the constables are conducting the removal." The butler cleared his throat and offered a buff-colored square of paper. "Also, a messenger delivered a telegram from his lordship. He plans to arrive by early evening."

"Thank you, Mr. Paxton."

Gideon never relished informing anyone of a family member's death. Lord Becknell would have questions, and as yet he had no answers.

But he had a starting place. After the rest of the staff, he needed to speak to Lord Ballinger, who'd apparently been the last person to see Lady Becknell alive. And he'd rowed with her. Lady Ashcombe and Mrs. Ellsworth might have more information about Helen Becknell too. Though he felt certain the staff themselves knew more. The question was whether they'd reveal the family's secrets.

Most disturbingly of all, he needed to seek out Electra Poole, the young woman who'd been many things to him—the daughter of his mentor, the most loyal childhood friend he'd ever known, and an exasperating enigma who he could never quite understand.

Chapter Three

Electra slept fitfully, her dreams full of shadows. When she woke late in the morning, her limbs felt heavy, as if the gravity of the vision she'd seen at Becknell House weighed her down.

The images haunted her, and as she sat up in bed, her mother's voice echoed in her mind.

Some things the mind cannot unsee.

She'd said it shortly before they had taken her away. Electra's father had grown weary of "the fancies" in her mother's head and insisted she forget them. How many times had he demanded she simply put them out of her mind? But her mother never could, and she couldn't pretend that she had. The doctors promised they could make her well, but they'd done the opposite.

And her mother had been right. Even if a vision was conjured solely in Electra's mind, she *had* seen it and could not easily push it away.

She rose and dressed quickly, all the while wondering if the hastily scribbled note she'd sent off with a messenger last evening had reached Lady Becknell. She'd stayed awake, pacing her threadbare rug like her mother used to do—like a madwoman, her father would have said.

All her life, she'd feared that her mother's madness had passed down to her too. But was it madness? Or was it a gift, as her mother's family back in Ireland called it?

Near midnight, she'd gone out into the streets, searching for the messenger boy who'd taken her note, praying he could tell her if he'd put it into the hands of someone in the Becknell household. But she'd never found the boy.

Now, going back to Mayfair uninvited was her only option.

Etiquette was well and good, but she'd risk being rude in order to ensure Lady Becknell knew what she'd seen.

The vision disturbed her as none ever had. She'd never foreseen the death of anyone. Indeed, less than half a dozen premonitions of future events had ever come to her at all. Because they were so rare, she felt deep hesitation about revealing the details. Especially since some visions never came to pass. She often did not trust what she saw.

Still, if she failed to warn someone, she would be partly responsible if the worst came to pass.

She put on the same black wool skirt she'd worn the night before and felt a lump against her thigh as she settled the fabric. Slipping her hand inside the skirt's deep pocket, her fingers brushed metal. Her body jolted, and she felt that juddering pull toward her second sight. Her mind filled with images—Lady Becknell sliding the locket across the mahogany table, watching as Electra flipped it open to see the strands of hair inside. Lady Becknell pulling her in for an embrace and slipping the necklace into her pocket.

That's why she'd held her so awkwardly.

But why?

Electra lifted the locket out and rubbed her fingers over its burnished surface, but no other insights came. She quickly finished dressing, then fastened the buttons of her black gloves with trembling fingers. The ticking of her mantel clock seemed louder than usual, like a drumbeat urging her to move faster. At least returning the locket gave her a proper reason for going back to Mayfair.

A carriage rolled up outside her building, and Electra glanced through the slit in her curtains. Dread gathered in her chest when she recognized the crest on the side of the vehicle. Lady Cordelia Redmayne, like most ladies of polite society, never made calls in the early morning hours.

Electra rushed from her room, down the stairs, and out the front door, meeting Cordelia as she descended from her carriage.

She strode forward and pulled Electra into a quick embrace. "Thank heavens you're well, my dear." Cordelia pulled back but kept hold of Electra's gloved hand. "I've had the most terrible knot in the pit of my stomach since I read of Lady Becknell."

The dread in Electra's chest spread like an inky darkness through her veins. She clenched her teeth to steady herself, to contain the sensations so they didn't overwhelm her.

Only a few years older than Electra, Cordelia was clever and spirited and tended to see good in every situation. Not today. Electra had never seen her so serious and grim.

Cordelia drew a folded news sheet from her reticule.

Electra could read the headline as soon as she withdrew the paper.

SHOCKING DISCOVERY IN MAYFAIR

A sound like the clanging of a bell rang in Electra's ears, and she felt, for the first time in life, as if her knees might give out. She squeezed Cordelia's hand.

Then she was no longer standing in the street but somewhere darker—ten years old again, watching as men in white coats led her mother away. She had screamed that day, but she didn't scream now.

"When I saw this," Cordelia said breathlessly, "I feared something awful might have happened to you too."

"I sent her a note," Electra heard herself say. "I tried to warn her. I should have told her the moment I saw it."

"Good heavens, Electra." Cordelia leaned closer. "Did you foresee this?"

Her mouth had gone dry; her mind had stalled, shocked into blankness.

"Come with me," Cordelia said. She wrapped an arm around Electra's and guided her toward the waiting carriage.

Woodenly, Electra climbed inside and settled onto the velvet squabs. She sat up straight, unable to let herself rest against the cushions. The tension in her body had her balling her fists, clenching her teeth.

She'd reacted this way three years ago—when she'd received word of her father's death. Emotions had been at a higher pitch then, the feelings too overwhelming to sort out for months.

But it was a shade of what she felt now—a mix of guilt and fear and anger.

Though she did not hear Cordelia offer the coachman instructions, the horses started on their way. What seemed like a moment later, the vehicle slowed as they approached Cordelia's townhouse.

"Electra," Cordelia said softly as she reached across the carriage and gathered her gloved hands, chafing them as if to keep her warm. "You're frightening me, my friend. Please tell me what happened."

Her pleading tone broke through to Electra. Cordelia had always helped her, just as she was trying to do now.

"I went to her last night as arranged."

"And then?"

"Our session was interrupted by a visitor. She sent me away and said we'd meet again."

Cordelia tipped her head. "Who was the visitor?"

"I don't know. A gentleman of late middle age. Blond hair. Square jaw. I only got a glimpse." Electra lifted her eyes to Cordelia's. "She embraced me before I left. It stunned me. We'd only just met and she'd seemed more frustrated with my failure to help her than anything." Focusing her mind, Electra summoned the vision she'd seen last night. "But when she touched me, I saw her. Dead. I saw Lady Becknell lying dead."

Cordelia's eyes widened. "Lying where?"

"At the bottom of the house's staircase." Electra flicked her gaze to the newspaper lying on the seat next to Cordelia. "Is that how she was found?"

Cordelia inclined her head.

"Sometimes I see a future that never comes to pass," Electra said. "But I saw this one. And I did not stop it."

That was the curse of it—not knowing which threads to pull, which to let lie. For most of her life, to speak of what she saw was to risk people thinking her mad. Yet to stay silent was to risk guilt.

"Did you...see how she came to fall? Did someone push her?" Cordelia asked softly.

"No, I only saw her lying there. It was brief. A flash." Electra closed her eyes, locking her hands together in her lap. "When it happened, we were parting. Then she embraced me and went off to her visitor. But I sent a note via messenger as soon as I returned to Bloomsbury."

Electra met Cordelia's worried gaze. "I do not know if she received it. I was preparing to go to Becknell House when you arrived. And then I found this." She pulled the locket from her skirt pocket.

"Whose is it?"

"It's Lady Becknell's. She slipped it into my pocket, but I didn't find it until this morning. Should I not return it?"

Her friend's forehead pleated between her blonde brows the way it always did when she was mulling some difficulty. "Well, we cannot go there now."

Cordelia gestured to the newspaper beside her. "According to the article, the police have closed off the house while they investigate."

Electra snapped her eyes to her friend's. "So it wasn't an accident?"

"The papers don't say."

"I don't think it was an accident," Electra admitted.

Cordelia tapped her fingers against the seat beside her. "I could always ask Kit to see what he can discover."

Sir Christopher Redmayne, Cordelia's estranged husband and an MP, had championed a policing bill in the House of Commons and was acquainted with several high-ranking police officers. Before his death three years past, Electra's father, a detective chief inspector of the Metropolitan Police, had been one of those acquaintances.

"I invited Kit to the sitting this evening." Cordelia said, her voice gentle and uncertain as she smoothed the satin trim at her wrist. "That is assuming you do not wish to cancel."

For a long moment, Electra said nothing. Last night, she'd questioned the wisdom of continuing to use her strange gifts at all. Every time she did, she felt trepidation.

Her mother had been *gifted*. Her father had called it delusional. The doctors at the asylum called it madness.

"Perhaps I should stop altogether," she said quietly, "and never seek to see such things at all."

"Don't say that." Cordelia's leaned toward her across the expanse of the carriage. "I know you must feel guilt, but if this was not an accident, whoever did this to her is the only guilty party."

Electra met her eyes but said nothing. She would not refute her friend, but the guilt she felt was as undeniable as the vision she'd seen.

"Of course, this has unsettled you, and I know you feel fear whenever you use your gifts." Cordelia's expression softened. "But you're brave, and I know what you've done for others. And for me."

Electra's throat tightened, and she looked out of the narrow carriage window as they turned into the neat green square on the approach to Cordelia's townhouse.

When Electra lost her father, Cordelia had taken her in and then funded a trip to Ireland, so that she could meet and spend time with her mother's family.

She couldn't bear to disappoint her, nor those Cordelia had gathered for the sitting. Often, they were her friends or acquaintances—or the husband she loved but couldn't seem to live with. Electra didn't wish to fail any of them—as she'd failed Lady Becknell.

Gideon had passed a long day of thwarted attempts to obtain solid facts in the case of Lady Helen Becknell by the time he alighted from a hansom cab in front of the Russell Square address printed on Electra Poole's calling card.

Most of the Becknell staff could offer nothing about the night of the event, since they'd been released from their duties. And few wished to tell him any of the family's secrets. According to his London staff, Lord Martin Ballinger had departed London for his country house, and her ladyship's sister, Beatrice, was so distraught, the lady could not stop crying long enough to answer any of his questions. He'd even sought out Lady Rosalind Ashcombe, but her staff claimed she was abed with a fever. Her butler conveyed that she'd not attempted her usual visit to Becknell House the previous night due to illness and had sent a note to that effect.

He'd returned to Becknell House, but none of the servants could confirm any note's arrival.

Perhaps, most disturbing, Lord Philip Becknell had not returned to London and the family's household, and at the moment, could not be located.

Descending to the pavement, Gideon halted. He recognized the townhouse, having visited the residence once with Erasmus Poole to meet Sir Christopher Redmayne, an MP who'd penned a police reform bill.

Did Electra reside with the Redmaynes?

He rapped on the door and a servant answered a moment later.

"Inspector Pierce to see Miss Electra Poole," he told the young woman.

The girl's brows pinched. "Were you invited, sir? If so, the sitting has begun. No guests can be added."

"I was not invited. I'm here on police business." It was late in the day. He'd put off this eventuality as long as he could. "It won't take long, but I'm afraid I must speak to Miss Poole. Is she in?"

He wouldn't be put off again today.

"Of course, sir. Come in." She stepped back so that he could enter the Redmayne's foyer.

Gideon removed his bowler and clutched it in his hands.

"Please wait here, sir."

Gideon heard music playing faintly as the girl strode off. A soft, slow piano melody. Then the music stopped, and he heard a voice that sent a charge of tension through him.

Electra was here.

He followed the path the servant had taken to a door that stood cracked open. Peering inside, he saw a dimly lit parlor. The lamps had been turned low, though candles dotted the room, their flames dancing as if in a breeze.

In the center of the room, nine people were seated at a round, black-draped table. At the table's center, a tall, thick candle blazed, lighting up a face he knew as well as his own.

He'd never attended a seance, a fad among the upper crust, but what he saw before him was much as he'd imagined one might be. Though, admittedly, he detected none of the theatricality seances were known for. As he understood it, mediums put on a dramatic performance, and such gatherings were viewed as entertainment.

Gideon couldn't stomach such nonsense.

Yet these individuals didn't seem entertained. They sat in somber quietness, and a strange energy seemed to fill the room. Electra presided. That was not in question—even in her stillness, she exuded a magnetic pull as if all the light in the room bent toward her.

Her ink-dark hair was loosely bound, and her black gown contrasted sharply with her pale skin. He felt a flair of disappointment that her eyes were closed. They were unusual eyes. Not precisely blue, not entirely green, but shifting with the light like a dragonfly's wing. Children had teased her. Called her a witch.

"You feel guilt, my lady," she murmured in a hauntingly low tone.

Her voice hadn't changed—still deeper than other ladies, still measured and cool.

"Yes," a bejeweled woman to her right replied, her voice taut with emotion. "Enduring guilt."

"You may let that go," Electra told her firmly. "He would wish you to."

Gideon balled his hands into fists, and anger simmered past his usual control.

Trickery disgusted him, even if this gathering seemed sober compared to others. He could not stomach conjurers and fortune tellers. They preyed on the desperate and the gullible.

Electra was clever and eminently capable. He could think of half a dozen professions she might step into and conquer, even with the restraints on a gentlewoman's options for employment.

Yet here she sat orchestrating a sham as brazenly as some fraudulent table rapper or mesmerist. Part of him wanted to look away. He'd always thought so much better of her. Indeed, there'd never been a woman in his life he thought of the way he did Electra—despite years of attempting to put his feelings aside.

Now, he had to ignore his feelings. He had a murderer to find, and Electra might know details that could aid him.

The young maid who'd admitted him stood anxiously at the side of the gathering, her eyes fixed on a woman Gideon recognized as Sir Christopher's wife.

As if she felt his regard, the girl glanced at him and gasped. "Sir," she whispered, then shook her head.

Her voice caused the solemnity of the room to shatter. Those at the table turned his way.

Finally, he saw those arresting eyes—Electra Poole stared straight at him, her black brows bent.

"Gideon," she breathed in that smoky voice of hers.

A man at the table pushed back his chair and got to his feet. Gideon recognized him as the baronet who owned the townhouse.

"Inspector Pierce," Sir Christopher Redmayne said. "I suspect I know the reason for your visit."

"Good evening, Sir Christopher." Gideon flicked his gaze to Electra. "I see I've interrupted your..." He didn't know quite what to call it. "It is Miss Poole I've come to speak with."

"Must it be now?" Lady Redmayne asked. The baronet's pretty wife remained seated next to Electra.

"Yes, it must be now," Electra answered before he could. "Forgive me, everyone." She swept her gaze at those around the table. "Please excuse me."

When she stood up, a cloudy round stone the size of a hen's egg fell to the carpet at her feet.

A gentleman at table shifted to retrieve it for her, but Electra beat him to it. She dipped and scooped it up in one nimble movement.

Then she turned her gaze to Gideon's as she strode past him. She moved so quickly, he immediately turned to follow, lest he lose her in the Redmayne's spacious townhouse.

In the hallway, he trailed her to a room at the far end of the house, which she entered without a single glance his way.

Gideon stepped inside the yellow-papered room and found Electra standing before the fire with her back to him. He remembered that ramrod straight posture well. All that teasing from other children had turned her into a young woman who carried herself with confidence, though he knew it was sometimes feigned.

Electra Poole had an otherworldly air about her and more mettle than most ladies of his acquaintance, but he'd also seen her cry. He suspected she hated him for it.

"This is regarding Lady Becknell, I take it," she said, her voice softer than the one she'd used in the parlor.

"Yes."

"Was she murdered?" As soon as the question was out, she turned to face him, watching him so intently that Gideon felt uneasy under her scrutiny.

"She was," he admitted. The papers would print as much in the morning editions, no doubt. "I have some questions for you." He gestured toward a pair of chairs not far from the fire.

Her expression changed. Gone was the cool, inscrutable mask. Her lips trembled and she lifted a hand to lay it across the base of her throat, a gesture he'd seen her use countless times to steady herself.

"Let's sit," he said, his voice gentling to a degree that shocked him.

As she moved to do so, her beaded gown rustled. Settling into the chair on the left, she sat stiff and straight, hands clasped tight in her lap.

Gideon sat opposite her and opened his notebook on his thigh.

"Tell me how you knew Lady Helen Becknell," he said, falling into the emotionless tone he used when conducting interviews.

Though it did not feel like a typical interview, he was determined to make it so.

"I only met her once, at her request. She sent a letter to me at Cordelia's address three days ago, setting the time and day for a private session. I went to her home at the appointed time for that consultation."

"What sort of consultation?" He steeled himself for whatever spurious claims she would make.

Her clasped hands tightened, and her knuckles whitened. "Not what I suspect you imagine. I do not put on a performance to entertain. I see things. Feel things. I use my abilities to offer assistance, usually reassurance."

Gideon ground his teeth and stared into those extraordinary eyes that were as opaque as armor.

"Did Lady Becknell pay you for your *abilities*?"

"Yes. She sent a sum with her letter and was to pay the remainder after our session."

"Was to? She did not?"

"Our session was cut short when a visitor arrived."

Gideon noted that. It squared with what Grace Dobbs had said too.

"Did you see the visitor?"

"Very briefly. He was a middle-aged gentleman with blond hair and a square jaw."

Lord Martin Ballinger, who Gideon was determined to speak to next, even if it meant a trip to the man's country estate in Hampshire.

"Tell me what occurred at your session."

For the first time, she hesitated.

Gideon arched a brow at her.

After drawing in and releasing a breath, she said, "It feels odd to reveal her private concerns."

"The lady was murdered. All facts I am able to gather must be collected, and I cannot predict what will prove relevant."

"I know how investigations work," she snapped, every inch Erasmus Poole's only child. "She seemed to believe that someone might be deceiving her. A gentleman, I believe." She quieted and stared at the fire, then started again more quietly. "She was also struggling with grief. She asked about a brother, who I assumed had passed."

"When?"

"A long while ago, I believe. I sensed grief and affection from her, along with fear."

Gideon gripped his pencil in a clenched fist. "I want facts, Miss Poole, not what you claim to have *sensed*."

She let out a little scoffing sound. He knew it was because he'd addressed her formally, but he preferred any distance he could get.

"Well, *Inspector Pierce*, what I can tell you is that she invited me, I went, and our session was cut short."

Gideon lifted his gaze to hers, narrowing his eyes. "What else did you observe about Lady Becknell? With your eyes, not your...*metaphysical* talents. "

"She appeared ill at ease. She was fearful. Anxious. She showed me a locket with a cutting of hair in it. And once her visitor arrived, she sent me off."

"And did not pay you?"

"No, but..."

At her hesitation, he stilled and then looked up at her. "But?"

"She embraced me. It surprised me." She pulled her shoulders back the merest inch, seeming to steel herself. "When she touched me, I saw her lying dead at the bottom of her stairs."

Gideon froze, his pencil digging into the paper. His stomach felt as if it had been tied in a knot.

"Why would you say such a thing?"

"Because it's true," she said fiercely.

"Are you saying you were at Becknell House after Lady Becknell died?"

"No, I'm saying I saw her dead while she embraced me. In my mind."

Gideon stared at her—shocked and horrified all at once. "That's impossible, Electra."

Whatever her role as a medium might entail, Gideon struggled to see Electra as dishonest. She'd been secretive, yes, and often reticent to confide in him. But he knew of only one bald-faced lie she'd told, and that had been for his sake. It was why seeing her holding court in the Redmayne's parlor had been so disturbing.

Yet despite how he trusted her, there was no logical way she could have seen what she claimed.

She shot up from her chair and looked down on him with a sort of regal poise. "No, Gideon, that is the God's honest truth. Are you calling me a liar?"

Chapter Four

He didn't believe her, just as she'd known he wouldn't. It was why she'd cut ties with Gideon Pierce after her father's death—one of many reasons. He reminded her too much of her father, a man she wasn't certain she could ever forgive. A man Gideon would always revere. She didn't blame him for his loyalty. Her father had saved Gideon. But the same man he saw as heroic had condemned Electra's mother to a terrible end.

"I've never known you to a be liar," he finally admitted. "But I believe in facts, Electra, not mysticism."

He worked his jaw and stared at the carpet before looking up again, his whiskey-brown eyes far colder than she remembered them.

"I cannot fathom how you've become a...*fortune teller*." He grimaced as if the words were vile to utter.

She'd closed herself off after leaving the parlor. She had no wish to read Gideon's thoughts, yet even without effort, his frustration came at her like a pulsing wave. And another emotion rippled off him too—relief. As if he'd missed her.

That put an unwanted lump in her throat.

"Do you have any further questions, Inspector?"

"Who else was at Becknell House when you arrived?" he asked, his voice a bit raspy.

"A maid admitted me and told me no one else was at home. I saw only the maid, Lady Becknell, and her visitor."

His pencil moved quickly across the page of his pad as he noted her reply.

"When you say Lady Becknell seemed unwell, what gave you that impression?"

Before she could reply, he added, "Through your empirical senses only, please."

"She looked pale and gaunt. There were shadows beneath her eyes."

"Did she seem inebriated or sedated?" His brows arched as if she'd said something that intrigued him.

"No, not at all."

He nodded. "And when did you arrive and depart?"

"I arrived by six in evening and left perhaps twenty minutes later."

"Was she upset by whatever you conveyed to her?"

"She was frustrated that I could not give her the answers she sought." Electra had sensed distress from the woman the moment she met her, but she didn't know whether their brief sitting had heightened the lady's worries.

"Not despondent?"

"No. She didn't seem so."

After noting as much, he flipped his notebook closed and slipped it into the pocket of his coat.

"Thank you for your time."

"Of course." Electra stood, and he followed suit.

As he looked at her, a bit of warmth entered his eyes. "I wondered where you'd gone."

The distance she'd put between them was purposeful. He

could never understand her, never had, even when they were children. How could he? His logical mind rejected anything his eyes could not see, his fingers could not touch, and scientific instruments could not measure.

"I went to Ireland for a time, then returned to England. But I'm well, as you see."

"Yes." His gaze hardened again, and he gave her a sharp nod. "I bid you good evening, Miss Poole."

It seemed they'd return to being strangers, and that suited her, even if it put an odd hitch in her chest.

"Good evening to you, Inspector."

After he'd gone, Electra settled on the chair again and stared into the waning flames in the fireplace grate.

"Everyone's gone," Cordelia said softly as she entered the room a while later and took the chair Gideon had briefly occupied. "Since your inspector came, it must be murder. Does he know who did this?"

Electra eyed her. "He is not *my* inspector, and I daresay he wouldn't share such details with me, even if he was on the cusp of an arrest."

"But he is the man your father mentored, is he not? The mudlark... The urchin he took in."

"He is."

"Were you two not like siblings once?"

"No." Electra had never thought of Gideon as her brother. When he'd first come into their home, he'd claimed a bit of her father's affection, and then he'd won a piece of her heart too. "We were...friends."

"And now?"

"I don't know what we are. Tonight was the first time we'd seen each other in years."

Cordelia exhaled a thoughtful sigh as she assessed Electra. "I wonder how long it will take him to find Lady Becknell's killer."

"Gideon Pierce is driven and unrelenting." Electra cast a look at her friend. "However long it takes, I'm certain he will."

Cordelia arched a brow. "Then why do you seem so troubled?"

"Because I saw what was going to happen to her and said nothing. If only I'd warned her in the moment—"

"My dear, you cannot know if it would have changed a thing."

But Electra believed it would have—not with her empirical senses or even her inexplicable ones. The certainty came from someplace deeper.

"There must be something I can do now to make up for it. To ensure she gets justice."

"Did you give him the locket?"

"I didn't." Electra shook her head. "Seeing him...surprised me. And Lady Becknell gave it to me. But maybe I should have at least told him about it."

"Mmm." The pensive sound was one Electra often heard from Cordelia when her clever mind was churning. "You still could, and I think perhaps there are other ways you could aid the investigation too. After all, you possess abilities to see the truth that Inspector Pierce does not."

Electra snapped her head toward her friend. "If I could touch whoever did this, perhaps I'd know."

Cordelia sat forward on her chair. "The gentleman visitor. If only you knew who he was."

"Gideon would never forgive me if I meddled in his case."

Cordelia nodded, then crossed her arms. "But you're already involved. His coming here proves that, and whether he accepts your gifts or not, they could prove useful."

"Yes." Energy built in Electra until it was difficult to remain seated. "And I think I know just where to start."

WHEN ELECTRA alighted from a hansom in Mayfair the next morning, she noted the black-ribboned wreath on the front door of the Becknell townhouse. The house had struck her as quiet the evening before last, but now all the curtains were pulled as if to emphasize its solemn separateness.

She approached the door and rapped, hoping Grace would be the one to answer. When she did, the young maid's eyes widened in recognition.

"Oh, Miss Poole. I'm afraid Lady Becknell..."

"Yes, I saw the papers and I've come to offer my sincere condolences."

Grace's lips trembled. Electra thought she might burst into tears.

"No visitors but family are to be admitted, miss, while the house is in mourning."

"I do understand." Electra offered the young woman a smile. "I sent a note around last evening after I departed. Do you know if it was received by her ladyship?"

The maid shrugged. "Don't know about no note. I left shortly after you did."

"May I speak to you, Grace? Privately?"

"I..." She wrung her hands and glanced behind her. "Mrs. Evans wouldn't wish me to." When she looked as if she might shut the door, Electra slid her boot across the threshold and took a small step forward.

"Lady Becknell," she whispered to Grace, "said you're the one who referred her to me, but I don't recall us ever meeting. Have we?"

Grace shook her head, then glanced behind her once again before turning frightened eyes back to Electra. "Come to the parlor, miss. I can only spare a few minutes."

Electra stepped inside and followed the young woman into a finely furnished room at the front of the house. After pulling the door shut behind her, Grace stared at Electra. Then she pointed towards a settee. Electra settled herself on the edge. Grace sat in a straight-backed chair.

"No, we never met before, miss," she rushed. "It was Sarah who told me of you."

"Sarah?"

"Lady's maid to Lady Ashcombe."

"I see." That name was one Electra knew. She'd attended the very first seance she'd ever held at Cordelia's Russell Square townhouse. "I do recall Lady Ashcombe."

"Sarah said you helped her mistress find an heirloom she'd lost. Her ladyship spoke of it often."

Though it seemed a small thing at the time, Lady Ashcombe had been thrilled. And Electra had been so stumbling and uncertain of her abilities, it had seemed a little victory for her too.

"Had Lady Becknell lost something? Was that what caused you to recommend me?"

"No, miss." The young maid stared at the carpet. "She fretted overmuch about many things."

"Who was the man who came to visit her last night, Grace?"

Her head came up sharply, eyes wide again. "Lord Ballinger," she said quietly.

Electra bit her lip, unsure how far to push. If he was a nobleman, Cordelia would likely know who he was and where to find him. "Do you know why he came?"

Grace hesitated, then lifted a shoulder. "He visited often, miss."

"To see Lady Becknell?" Electra didn't have to read the girl's thoughts. It was all on her face, the same thing Electra had sensed last night. Lady Becknell and Lord Ballinger had been lovers.

"They rowed fiercely after you'd gone," Grace whispered, her breath coming in quick pants, as if her heart was racing.

"Did he...harm her?"

"Oh, I've no notion, miss. Honestly. Mistress bid me to leave for my half day."

Electra couldn't read anything from the girl's mind. Unlike last night, she was closed off, trying to keep her emotions in check. "I'll be forthright with you, Grace. She intended to have me back, and though I only met Lady Becknell briefly, I do wish to help her."

Grace's skin paled. "Can you speak to her now...on the other side?"

"No." Electra noted the girl's obvious relief. "But I still wish to help her." Perhaps if she revealed more, it would induce the maid to do the same. "She seemed distressed about others deceiving her. A gentleman or perhaps a lady. Do you know who that might be?"

"Oh, I..." Ducking her head as if sheepish, she finally said, "I shouldn't say, miss."

"But you know who she meant?"

Grace pressed her hand to her middle. "Might have been Lord Becknell." The young girl drew in a breath and added, "Might have been that artist she'd visited these past weeks. Lucan Fox is his name."

"Do you know where I can find him?"

"No, miss, I—"

Before she could finish her thought, footsteps sounded outside the parlor door.

"You may use this room, Inspector," a woman's voice said from the other side of the panel. "I'll send Finch to you directly."

Electra held her breath, knowing the voice she'd hear reply.

"Thank you, Mrs. Evans," Gideon said.

Grace and Electra both stood and swung to face the door.

The middle-aged woman who opened it cast a fierce look Grace's way. "What on earth are you doing, Grace?" Then her bespectacled eyes turned to Electra. "What's the meaning of this?"

"I'm Electra Poole. I visited last evening and forgot my gloves." Electra lifted her gloved hands. "As you see, Grace helped me find them."

Mrs. Evans looked only slightly mollified by Electra's fib, but, of course, that wasn't the end of it. Because there was a tall, broad-shouldered detective glowering at her from just over the woman's shoulder.

"Fortuitous to find you here, Miss Poole," he said, sharpening each word as if he was clenching his teeth while he spoke. "May I have a word with you, please?"

He looked expectantly at Mrs. Evans, who nodded and withdrew. Grace all but raced after her.

Gideon stepped inside and pushed the door shut behind him with the heel of his boot.

For several unsettling moments, he merely leveled her with his dark stare. She imagined him using the same technique when questioning a suspect.

But Electra was immune to Gideon Pierce's glares.

"Say what you must, Inspector. I have places to be this morning."

"Do you indeed? If only you'd gone there rather than come to meddle in this investigation." As soon as she took a breath to reply, he took a step closer. "And don't give me some faddle about your gloves."

"But I'm so pleased to have them back." Electra shot him a glare of her own and tugged at the edge of one glove.

His jawline softened as he shot her a half-smile. "Yesterday I said you weren't a liar, but it's only because you can't believably pass off a falsehood to save your life."

She stared at him, perhaps thinking of that one convincing lie she'd told her father.

"If you'll excuse me, Inspector." Electra offered him a nod of leave-taking and started past him.

He took a step to block her way. "What did you want with Grace Dobbs?"

Electra turned to look at him. They were so close, she could see the scar above his lip and the other at the edge of his jaw. "To know the name of the man who visited last night."

Gideon closed his eyes. His expression had chilled even more when he opened them again. "Stay out of this, Electra. A woman was murdered after speaking to a psychic medium." He swallowed as if the words themselves were bitter. "I may not believe in such nonsense, but the man who did this might."

A heaviness pressed on Electra, darkness like a shroud choking her senses. It was fear—Gideon's worry for her.

She'd never considered that the killer would assume Lady Becknell had conveyed anything that would cost the lady her life. Could whoever killed her believe they'd silenced her? Gideon's notion wasn't completely illogical.

And, of course, no killer who hoped to conceal their crime would be pleased to know the victim had recently spoken to someone with second sight.

"I shall heed the warning, Inspector."

He studied her, assessing, as if he was the one who could read thoughts and was trying to determine what she might do next. Then, finally, he stepped aside, gesturing toward the door.

As Electra strode past him, he bit out, "See that you do."

After exiting the room, Electra collided with a tall, russet-haired young man in a dark suit. He reached out to steady her, then quickly removed his hand.

"Pardon me, miss," he said. "I was sent to see Inspector Pierce."

"He's in the parlor, awaiting your arrival," Electra told him. "You must be Mr. Finch."

The young man seemed pleased she knew his name. "Jacob Finch at your service."

"Don't let me detain you, Mr. Finch."

He looked toward the parlor door with a bit of trepidation.

"Suppose I mustn't keep the inspector waiting. Good day to you, miss." He bowed his head, and Electra side-stepped so that he could rap on the door.

Then she strode quickly down the hall toward the front foyer of Becknell House.

She looked over her shoulder and down the long hall to ensure no one might observe her, then she stopped near the foot of the stairs and quickly tugged off one of her gloves. Checking again to make sure no one saw, she reached out and touched the banister. Nothing. Then she knelt and touched the edge of the bottom step.

Her breath stalled in her throat and she felt the shift that took her from the present into some other place. A hazy vision—Lady Becknell beseeching someone, her body racked with pain. *Please.* She begged for their help, then her body convulsed so fiercely she couldn't speak at all. The vision shifted, merging with last night's——Lady Becknell lying stiff and straight at the bottom of the stairs.

Electra snatched her hand back and fumbled to replace her glove when she heard the clip of someone's footsteps.

The vision hadn't been enough. She could not see the face of the person Lady Becknell had called out to.

Electra stood and left the house without any of the staff

attending her, then kept walking until she was near the edge of the square's green space. Every vision left her a bit off-kilter, a bit diminished, as if something had drained from her. And there were the moments of sensing others' feelings too—Gideon's worry for her and she'd gotten something from young Jacob Finch too.

Though he'd been nervous about speaking to a Metropolitan Police detective, she'd sensed something more. A clear, unmistakable aura of guilt.

As GIDEON EXPECTED, Jacob Finch, the viscount's valet, confirmed that he and Lord Becknell had been away from Becknell House at the time of her ladyship's murder. He also insisted his employer's return had been delayed beyond their control due to a congested line on the Great Western line.

Simple questions. Quick answers. And yet the redheaded young man was sweating as if he'd just run the track at Epsom Downs. He darted his eyes, twisted his hands.

"Did you retain the train tickets?"

His already pale, freckled skin whitened more. "No, sir. Never thought I'd need them."

"So you discarded them?"

"Must have."

"During your time with the Becknells, how often have you observed Lord and Lady Becknell quarreling?" Gideon dipped his head once to temper the switch of direction and the directness of the question.

"Oh, uh, I've not been with them long."

"No? How long then?"

"Six months, give or take."

Finch was quite young to serve as a valet, but domestic staff sometimes retired or sought other posts and nobles preferred younger replacements, who might be relied on for years of future service.

"Any idea what happened to the last valet or their name?"

"Nettles, I believe his name was, sir. Cannot say when he left." Finch lifted a hand to tug at his collar. Perspiration dotted his forehead.

The young man was withholding information, and the fear of revealing it seemed greater than his unease at being questioned by a detective.

"In your six months, give or take, of service, did you often observe quarreling between Lord Becknell and her ladyship?"

"Once or twice, sir."

Gideon tipped his head and assessed the nervous lad anew. He'd expected an outright denial. Loyal servants tended to deny anything that might besmirch their employer.

"What did they quarrel about?"

Color rushed into the young man's cheeks.

"Dalliances?" It wasn't wholly a guess on Gideon's part. Grace Dobbs admitted that Lord Ballinger visited frequently when Lord Becknell was not at home.

Finch suddenly found the floral rug under their feet fascinating, his cheeks heating to a feverish red.

"His lordship or her ladyship?"

"I could not say, sir." Yet he nodded his head as if reflexively.

"I appreciate the position such an inquiry puts you in, Finch, but any detail might help me find the culprit who did this to her ladyship."

"Will his lordship know what I say?" the young man asked in a near whisper.

"No." Gideon wouldn't promise not to use the information he collected in his imminent meeting with Philip Becknell, but he wouldn't tell the nobleman which servant told him what.

"Both." The word came out on an exhale and the young man shifted on his chair as if he couldn't bear to sit still.

Gideon waited. "Tell me more, Mr. Finch."

"I'll lose my post, sir, and don't wish to leave on bad terms." Fear had tightened the young man's features. "His lordship always bids me to be discreet."

"But?"

"As you say, sir. His lordship has...dalliances. Lots of ladies admire him."

"And her ladyship?"

Finch jaw clenched and he dipped his head. "Her ladyship did wrong too, but she was a troubled sort. Told me she had lots of regrets?"

Gideon stilled his pencil. For a viscountess to confide such personal feelings to her husband's valet seemed odd. "Were you and her ladyship—"

"Good God, no. Never. How could I?"

"Understood." Gideon knew that such liaisons were not unheard of, despite how appalled Mr. Finch seemed by the prospect.

"Do you know of anyone else who quarreled with her ladyship or wished her ill?"

The young man seemed to seriously consider the question. "She rowed with her sister at times." He swallowed deeply. "Can't say why."

"As sisters do, I suppose."

"Yes, sir."

"Anything else you think I should know, Mr. Finch?"

The valet shook his head, though haltingly, as if forcing the movement. "I don't, sir."

Gideon laid his notebook aside and stood. "Thank you,

Finch. Please let his lordship know I'd like to speak to him next."

The young man's eyes widened. "He's not here, sir. I believe he went to his club."

The viscount's determination to avoid Gideon's questions had passed odd and moved straight on to suspicious.

"Then I shall arrange to speak to him later. That's all, Finch. You may go."

The young man gulped audibly, stood, and bolted from the room.

Murder put everyone in a household on edge, but the young man's demeanor made it clear he was hiding something. Gideon's only question was whether it was his own secrets or his employer's.

Chapter Five

When Gideon entered Vine Street station on Tuesday morning, the duty sergeant informed him that the coroner, Dr. Tate, awaited him. He found the doctor sitting in his office, lifting a steaming cup of tea to his lips. The man winced after taking a sip.

"They make it strong here," Gideon told him as he strode into his office.

"And scalding." Dr. Tate shot a grimace his way.

"I wasn't expecting you to deliver the postmortem findings personally." The surgeon who carried out the examination usually sent his report via messenger or post rather than coming in person. And Dr. Tate never came to personally deliver a post-mortem report, not as long as Gideon had been at Vine Street.

The coroner lifted a bushy white brow. "This entire matter is proving unexpected, Inspector. And sensitive, considering the family involved. The case is of great interest. I thought you might have questions once you read the report, so I came to provide answers."

"I'm much obliged to you. Any insights would be welcome."

As of yet, everything related to the case was far too murky for Gideon's liking.

The man lifted a document from his satchel and handed it over. Before Gideon could read more than a few lines, Tate leaned forward.

"As we suspected yesterday morning, the lady was throttled at the hands of a strong assailant. But from what Farringdon found, I believe the assault was antemortem—prior to the time of death. It likely happened hours before and was doubtlessly traumatic, causing the bruising and abrasions you saw. Though it was not fatal."

"The fall down the stairs then?"

"No." Tate worked his jaw.

"But the wound on her head."

Tate nodded and looked grave, even for a man who was mirthless as a rule. "When she fell, I believe the lady was already on the cusp of death. Which explains the small amount of blood from the cranial blow."

"I don't understand." Gideon lifted the coroner's report. "What did Farringdon find?"

"Strychnine," Tate uttered the word, then arched a brow as if waiting for Gideon's reaction.

Gideon stilled, his jaw tight. "Poisoned?"

"Yes. The condition of Lady Becknell's body—the clenching of her fists, the grimace, the locked limbs—caused me to suspect as much. So I asked Farringdon to consult a chemist, and he confirmed its presence in her stomach."

"Someone fed it to her." Gideon pressed two fingers to his temple.

"Or she drank it."

"So, why did she fall down the stairs?"

"The poison causes convulsions, stiffening of the body," Tate clarified. "If she was near the stairs when the poison took effect, she'd have little control." Tate tapped the report with his forefinger. "I believe that may be how she came to tumble down the stairs."

"Then likely not pushed?"

"There were no signs that she attempted to break her fall." Tate held his hands out in front him, palms up. "And you saw the straightness of the body as it lay at the bottom of the stairs."

"But she still might have been pushed."

"It is possible, but the person would have done so to a woman in the throes of a violent seizure and in a great deal of pain."

"And the tonic that she took to sleep?"

Tate shook his head. "The surgeon found no indications that her ladyship had taken the laudanum-laced tonic, though it is difficult to detect." Tate gestured toward the report. "What we can confirm is strychnine poisoning, and it would have taken swift effect. No more than thirty minutes and likely much less."

"So the note in the typewriter was unrelated." Gideon tapped his fingers against his thigh.

"Possibly," Tate affirmed. "Likely. If you're at all considering her ladyship's end was self-inflicted, I would disregard that hypothesis. If one chose to ingest poison, no one would choose strychnine. It's exceedingly bitter."

"So she was throttled earlier in the evening, ingested poison, and might have been pushed down the stairs." Gideon dropped into his desk chair and steepled his fingers in front of him, staring at a spot on the opposite wall.

How could such a lady have been so abused as to suffer so much violence on the same night? Did that mean two assailants? Or a single killer who'd failed at strangulation, but then had easy access to poison?

If he was now looking for two attackers, each would have their own secrets. Their own lies. Their own motive. And both were likely known to the poor woman. There'd been no sign of forced entry into the Becknell townhouse, and the poison was most logically administered in her food or drink.

"It's been years since I encountered a strychnine poisoning case." Gideon recalled a man early in his career who'd poisoned his wife. "It's easily obtained, I take it."

"Quite. In small doses, it's included in some medicinal tonics. A chemist or apothecary could provide it. Or a mail order pharmacy. It is often sold as rat poison."

Gideon scraped a hand through his hair.

Electra's involvement already made this case a tangled one. Now it felt labyrinthine, and Gideon wasn't certain which line of inquiry to follow. Lack of certainty gnawed at him, but it also fueled him.

"It seems I have a great deal of work ahead, Coroner. Thank you again for coming."

Tate didn't stand or make any move to depart. Instead, the man studied him with what Gideon thought might be a flicker of sympathy.

The snow-haired doctor cleared his throat, then added, "There's more, Inspector Pierce."

"Go on." Gideon rolled his head on his shoulders against a sudden tightness there.

"Lady Helen Becknell was with child. By the surgeon's estimate, about ten weeks along."

"I see." A possible motive and a multiplying of the tragedy of the case.

What was done to the woman was monstrous, and he couldn't help but feel pity for Helen Becknell and her child. But emotions did not solve murders, even if they often inspired them. He'd long ago schooled himself to channel sympathy into persistence.

The coroner stood, though he hesitated. "I'm at your service,

Pierce, and have the chemist, Dr. Gregson, at my disposal if you should need further tests conducted."

"Could he examine the sleeping tonic bottle taken from the scene? I'll send constables back to Becknell House to collect any other tonics or medicinals the lady might have used."

"I'll see that he does and have the results sent to you."

"Thank you, Coroner. I'll see you at the inquest tomorrow."

"Until then, Inspector."

After he'd gone, Gideon called Constables Clegg and Thacker into his office, providing them with the list of Becknell staff and tasking them with looking into each individual on the list. As well as Helen Becknell's family history and what they could find out about the brother she seemed so determined to contact.

Gideon needed to speak to two men before tomorrow's inquest—Lord Martin Ballinger, who he suspected had been Lady Helen Becknell's lover and the last man to see her alive, and Lord Philip Becknell, the woman's husband, who'd have easy access to any food or drink she'd been served in their shared home.

Since Cordelia had far more knowledge of London society's goings-on, Electra returned to Russell Square first to consult with her before attempting to find Lord Martin Ballinger or the artist, Mr. Fox. If his clients were mostly among London's upper crust, like Lady Becknell, Cordelia might very well know him personally, and she'd certainly know of a nobleman like Ballinger.

After the Redmaynes' housekeeper, Mrs. Hurst, informed her that Cordelia was still in the morning room, Electra headed there. But she slowed her steps when she heard Kit's voice blended with Cordelia's as they conversed.

Apparently, he'd either remained overnight or returned early this morning. Electra suspected the former. The Redmaynes were a mercurial couple with wounds between them, but one thing Electra never doubted—the two loved each other fiercely, even if they couldn't seem to live together peaceably at the moment.

"We must protect her," Cordelia said with her usual vehemence.

Kit's low voice was harder to catch.

Electra stepped forward to rap lightly on the half-open door.

"Come in," Kit called.

"Who needs protecting?" Electra asked as she entered, though Cordelia's thoughts were clear. Whether because of familiarity or Cordelia's eagerness regarding Electra's abilities, she was the easiest person in her life to read.

Her friend believed Electra needed protecting.

"You, my dear," Kit confirmed. "Cordelia told me of your meeting with Lady Becknell on the day she died."

"Tell her the rest." Cordelia's voice was taut with worry, her green eyes fretful.

Kit gestured to a news sheet on the side table near his chair. "Someone in the house has been speaking to journalists, it seems. Your presence that night has been noted."

Electra reached out for the paper. "Let me see."

Kit arched one brow at his wife. She twined a finger nervously around a strand of her honey-blonde hair, then nodded at her husband.

"The usual sensationalism," Kit said as he handed her the news sheet.

Electra read the headline, tightening her hold on the newspaper.

NOBLE LADY FOUND DEAD AFTER SPIRITU-
ALIST VISIT

The article's content was even worse.

*Confidential sources say Lady Becknell had, on the evening
of her demise, attended a private séance conducted at her residence by a certain Miss Poole, a self-styled clairvoyant, whose
name has gained some notoriety among those given to spiritualist
entertainments.*

"Judas." Her mother's favored exclamation burst from Electra. "They have my name."

Will they come for me? The thought wasn't born of ratio-
nality but the memory of what had been done to her mother. It
was one thing for a few ladies of London society to know of her
abilities, but now her name and activities were in print for all of
London to see.

"What will happen?" Her gaze sought Kit's and then
Cordelia's.

"First, I think you should remain here with me until this all
blows over," Cordelia immediately replied.

"And, of course, we'll accompany you to the inquest tomorrow," Kit put in. "A constable came round with a summons this
morning while you were out." He pointed to a piece of paper on
the low table between the settees.

"And if anything scurrilous is printed," Kit added, "I shall
engage a solicitor on your behalf."

Electra strode over to read the summons. "Do I tell them
what I saw in my vision?"

Kit and Cordelia exchanged a look.

"No, I would advise that you do not," Kit said, his tone firm
and full of a certainty Electra did not feel. "The coroner won't
accept it as fact, nor would the jury. You can only relay what
you observed while at Becknell House."

"Unfortunately, it seems you saw little that might aid your inspector," Cordelia said.

Her inspector. Gideon would be at the inquest, of course. And he'd no doubt look at her with the same combination of horror and disappointment as he had last night. Or the flare of irritation she'd seen in his eyes this morning.

At her silence, Kit tipped his head as he studied her. "Do you know more than you've told us, Electra?"

"Kit," Cordelia chastised.

"There is something," Electra admitted, then strode over to sit on the settee next to Cordelia.

Cordelia turned and immediately took her hands. "Tell us."

"I returned to Becknell House this morning."

"Bloody hell." Kit sat forward in his chair. "We mean to keep you far from this investigation, Electra. Protect you from whatever infamy will come to Lord Becknell."

Electra lifted her gaze to his. "You think her husband killed her?"

Kit immediately squared his jaw and flicked a look at Cordelia.

"It seems the two of you have something to tell *me*." Electra cast a glance at each of them.

"They're just rumors," Cordelia finally said, her voice soft, hesitant. "The gossip is that each of them had affairs, but while he expected her to take his infidelities in stride, he punished her for hers."

"Punished her how?"

Cordelia lifted her teacup and took a gulp of tea.

Electra sought to sense her thoughts, but surprisingly nothing came.

"Helen and I were both part of a charitable trust run by Mrs. Charlotte Ellsworth." Cordelia drew in a breath. "At one meeting, Helen had bruises on her wrists, and I noticed a mark on her neck. Charlotte inquired, and she gave an odd look." Cordelia nibbled at her lower lip. "I asked Charlotte privately later and she told me in strictest confidence that she suspected Philip Becknell was violent."

"Suspected?" Kit clarified. "Helen did not confirm that?"

"No." Cordelia shook her head. "She put Charlotte off. But there were whispers among servants about fierce rows between Helen and Philip."

"Rumors will get us nowhere." Kit settled back in his chair, then turned to look Electra's way. "What happened when you went to Becknell House?"

Electra knew Kit would bring his power to bear to protect her, as his wife's dearest friend. But though Cordelia championed Electra's use of her abilities, she knew Kit harbored doubts.

"I spoke to Grace Dobbs, the Becknell's maid."

Cordelia leaned closer, eyes wide. "And?"

"She implied that Lady Becknell and Lord Ballinger were lovers. She mentioned that Lord Becknell may have been deceiving his wife, but about what, I do not know. And she mentioned another man. A painter called Lucan Fox."

Cordelia drew in a sharp breath. "I knew it."

"Mmm." Kit's murmur was not a pleased sound. "The man would have taken you to bed if you'd let him." He'd fixed his dark-blue gaze on his wife. "Did you?"

Cordelia narrowed her eyes until they were slits. "Of course not, foolish man."

Kit nodded, his lips tilting up slightly, seemingly pleased, and convinced, by his wife's insistence.

"I take it Lady Becknell wasn't his only lover," Electra said.

"Heavens, no," Cordelia affirmed. "He's...charming. Almost painfully handsome."

Kit made a sound somewhere between a scoff and a growl.

"There's more," Electra said, hoping to cut through the

growing tension in the room. "Before I left, I touched the spot where I saw Lady Becknell in my vision."

"Heavens." Cordelia clutched at her middle.

"I saw much the same as I had when she embraced me, but..." Electra swallowed against the tightening in her throat that came the moment she recalled Lady Becknell's pleas.

"What is it?" Kit pressed, his voice low.

"I saw her reaching out, begging someone to help her, and then her body went rigid, as if she'd been shocked or suffered a seizure."

"Gracious, who did she reach for?" Cordelia whispered.

Electra shook her head, pushing away the images. "I saw no faces. I don't know, but I don't think she was alone when she fell down the stairs."

"Should you tell the inspector?"

"Absolutely not." Electra stood and smoothed the fabric of her skirt. "He doesn't believe me, and he never will." Cordelia dipped her head. Kit arched a brow but said nothing. "Now, if one of you would be so good as to tell me where I can find Lord Ballinger and Lucan Fox."

GIDEON STOOD IDLING in the Becknell foyer long enough that he'd begun to gnash his teeth. When he was on the verge of heading down the hall to find Lord Becknell himself, Mrs. Evans finally approached.

"His lordship will see you in his study, Inspector. I can show you the way."

Gideon followed her down the long, dark-paneled hallway. The study was on the opposite side of the townhouse, and when Gideon stepped into the nobleman's domain, Lord Becknell stood much as Electra had the night before when he'd entered the Redmayne's sitting room—back ramrod straight and facing the fireplace.

The room smelled of whiskey and leather and Gideon noticed a cut crystal glass of amber liquid at the edge of an enormous desk. A vivid, bold-hued portrait of Helen Becknell dominated one wall.

The sight of it caused him to narrow his eyes.

Gideon stepped forward. "Lord Becknell."

The tall, dark-haired nobleman turned almost theatrically, a slow, meaningful pivot. Becknell was known for his charm, for being a gracious host, for being a mediator who could bring opposing sides together in the House of Lords, according to the newspapers. What struck Gideon was the man's impressive size —quite tall, broad-chested, wide-shouldered—and his age. He seemed older than his wife, perhaps by a decade or more. Not unusual, but Gideon noted it just the same.

"Inspector Pierce." Becknell's voice was gravelly deep, his expression somber. "Can you tell me who did this to my wife?"

"Not as yet, my lord." Gideon searched the man's face, noting his pinched brows, lips pressed together. "But I won't stop until I know the answer to that question, I assure you."

"An awful, dastardly end for her." He shook his head, then cast a look at the portrait. "My poor darling Helen."

"Shall we sit, my lord?" Gideon gestured to the wingbacks arranged before the fire on either side of where Becknell stood.

"Do you mind if I stand, Inspector? I fear if I let myself settle, I shan't want to get up ever again."

Gideon gave no reaction to the rather melodramatic comment, then settled on the edge of a straight-backed chair against the wall that allowed him a good view of the viscount.

"I understand you were in Oxfordshire for the last three days for a hunting party."

A muscle in Becknell's jaw flickered. "Indeed."

"Who hosted you, my lord?"

"Lord Richard Ansley. Do you know him?" His tone had turned haughty, almost sardonic. He wasn't a man used to or fond of being questioned, it seemed.

"I do not, my lord." Gideon didn't rise to such bait.

He'd been looked down on by some in the police force. Mostly cronies of Erasmus Poole who knew of his history. But he'd proven himself, polished up so well that those he encountered in his work now saw him as respectable. Yet with noblemen like Becknell, he sometimes wondered if they could see past the polish and somehow sniff out his guttersnipe past.

"Your return to London was delayed." It was not a question, though Gideon wanted to hear Becknell's explanation.

"Unfortunately, yes." His mouth tipped in disgust. "Damned trains. Never bloody reliable. Some accident clogged the line."

The man hadn't altered his stance—legs braced, hands behind his back, a position that allowed him to look down on his interrogator.

Gideon pulled out his notepad and pencil. "Forgive the bluntness, my lord, but who might have wished your wife harm?"

Becknell drew in a long breath and exhaled slowly. "A question I've asked myself repeatedly." The man pressed two fingers to his lips and then looked long and hard at Gideon, as if sizing him up.

"In our circle," he began in a quiet voice, "there are ongoing squabbles. Petty jealousies. Gossip. It's the way of London society, but I cannot think she would have admitted anyone last night who would have toppled her down the stairs."

Gideon cleared his throat, and Becknell tipped his head.

"You're certain she was pushed down the stairs, are you not?"

"She did fall down the stairs, my lord, but there were also marks on her ladyship's neck."

Becknell arched a thick, dark brow. "I beg your pardon."

"The marks seem to have been left by someone's hands, possibly hours before her death."

Becknell's olive-hued skin paled and the shock in his eyes did not seem feigned.

"But I thought the fall..." The nobleman trailed off and fell silent.

"Yes," Gideon said into the quiet, "but shortly before that fall, she seems to have sustained a violent attack."

The man's brows dipped and he clenched his hands into fists. "Ballinger came here last night."

"Yes, and I plan to question him next."

"Perhaps you should have questioned him first," Becknell bit out, then finally shifted, striding over to scoop up the glass on his desk and knock back the liquid inside.

"What can you tell me about her ladyship and Lord Ballinger?"

Becknell narrowed his eyes and stared at Gideon. "May I trust in your discretion, Inspector?"

"Discretion, yes. Secrecy, no. I am collecting facts to find the answers you seek, and at the inquest tomorrow, I must answer honestly."

Becknell scoffed as if Gideon's answer vexed him. But after a moment, he let out a shuddery sigh and admitted, "The man seduced my wife." He ground his teeth, flexing his jaw. "She ended it. She swore as much to me, and I believed her. It was all forgiven, but Ballinger..." He grimaced after speaking the man's name. "The bastard would not let her go. He pursued her relentlessly." Flicking a look Gideon's way, he added, "And without a shred of discretion. Thought a scandal would force her hand. Or mine. And then I'd let him cuckold me as he pleased."

Gideon had to weigh how much to tell a family member at such a crucial point in a murder investigation—such as the matter of poison and her ladyship's pregnancy—though at the inquest in the morning, Becknell would hear it all.

"Beyond Lord Ballinger, is there anyone in the household—"

"Good God, man, no. Helen got on well with the staff."

"And did she get on well with her sister?"

Becknell waved a hand. "They bickered as sisters do, but they were close. Confidantes. If they did not have affection between them, Helen never would have insisted Beatrice live with us."

"And when did she?"

Becknell blinked. "I can't honestly recall. Perhaps two years after we married. She's been with us for over a decade."

"And she was from home last evening?"

Becknell shrugged. "As I understand it. I pay no notice to Beatrice's social calendar, but she's keen on charity doings and has a sickly cousin she visits."

Becknell emptied his glass and then slumped onto the edge of his desk, staring into the fire. He'd unraveled a bit from the man Gideon faced when he'd stepped into the study.

"Who is Edward? Someone who was dear to Lady Becknell?"

"I've no idea." Becknell's reply didn't sound truthful. His voice quavered, and it was a noticeable chink in his otherwise composed demeanor.

"You know of no one named Edward among your wife's acquaintances?"

"I said I did not."

"Do you know of any means by which Lady Becknell might have ingested poison?"

The viscount's jaw slackened and his eyes widened. "Poison?"

"Strychnine. The coroner confirmed its presence in her ladyship's stomach and will state as much at tomorrow's inquest."

The viscount shook his head and stared at the carpet. The news *seemed* to stun him.

"She...took tonics. Medicinals. She wasn't careful about it. Could she have taken it in one of those?"

"I don't believe so, sir. Not at the levels detected in the postmortem."

"Dear God. Who would have done such a thing? And how?"

Gideon gave the man a few moments to collect himself, but not too long. When Becknell stood again and went to refill his glass from a decanter on a side table, Gideon drew in a breath and prepared to offer the final revelation.

"I must broach a delicate topic, my lord."

"Have we not gone far beyond delicacy, Inspector? Out with it, man."

He waited until Becknell's curiosity caused him to turn and face Gideon once more.

"Were you aware that her ladyship was with child?"

Becknell froze, his newly filled glass halfway to his lips. The man's face transformed. Blood rushed into his cheeks, perspiration dotted his brow, and he gripped the cut crystal so tight, Gideon thought he'd surely shatter it.

"Lucan Fox," he bit out. "That's the man you should be questioning, Inspector. The man's a debaucher, and I dare say if he knew Helen was..."

That Becknell assumed the child was not his own struck Gideon as an enormous insight.

"You have reason to think Mr. Fox would have done her harm?"

"I do," Becknell said, squaring his shoulders. "And she was besotted with the man. No doubt, she'd admit him at any hour, especially since I was away. Find out where he was last night."

"I'll endeavor to do so, my lord." Gideon stood. "I shall see you at the inquest tomorrow."

The man's only response was a sharp nod. His skin remained mottled with red, his knuckles still blanched as he held his drink.

Gideon stepped out of Becknell's study, and the case and its suspects began to take shape in his mind. Beyond Becknell's reactions, one thing stood out. On Monday, when he'd arrived at Becknell House, the portrait of Lady Becknell had been hanging in the hallway.

One could argue that Philip Becknell, in his grief, wanted the portrait of his beloved wife near him in his study. But Gideon couldn't help but wonder if it was moved for a different purpose—as a set piece for the performance he'd just witnessed.

Chapter Six

C ordelia insisted on accompanying Electra to seek out Lord Ballinger, but his butler claimed his lordship was away from home. Then, after much persuading, and a promise to return to the townhouse, Cordelia agreed to part from Electra. Outside Ballinger's townhouse, Cordelia headed off in her carriage to a call on a lady friend, and Electra secured a hansom cab, ostensibly to take her back to Russell Square.

But the minute she closed over the cab's half-door, Electra directed the driver to take her to Soho. Cordelia confided that it was where Lucan Fox's studio-townhouse could be found. The streets were bustling in the district in a way the streets of Mayfair were not, and it took only a brief inquiry at The Devonshire Arms public house to get directions to the artist's home. He was well known in the neighborhood, apparently.

Though his townhouse was far less fashionable than Becknell House, the building's red bricks and climbing ivy struck Electra as far more appealing.

She lifted the weathered lion's head knocker and waited a long while for a response before knocking again. Squinting upward into the bright sky, she noticed a drapery twitch aside on an upper floor window. Not long after, the front door swept open and a barefoot man in trousers and a half-open, billowing white shirt leaned on the door's frame.

Cordelia's description of "almost painfully handsome" suited him well.

Waves of gold-blond hair tumbled over his forehead and dusted his chest, his face was chiseled and perfectly proportioned, and his blue eyes, lightened by the sun, glinted as he assessed her from boot to brow.

"I don't believe we're acquainted, love," he said, his voice rough as if he'd just awoken. "But let's not stand on ceremony. Lucan Fox, at your service. And you are?"

"Electra Poole." She wondered if he was one of the many Londoners who'd read her name in the newspaper this morning. "May I come in and speak with you, Mr. Fox?"

He arched a brow and smiled easily, which sharpened the perfect lines of his jaw. "With a name like that, I fear you've come for revenge," he teased.

Apparently, he only recognized her name from Greek myth and not from the London papers. Relieved, Electra lightened her tone to match his. "No, sir, just curiosity. Might I take up a few moments of your time?"

He assessed her, studying the features of her face, lingering on his lips. "I'll offer you as many moments as you like, Miss Poole. You find me with a free afternoon. Come in, love."

Stepping into the townhouse, Electra was assailed by colors and scents. Art covered nearly every inch of the walls—florals, nudes, richly garbed ladies. Through an open door, a cluttered parlor was strewn with furnishings covered in bold-hued fabric in half a dozen different shades. Perfume lingered in the air and something deeper and woodsy created an odorous haze.

"Come, Electra." He tipped a look her way. "May I call you Electra? You must call me Lucan."

He led her into the disordered parlor that looked as if it served as both studio and sitting room. She noticed an ornate brass pot wafting incense smoke. A half-covered canvas sat on an easel, and all Electra could make out of the painting were a pair of lady's shapely nude legs.

Was it Helen Becknell?

Lucan Fox immediately approached a drinks cart teeming with bottles. "A bit of port? Brandy? Or shall we be truly decadent and go straight for absinthe?"

"No, thank you." Electra abstained from liquor as a general rule. It dulled her senses, blocked her abilities, and had been her father's means of retreating from grief too often for her to take much pleasure in it.

Lucan Fox poured himself a generous glass of blood-red port.

"So, who sent you, Miss Ravenlocks?"

Electra wasn't used to such brazen flirtation from a man, nor to a man who so fully embraced his own obvious appeal. Lucan Fox was pleasing to the eye and definitely knew it.

"No one sent me, Mr. Fox." Electra couldn't bring herself to address him informally. "I came for information." As she spoke the words, she sought to open herself to anything she could discern about the man. All that resonated from him was a sort of blithe self-confidence and curiosity. His thoughts themselves remained stubbornly opaque.

He flashed an appealing smile. "What sort of information? Do you wish to know my fee to have your portrait painted?" Approaching a few steps, he reached out and swept a finger along her cheek before she could rear back.

She sensed nothing from the contact, though it had been brief.

"I quite like your face, Electra." He pursed his lips and swept his gaze downward. "And your figure. I'd paint you gratis, lovely."

"I don't want a portrait, Mr. Fox, but would you tell me about Lady Helen Becknell?"

For the first time since her arrival, he abandoned his loose posture and straightened to his full height, a head above hers. He knocked his shoulders back as the slightest tremor caused his lips to wobble. "Terrible business. Poor Helen. I was sorry to hear the news."

So he *had* read the papers—or heard the news from someone else. Or from his own involvement.

Electra sensed a flash of genuine grief. It dimmed his brightness.

"You were well acquainted with her?"

He reached up and gripped the back of his neck, then looked at her from under his brows. "Are you asking if she was a paramour?"

"Yes."

The edge of his full lips quirked. "I do like your plain-speaking manner, so I offer the same. For a time, yes, we were lovers." He swept a hand over his mouth, then dropped his gaze to the thick multihued rug under their feet. "Are you a friend of hers? Or family?"

"Neither," Electra admitted. "But I'd like to see her get justice."

He inched up a brow at that and flashed a smile. "A crusader then." Tipping his head, his grin widened. "Are you one of those fearsome lady detectives?"

Electra couldn't help but scoff. "No, Mr. Fox." She forced a brief smile to match his more potent one. "When did you last see her?"

He swigged back half of his port. "On Saturday. The day

before she died. Though I didn't plan to. I was surprised by her visit."

"Why?" Electra prompted when he said nothing more.

"Because I'd ended things between us weeks ago." In one long swallow, he drained the rest of his glass. "I always know when it must end with a lover. Things become stifling, you understand. I never lie to them, Electra. I set out the rules and tell them how it shall be." A smirk of what looked like arrogance curved his lips. "Invariably, some wish for more."

"She wished for more?"

Rather than answer, he turned his back on her and refilled his glass nearly to overflowing. "Worse than that. She attempted to snare me."

"Snare you? In what manner?" Electra stepped a bit closer, frustrated that the man was so difficult to read, despite how open he seemed.

"Not for marriage, obviously," he said when he turned back to face her. "There was the great and mighty Lord Becknell, of course. But she claimed—" He swallowed as if the next words had lodged in his throat.

Electra waited, hoping she'd not encountered the end of his easy-speaking manner.

"She claimed to carry my child in her belly." Gripping his port glass, he lifted one finger to point at her. "I take care to prevent such things, Electra. I swear it was not mine."

"Did you argue?"

"Of course we did." He took a few steps closer. "I want no by-blows and told her as much." He pursed his lips, then looked past her as if recalling the conversation.

So close to him, Electra expected to feel something, sense something, or see his thoughts, and yet she could not. Impulsively, she took a few steps and then feigned tripping over one of the swaths of fabric that hung off a low settee.

She reached for him, gripping his bare wrist, and he immediately drew her closer. Too close. Images arose, though they were dim, as hard to grasp as smoke—as if perceiving through Lucan Fox's eyes, she saw a murky view of Helen in tears, speaking adamantly, then striking out at him as he wrapped his hands around her throat.

"Steady on, Ravenlocks." Lucan Fox had leaned into her until his chest brushed hers, and then he wrapped an arm around her waist. "You smell like violets. How modest for someone who was given a face such as yours."

"Forgive me, Mr. Fox." Electra immediately stepped away from his embrace.

"Nothing to forgive, love. I'll catch you whenever you like." He winked.

Electra felt a blush scorching her cheeks, her neck, the tips of her ears, and she laid a hand across her middle to steady herself after the vision.

She couldn't help glancing down at the painter's hands. A little shiver skittered down her back at the image of him wrapping them around Lady Becknell's neck. They'd fought, but had he killed her?

When she looked over at him, he was opaque again. No feelings or images arose.

"You rowed with her," she heard herself say before she could think better of it.

"I did admit as much, love." He tipped his head. "You look a bit peaky. Sure you don't want a drink?"

"Yes, perhaps I will. Just a sip or two." Electra didn't want a drink, but she wanted to know whether he had killed his lover.

When he went to the cart to pour port into a diminutive glass, she laid her hands on a jar filled with pencils and paintbrushes. She touched her fingers to a paintbrush's handle, hoping to summon the same moment again. Their argument had taken place in this very room.

"A tipple for the lady," he said, his voice low and warm.

Electra wrapped her hand around his where he held the stem, lifting her gaze to his.

Flickering images took shape as her body jolted. Lady Becknell pushing him from her, tears streaming down her cheeks. Than an image of him pushing her. Not downstairs, but out the front door of his townhouse.

"Drink, Electra." His tone had turned firm. "You look as if you might swoon."

"Thank you." She lifted the glass and took the tiniest of sips.

He eyed her warily, as if convinced she might collapse in front of him, as he quaffed from his own glass.

"How did matters conclude between you?" Mostly, she was curious whether he would tell her the truth or reveal anything more than she'd seen in his memories.

"Right back to the interrogation, are we?" He grinned, then shrugged. "She had other lovers. The brat was one of theirs, I assure you. But I regret to say I wasn't kind. I accused her of lying and attempting to trap me." Inclining his head, he took another long pull on his port. "You must understand, I aim to send ladies away thoroughly satisfied, so I regret how Helen and I ended."

Electra could no longer read anything from him. Even when she'd seen his memories of the confrontation with Helen Becknell, she'd felt no emotions from him, as she usually did with people's thoughts or remembrances.

But now, his eyes reflected genuine sadness. True regret. Unless, of course, he was a grand actor. Before she could ask more, a knock sounded at the townhouse's door.

Lucan Fox frowned. "Who the hell could that be? I expected a quiet afternoon." Setting his glass on a nearby table, he cast a look over his shoulder. "I'll see who it is, but please stay. I'm determined to sketch that striking face of yours at the very least before you go."

Electra nodded, though she had no intention of sitting for a sketch.

After he swept from the room, she set the glass of port down and approached the easel, lifting the cloth to see the rest of the painting. It was most definitely not Helen Becknell. The lady in the painting had pale blonde hair, voluptuous curves, and dark eyes.

As Lucan Fox greeted his visitor, Electra stepped toward the threshold, listening to the exchange.

"Most unexpected, but come in if you must, Detective Inspector."

Electra groaned, clenched her teeth, and cast a look around the room, considering whether to hide behind the drapery.

But it was too late.

"Please join us, Inspector," Lucan Fox said as he entered the room again with Gideon on his heels. "Port? Brandy?" Mr. Fox asked, glancing at the tall, dark, scowling detective over his shoulder.

But, of course, Gideon paid him no heed.

He'd spotted her, and his gold-brown eyes turned glacial. Electra imagined he was considering whether to clap her in irons or toss her over his shoulder and remove her from Lucan Fox's townhouse bodily.

"Miss Poole," he said, his voice that low rasp she knew meant he was doing his best to keep every emotion rioting through him under tight control. "What a surprise to find you here."

～

Gideon could feel Lucan Fox's curiosity pique as he watched the exchange with Electra. The infuriating woman refused to look even the slightest bit chagrined to be caught—again—interfering with his investigation.

"You know each other, I take it." The tall, blond painter sounded amused.

"We used to," Electra retorted blithely.

Gideon forced himself to turn his attention to the man whose untidy townhouse he stood in. "I have a few questions for you, Mr. Fox, but would you give me a moment with Miss Poole?"

"By all means. As long as you don't send her off. I mean to sketch her." The young man stepped back and performed a dramatic bow, then exited the room, pulling the door shut behind him.

"Are you not afraid he'll abscond before you have the chance to question him?"

Gideon remembered that inky brow pitched high look she shot him all too well. Worse, he'd missed it.

"He'd have to find a pair of shoes and put on some clothes first."

"Fair point."

"Do I even need to ask—"

"What I learned from Lucan Fox? I'd be happy to tell you."

Gideon let out a sigh and gestured toward her. "By all means. Please divulge." If she'd learned anything of use, it might actually save him time, though he'd never admit as much to her.

"Mr. Fox and Helen Becknell were lovers."

"Yes, I was already aware."

Her blue-green eyes flashed with irritation. "He told me that she visited him the day before her death."

Gideon must have given something away in his expression

because her chin notched up almost pridefully, as if she'd recognized that was a new bit of information.

"He says Helen told him she was with child," she said in a quieter tone, as if the topic should be treated with delicacy.

"Yes, I know of her condition too."

Electra perched her hands on her hips. "She said it was *his* child. Did you know that?"

Gideon twisted his bowler in his hands. "No, but based on my last conversation, I suspected as much." He tipped his head as he watched her. He couldn't seem to stop and told himself it was because he was trying to reconcile the woman before him with the girl he'd once known.

"You interrupted us, so I didn't get a chance to ask if he has an alibi for Sunday evening. You'll still need to do that."

Gideon choked out a laugh. "Anything else you've left for me to do in *my* investigation, Miss Poole?"

She crossed her arms and tapped her boot against the carpet. "I think you should question Grace Dobbs further. Mr. Fox mentioned that Lady Becknell had other lovers, and Grace knows more than she's saying."

Gideon thought the same.

"Lord Ballinger for one." She pursed her lips, then asked quietly, "Who do you suspect?"

"You know I won't discuss that with you."

Electra shocked him by striding closer until they were inches apart. Then she lifted her fist out before him and released her fingers, letting a chain drop with an oval locket swinging from its length.

He reached out to examine it more closely and his hand brushed hers. The contact caused his breath to hitch. All his buried feelings threatened to well up like a tide, and he fought to keep them at bay.

"I told you that the night I went to her, she embraced me

before I departed. She held me overlong, and I didn't know why. But the next morning, I found this in my pocket."

"You didn't tell me that." Gideon's voice rose in irritation.

Electra merely shrugged.

He took the locket in his hand, though she still held the chain. With his thumbnail, he sprung the fastening. A curl of reddish hair lay nestled inside.

"She offered it to me during the sitting. Sometimes I can read things from objects."

Gideon's muscles tensed at mention of her supposed spiritualist skills and he released the locket. "And did you?"

"Not as much as she wished me to."

"Are your...abilities fallible then?" Despite himself and everything he believed about the world and science and reason, he was curious what she believed.

"Do you really want to know, Gideon?"

His mouth went dry because there was a flicker of something like hope in her green-blue eyes. A nod was all he managed; he didn't want to snap what felt like a fragile string of connection between them.

"I don't trust them, to tell you the truth." She looked away and then back at him. "My mother was made to distrust what she saw. And I have no control over what I see and feel. I'm not at all certain why or how it works. Often, it fails me when it would be most helpful. So, yes, my abilities are fallible."

She'd rushed the words out and breathed heavily as she waited for him to react.

The mention of her mother shocked him; Mrs. Poole was a topic both Electra and her father had protected with unremitting silences. Not only did neither share much about her with Gideon, but he never observed them mentioning her with each other. Electra's mother was forbidden territory.

He swallowed, fighting the urge to step closer to her, to

comfort her if that's what she needed. But they'd been strangers for three years, and she wouldn't welcome such presumption from him.

What he knew for certain was that there was no artifice in her words. Whatever talents she claimed to possess, she believed what she saw was true and accurate. But her abilities disturbed her too.

They fell into an awkward silence. Arguing would accomplish nothing, and Gideon was already running out of time prior to the inquest in the morning. Before he could form any sort of reply, Lucan Fox opened the door.

"Are you two finished? All went quiet." He glanced at Gideon and then Electra.

Electra busied herself with replacing her gloves.

Gideon narrowed his eyes at the too-pleased-with-himself Lothario. "Do you have an alibi for Sunday evening and the early hours of Monday morning, Mr. Fox?"

His eyes widened. "Do I need one?"

"Yes," Electra said before Gideon could.

The artist's eyes softened as soon as she spoke. "I do have an alibi, love, but she wouldn't want me to tell you her name."

"You must," Gideon told him. "I'll need to speak to her in order to verify your alibi."

Fox let out an exaggerated sigh. "The Duchess of Malvern." Flinging a hand toward the large canvas on the easel, he added, "I've been commissioned to paint her, and she was here overnight."

Both Electra's brows winged up at that.

Gideon pulled out his notepad. "What time did she arrive and depart?"

"Perhaps eight on Sunday evening and near nine on Monday morning." Fox strode into the studio and approached the easel to pull a cloth across the half-finished painting of a voluptuous nude.

Gideon snapped his gaze to the man as he passed. "Where did you receive that scratch on your face, Mr. Fox?"

The painter turned toward a long mirror in the corner, then lifted a hand to his face.

"Other side," Gideon told him.

Lucan Fox turned his face to examine the other side. "Hmm. Hadn't noticed it. I honestly don't know when I got it. Perhaps on Sunday night." He lifted his gaze to Electra and had the audacity to wink.

She gave the fop no reaction whatsoever, and a little flare of satisfaction shot through Gideon.

"Did Lady Becknell have enemies?" she asked the painter.

The satisfaction was short-lived, and Gideon stepped forward. "If you don't mind, Miss Poole—"

"Enemies?" Fox asked, turning fully toward Electra as if Gideon wasn't in the room. "No. But there were many who smiled at her face and likely glared at her back."

"Why?" Gideon interjected, if only to regain control of his own damned investigation.

Fox turned back to him. "Ladies tell each other their secrets and then wish they hadn't. Helen told me about one—didn't give her name—who wished to off her vile husband. Another lady had debts. A secret gambler. Helen loaned her money so the noblewoman's husband didn't find out. Another took a fancy to Ballinger, but he only had eyes for Helen."

"Names?" Gideon asked.

"She was mum about names, for the most part. But Lady Ashcombe is the gambler." Fox twisted a ring on his forefinger. "Best not tell her I said so though. Will you?"

"Not unless I need to." Gideon assessed the young man, who seemed to not have a care in the world and whose eyes kept straying irritatingly back to Electra's face. "Who else may have wished her harm?"

"Have you spoken to Ballinger?"

"Not yet," Gideon admitted.

The young man looked suddenly uncomfortable and ran a hand through his hair. "The minute I read of Helen's murder, I knew he'd done it."

"You never told me that," Electra said as if offended.

Fox eyed Electra and smiled. "You never asked, Lady Detective. Besides I was hoping to keep you here a while and would have gotten there eventually."

Gideon strode to the center of the room, planting himself between Fox and Electra. "What made you think Ballinger murdered Lady Becknell?"

Fox smirked. "Probably because he said he would if he couldn't have her."

Chapter Seven

The blue sky and dazzling sunlight had slipped behind dense white clouds by the time Electra emerged from Lucan Fox's townhouse. She laid a hand against her throat, feeling the reassurance of the pendant there, and took in gulps of fresh air. Cloying perfume and incense seemed to linger on her clothes and skin.

"Thank you," she breathed.

Electra watched as Gideon grappled with hearing those words from her.

He scowled, then squared his jaw. Shifting uncomfortably, twisting his bowler hat in his hands, he looked away, then looked back to see if she was smiling or having him on somehow.

Finally, he nodded. "You're welcome."

They stood together on the pavement in front of Lucan Fox's residence, and she truly did feel a measure of relief that Gideon insisted on escorting her out. The artist had been determined that she should remain, and she found the man's bold, insistent charm far more unsettling than appealing.

"He wasn't keen on letting me leave until you showed up." Though she hadn't been able to read him, Fox had made her ill at ease. He was a contradiction—all outward amiability and yet he'd acknowledged that he and Helen Becknell had not ended well. Did that mean shouting and an argument? Or did it mean violence?

She wondered about Gideon inquiring about the scratch on Mr. Fox's face.

"Did Helen Becknell scratch her attacker?"

One of Gideon's brows climbed up his forehead, touching a dark curl of hair that had gotten dislodged when he removed his hat.

"I'll take that as a yes." Electra knew it from his eyes, not from any attempt to read his thoughts.

She'd set a rule for herself long ago that she would not attempt to sense Gideon's thoughts or feelings, though with her lack of control over her abilities, they'd sometimes come through regardless. Now, she couldn't decide whether she'd made the rule in order to respect his privacy or because she didn't truly want to know what went on inside his head.

"I won't confirm or deny such details for you, Electra. As you reminded me yesterday, you know how investigations work, and this case requires more discretion than most."

"Well, perhaps I'll hear *such details* during tomorrow's inquest."

He inhaled sharply. "I'm sorry that you must attend. That you're caught up in this matter at all."

"But I am, though I will have little to contribute." Of course, she might if she could lay her hands on the man who killed Helen Becknell, providing her abilities did not fail her in that moment. Or unless he proved to be one of those unreadable sorts.

"You'll return to the Redmaynes' house?" The words were more directive than question, implying that was exactly where she should go rather than stay and continue to interfere with his search for Lady Becknell's killer.

"Where are you going?"

He blinked as if she'd surprised him again. "To continue my inquiries, of course."

"To Cavendish Square?"

He lifted his cleft chin. "Why would I be going there, Electra?"

"Because it's where Lord Ballinger lives."

He pursed his lips, pushed his tongue against his cheek. "And how do you know that?"

"I have my methods."

He laughed, the sound bursting out as if it had snuck up on him. "Of course you do."

"What would it take to convince you to let me accompany you?"

"There's nothing that could convince me." He placed his bowler on his head and tapped it into place. "But do let me find you a cab."

"I could be helpful," she told him as she stepped a bit closer, daring to reach for the sleeve of his well-tailored suit.

She'd once teased him about spending half his salary to look like a toff, but, of course, that was the point—to look so impressive no one would ever guess the detective in Bond Street suits had once been as lowly as a mudlark.

He stared down at the spot where her fingers wrapped around his arm.

"Please, Gideon, I can...notice things you might not." His muscles shifted under her arm, and he studied her face.

"I cannot involve you in police business. You know that. Please go back to Lady Redmayne's, at least until this case is resolved."

"You believe that will be soon?"

He narrowed one eye, and then turned away. Electra searched her mind for anything that might persuade him. She could follow him, of course. Take a cab to Cavendish Square and wait until he departed.

Perhaps Gideon believed Lord Ballinger killed Lady Becknell. And he might be correct.

From Fox's description, the nobleman was obsessed with her. If he'd learned she was with child by another lover, what might he have done? Not to mention that the moment Lady Becknell stepped away from him and embraced Electra, she'd seen a premonition of the woman's death.

A hansom clattered to a stop at the edge of the pavement in front of them.

Gideon turned back and held out his hand.

"Electra?"

"I have a fancy to stroll in Hyde Park. We could travel together, and then the cabbie could drop you at Cavendish Square."

"No." He shook his head. "And you still can't lie worth a farthing. But I'll accompany you back to Lady Redmayne's just to make sure you get there safely."

She had one trump card to use with Gideon, though once used, she'd lose the leverage forever. After pondering, she decided this wasn't the time.

"No, it would only detain you further. I'll go." She strode past him and took the single step up into the hansom cab. He'd already opened the half-door and reached out to close it, as if determined to make sure she was secure.

Protectiveness from Gideon had never seemed as oppressive as her father's strict oversight, though if something had mattered to her enough, she'd rarely heeded either of them. Now, with a tenuous kind of truce between them beginning to take shape, she almost wished she wasn't about to do precisely what he insisted she not do.

After he'd given the cab driver the directions to Russell Square, he strode off to find a hansom of his own. Traffic was busy, and it took a few minutes for her cab to make progress toward Cordelia's house. Yet, of course, that's not where Electra intended to go.

When they'd travelled a mile or so, she rapped on the cab's wall, and the driver opened the little trapdoor above her head to look down.

"I beg your pardon, sir, but I've changed my mind. Can you take me to Cavendish Square?"

"Aye, miss."

It took a bit of maneuvering, but they soon changed course, and Gideon had enough of a lead that he'd reach Lord Ballinger's before her. She'd have to find a place to wait until he departed.

GIDEON PACED the pavement in front of Ballinger's townhouse as clouds filled the early afternoon sky, effectively ending the few hours of blue skies and warm sunlight Londoners had been blessed with in the morning.

Ballinger's staff still claimed the nobleman was away from home. Paying calls, according to the very upright and unfriendly butler he'd encountered before. Gideon suspected Ballinger was doing his damnedest to evade a police investigation.

The butler had offered a sitting room for Gideon to wait in, but sitting still had never suited him.

He pulled out his pocket watch, and strode off to find a hansom. He'd send a constable to await Ballinger and ensure that when the man did deign to return home, he'd stay there—or take a trip to Vine Street station—to answer his questions.

Even as he searched for a free cab, he couldn't help glancing back toward Ballinger's address. It would be just his luck to drive away as the man returned.

Then he swept a look across the green opposite Ballinger's townhouse, and one figure stood out.

Electra.

She stood near a clutch of plane trees, still as a statue, her head turned away as if that might keep him from noticing her. But he'd always noticed her. He feared he always would.

His first thought came with a surge of irritation. She shouldn't be here. He'd told her to go home.

His second thought came with a sigh of resignation. Of course she was here, right where he didn't wish her to be.

Gideon started toward her, his boots clicking on the pavement. She didn't look his way. She waited, as she always did, for him to come to her. As if she had all the time in the world, and none of it belonged to him.

"You were meant to go home," he said once he reached her.

She turned her head, calm and cool. "You know I rarely do what I'm meant to."

Rain began to drizzle down, and she looked up at the sky as if pleased.

She wore a dark burgundy gown today, the day suit elegant and tailored, with jet buttons at the wrists of her black gloves. Raindrops began to dapple her skirts, and he had the sudden urge to pull her beneath cover. As if that would protect her.

"He's not in, I take it." She nudged her chin toward Ballinger's home.

"No."

"You're at the end of your patience with him."

He stared at her, disturbed that she read him so well. That he failed to control his emotions as well as he thought he did.

"Am I so obvious?"

"To me, yes."

He didn't respond. Couldn't trust what might come out if he did.

"I'm going back to Vine Street," he told her instead. "Might I dare to hope you'll return to Russell Square?"

"Perhaps I should."

He tried not to show how much it relieved him. "If we ask the driver to go by way of Marylebone Road, we could share a cab."

"It's completely out of your way."

"For six pence?" Gideon held his arm out. "I'd call that peace of mind at a bargain."

She shocked him by actually doing as he wished her to, taking his arm and walking with him back toward Harley Street.

The cabbie tipped his hat when Gideon directed him to Russell Square, and then they were off in the open-front carriage. Luckily, the rain had decided to let up.

"Do you think he killed her?" Electra tried in a matter-of-fact tone.

Gideon arched a look her way. "I've not yet collected sufficient evidence to answer that question, though I wish I had."

"What does Lord Becknell look like?"

"Dark hair, dark eyes. He has an air of command about him."

"Not so unusual for a nobleman."

"Indeed." Gideon focused on the even, familiar clip of the horses' hooves on macadam to keep him from saying more. She'd always had a way of getting him to confess things, to reveal more than he should.

"I think Lady Becknell feared he was lying to her about something."

"Did she say as much?"

"She said she distrusted everyone but wanted the truth." She took a breath and added, "And when she spoke of deception, I saw a dark-haired, dark-eyed man."

"He was in Oxfordshire."

"Have you verified that?"

Gideon shook his head at her audacity, but it shouldn't have surprised him. "Would you prefer to run this investigation, Electra?"

Those extraordinary eyes of hers fixed on his face, and one black brow winged up the slightest bit. "If only women were allowed to do such things."

He had, of course, verified the trip via his lordship's valet, though he suspected Finch would say whatever was necessary to cover for his employer. It irked him that the valet could produce no train stub for the journey. He'd also had a telegram sent off to the hunting party's host, Lord Ansley, and was still awaiting the nobleman's confirming reply.

Electra fell silent.

Gideon found that almost as disturbing as quizzing him about the case. He'd spent many a day in his life curious about what thoughts were in her head. If he believed in the possibility of any human being seeing beyond the five senses, he might be inclined to believe it of Electra. She'd often noticed things others missed, but he'd ascribed that to being the daughter of a stellar detective. He could never accept that such knowing came from anything other than her curiosity and cleverness.

When the cabbie pulled along the pavement in front of the Redmayne townhouse, Gideon climbed out first to help Electra down.

"I hope you're able to locate Ballinger," she told him.

"I will."

When he made no move to return to the hansom, she eyed him warily.

"I'm fully capable of walking through the front door on my own, Gideon."

"I have no doubt, but indulge me. Let me escort you."

There had been hundreds of these battles of wills between them in the time they'd known each other. Gideon often won, not because he possessed some strength of character Electra did not, but because impatience made her view the battle itself as foolish.

"Very well." She started off without him and Gideon lengthened his strides to catch up to her at the same moment a gentleman approached along the pavement.

"Miss Electra Poole?"

The gentleman wore expensive clothes and carried himself like a man of consequence. Despite Gideon's presence a few steps behind Electra, the stranger all but ignored him.

"I am Electra Poole," she affirmed, then reached out a gloved hand to the stranger. "And I believe you are Lord Ballinger, are you not?"

She flicked a look Gideon's way. "This is Inspector Pierce. He has some questions for you, my lord."

The balding blond nobleman's sharp features tightened, and he assessed Gideon as if noticing him for the first time. "Inspector, I am content to answer your questions, but first I have a few that I must put to Miss Poole."

Electra didn't respond to the nobleman. She turned a look Gideon's way. To his very great shock, she was, in essence, giving him leave to decide how to handle Ballinger now that he had the man in his sights.

But then the edge of her mouth inched up, such a slight shift in her expression that someone who was not used to watching her closely might not notice.

Gideon noticed.

She was getting her way. It seemed, just as she'd suggested, they would be speaking to Lord Martin Ballinger together.

He gave her a nod as slight as her smile, and she immediately turned and ushered them into the Redmaynes' townhouse.

Lord Martin Ballinger looked like a man who'd been born to privilege. He wore a pinky ring with a diamond glinting at its center, a stickpin containing a flashing, faceted ruby, and a walking cane topped with polished gold.

Yet all of that contrasted with the tremor in his hands, the quiver in his mouth, and his inability to remain still when he took a seat. His knee began bouncing almost immediately.

The anxious energy that surged through him pulsed in the air around him too—anxiety and grief that seemed to tinge the air a dark green. What Electra did not perceive from the man was guilt.

"You were at Becknell House on Sunday evening, Lord Ballinger," Gideon said.

Ballinger drew in a breath and gritted his teeth. He'd wished to speak to her before Gideon had a chance to question him, but she would not allow him to avoid providing information that might assist Gideon's investigation any longer.

That was the priority.

Electra suspected all the man wanted from her was insight into Helen Becknell's thoughts, likely regarding himself, and she had very little to offer him on that score.

"I was, Inspector." With a palm braced atop his walking

stick, he lifted one finger to point at Electra. "Miss Poole saw me there, if briefly, and can confirm it."

"Miss Poole made herself available to assist the investigation immediately and has indeed confirmed it." It wasn't like Gideon to reveal emotion when conducting an inquiry, but he didn't wholly manage to keep the bite of irritation from his tone. "Tell me about your visit to Lady Becknell, Lord Ballinger."

"She is a close friend and had been suffering distress. I wished to offer my support."

"Support of what manner?"

"Well, reassurance, consolation, whatever she needed."

"What matter distressed her?"

The question caused Ballinger to snap his head up. He stared straight at Electra, and his thoughts came to her clear and unwavering. *Did she love him?* He meant Mr. Fox. Jealousy mixed with grief surrounded him. But was it jealousy deep enough to murder the woman he loved? And she did sense his love for her—it was there at the center of the other emotions. A needful, desperate sort of love that was never fully returned as he wished it to be.

"My lord?" Gideon prompted.

Ballinger shifted in his chair as if uncomfortable and wrestling with the answer.

"Helen was considering a separation from Becknell. I had offered to aid her in that goal, in any way she might require assistance. I even offered one of my properties for her exclusive use. But there was a complication."

"What complication?"

"Helen was with child." Ballinger arched both brows, notched his chin up. "Our child. I loved her. I still love her." The man's voice broke and his eyes went glassy.

Electra wondered if it was genuine grief.

"And that's what the argument was about?"

Ballinger's brows fell as he frowned. "What argument?"

"You were overheard, and Lady Becknell seemed disheveled after speaking to you."

Ballinger's grieved look vanished and he smirked, then let out a puff of laughter. "The housemaid told you, I take it."

Electra knew Gideon did not like exposing those who'd given him key information in an investigation. Her father had been the same. Too many times, one murder multiplied into others as the killer attempted to keep their secrets hidden.

Gideon refused to confirm Ballinger's assumption, but as Grace was the only one home after Electra departed, there could be no one else who'd overheard them.

"You know she's tupping Becknell, don't you? The housemaid. Fool girl fancies he's in love with her."

Gideon said nothing but bent his head to notate Ballinger's claim in his notebook.

Electra understood that it was more than a mere matter of recording facts. The pauses often prompted witnesses to fill the silence and say more.

"Becknell was unfaithful to Helen from the very night they were married. He confessed it to her once the vows were made. Once she was trapped. It's a wonder the man can keep track of all his trulls."

Gideon lifted his head and fixed the man with a stare, one brow arched. "Fidelity seems to be lacking on both sides, my lord, does it not?"

"No," Ballinger thundered back. "Not in the way you mean. What Helen and I had was the result of a decade of devotion on my part. Becknell made a bloody sport of infidelity, then had the gall to condemn Helen. We loved each other, and there was nothing tawdry in it."

Electra wished Gideon could read her mind because she was desperate for him to mention Lucan Fox, so that they could see Ballinger's reaction. If he and Lady Becknell rowed about anything, it was surely her entanglement with the young artist. Yet Ballinger acted as if he was the only man Helen Becknell had ever truly cared for.

"Did she not tell you as much, Miss Poole?" The nobleman's eyes were a much darker blue than Helen Becknell's but just as fretful.

"She did not, my lord."

That shocked him—a flash of surprise, then anger, tightened his features. For some reason, he believed that Helen Becknell had summoned a psychic medium to discuss her relationship with him.

"Well, what did she tell you? Why did she seek you out at all?"

Electra swallowed and glanced at Gideon. He dipped his chin once.

"She was concerned that a gentleman was deceiving her. And she wanted to contact her brother, who I take it had passed on."

Ballinger dropped his head, and his shoulders slumped a bit. "My God, she would not let it go."

"Let what go?" Electra leaned forward, sensing that this was the thread that would lead to answers.

"Helen had no brother. Confirm it with Beatrice if you like, but they had no brother." Ballinger gestured toward Electra. "This is about the bloody locket, isn't it?"

Loathing. That's the feeling that surrounded Ballinger like a fog at the mention of the locket.

Electra reached down into the folds of her skirt, into her pocket, and then extracted the burnished gold keepsake Helen Becknell had been determined to pass to her the night she died.

"This locket?"

Ballinger's mouth gaped open. "How did you come by that?" He glared at her. "Did you steal it that night?"

"I'm not a thief, my lord. Lady Becknell gave it to me."

Ballinger jerked his head back. "She'd never do such a thing. Never."

"Whose hair is in this locket?" Even after carrying it with her for days, holding it in her hands, trying to pull any further information from it, she'd felt and seen nothing.

The nobleman stilled, saying nothing. His whole body seemed tense, as if he was on the verge of striking out or breaking. Electra expected him to stand and storm out of the house.

"She told me the hair was her son's," he finally said, his voice pained. "A child she'd had in her youth, before her marriage. He did not survive long. Just hours after she delivered him."

Electra's mind shifted to the images she'd seen. The small grave. *I loved him then. I love him now.*

"Lady Becknell asked me about him, whether I could contact him beyond the veil."

Gideon let out an almost inaudible groan.

"She seemed relieved when I told her I could not."

Ballinger snapped his head up and locked eyes with Electra. "Damn you."

Gideon shot up from his chair and stepped toward the nobleman. "Mind yourself, Ballinger, how you speak to Miss Poole."

Electra felt a thrum of excitement at the base of her throat. "Why does that anger you?" They were close to something. Ballinger was some kind of key, but she wasn't certain how.

"Because you gave her hope!" he shouted.

Gideon stepped in front of Ballinger, blocking Electra's view of him.

Electra tipped her head to look around him. "Hope for what?"

"She'd become obsessed with the notion that her son still lived. That he'd been taken from her and hidden away. I told her it was nonsense. Hell, even Becknell told her as much, but she wanted to believe it."

Electra now understood that the deception Lady Becknell feared from husband was about whether the child was dead or alive.

"I begged her." Ballinger's voice broke, his shoulders curled inward, and he moaned as if he might weep. "I begged her to go away with me that night. We'd raise *our* child. Be happy."

"What time did you leave Becknell House, Lord Ballinger?"

The nobleman looked up at Gideon. "About eight in the evening. She insisted I go. Said she would not leave London until matters with her supposed son were settled."

"You went home?"

Ballinger nodded, then tightened his hold on his walking stick.

"Can your staff verify when you returned, my lord?" Gideon asked, his stoic tone a stark contrast to Ballinger's emotional one.

"You doubt me, Inspector?"

"It's a murder investigation, my lord. It is my prerogative to doubt everyone."

Chapter Eight

Gideon would not let Ballinger's emotional display or bursts of anger deter him.

The man had proven useful, if only in revealing this new thread regarding a son of Lady Becknell's. Gideon couldn't yet tell if it was a thread that would lead him anywhere, but it needed to be followed to its end, nonetheless.

If Ballinger was being honest, which Gideon would have confirmed with the man's staff, then he was likely not her ladyship's killer. Unless, of course, he'd placed strychnine in something she consumed long after he departed.

The only thing that seemed entirely believable about the man was that he loved Helen Becknell, though it seemed a rather grasping kind of love.

He gave Ballinger time to collect himself, then Gideon returned to his chair.

And immediately regretted it.

"Did she truly say nothing about me that night?" he asked Electra, the anger in his tone now more like beseeching.

"She did not." Electra watched the man intently and had done so since they sat down, as if trying to read him.

Despite himself, Gideon wanted to know what she made of Lord Ballinger. Did she believe his emotional displays were genuine?

"Are you acquainted with Lucan Fox, my lord?" Gideon spoke the words quietly, calmly.

"I do not keep company with such fools," Ballinger gritted out. "It's said he beds every woman he paints, but Helen vowed that was not the case with her."

Gideon felt Electra watching him.

"You doubted her," she said.

The nobleman's skin turned ruddy. "I tried not to, but I did want her for my own. That I will not deny."

Gideon assessed Ballinger, wondering about the man's obvious jealousy and what it might drive him to.

"Do you have any notion of who might have wished her harm?" Gideon hoped to reveal Ballinger's bias.

"Yes, Inspector, I'm afraid I do. Philip Becknell. He had done her violence in the past, and I fear he discovered Helen's plan to leave him."

Electra shifted out of the corner of Gideon's eye, standing up from the settee where she'd been seated and starting across the room.

"Thought I'd ring for tea," she murmured, but she didn't make it to the bell pull.

She tripped and reached out for Lord Ballinger's shoulder to steady herself.

Ballinger reached up to grip her arm. "Steady on, Miss Poole."

For a moment, she stood frozen, her hand on Ballinger, his hand on her. When the moment stretched on, Gideon stood and went to her, lifting a hand to her back.

"Are you all right?"

A glassy, dazed look had come into her eyes, then the sharpness he was used to returned when she dropped her hand from Ballinger's shoulder.

"I'm perfectly well," she said cooly, inching away from Gideon's touch. "Thank you, my lord," she told Ballinger.

The man made a sound of acknowledgement, but Electra didn't continue toward the bell pull. She took a seat at the far edge of the room. Gideon resumed his seat too.

When Gideon glanced at her to assure himself that she was indeed recovered from the odd moment, she shook her head with the slightest of movements.

"I have no more questions for you at this time, Lord Ballinger, but I trust you'll make yourself available if I do."

"Of course." Pushing up to his feet with his hand braced on his walking stick, Ballinger focused all his attention on Electra. "You truly have nothing to tell me? Is there no message Helen has for me?" he asked. "Or must I employ your services myself to contact her?"

Gideon resisted the urge to answer for her.

"I am not accepting commissions at this time, Lord Ballinger, and I do not believe I can contact Lady Becknell."

"You possess no genuine abilities then?" Ballinger demanded.

Rather than answer, Electra turned a look Gideon's way. It seemed she was on the verge of asking him a question, but then she faced the nobleman with an emotionless mask and a half-smile.

"None that would provide you with what you're seeking, my lord."

"I see." Ballinger tapped his walking stick on the carpet twice. "Then good day to you, madam."

With a nod in Gideon's direction, the man strode quickly toward the door as if eager to be done with both of them.

Only when Gideon shut the door behind him did Electra let

out the breath she'd apparently been holding. She stood and began pacing, then laid a hand at the base of her throat.

He expected her to explain, to divulge whatever was clearly troubling her, but she remained quiet. Gideon failed to remain patient.

"What is it?" he asked her, praying she wasn't about to claim some psychical nonsense.

"He didn't do it," she said as she paced, not even glancing his way. "He left when he said he did. Went home. Drank himself into a stupor."

Gideon drew in a sharp breath, closed his eyes, and willed himself not to say something that would offend or hurt her. "And you know this because, what? You touched him."

"Yes." She stopped, pivoted toward him, and held him in her blue-green glare. "I don't know all the rules of my abilities, but I know that I see the most when I touch a living person."

"I can't take that as factual."

"No, I understand that part, but if you trust me at all, or ever did, then I can only tell you that I saw it. And, more often than not, what I see is true." She crossed her arms. "Or comes true."

Gideon's leg bounced as he sat, considering all that Ballinger said and what he did not.

"He loved her," Electra affirmed, as if she knew the contents of the man's heart. "He would not have killed her."

"Even if he knew she was carrying Lucan Fox's child instead of his?"

"I don't think Lady Becknell ever told him that."

"You don't think? Your surmises are not based on fact, Electra." Gideon got to his feet, folded his notepad over, and placed it in his pocket.

"But the logical hypothesis is that it was someone in the household. Someone close to her." She tapped her bottom lip. "I need to speak to Lord Becknell."

"Good God, Electra. And do what? Stumble into him, lay hands on him, and know whether he's a killer?"

She actually blushed at that. It had been years since he'd seen a blush on Electra's cheeks, and it made him feel something he didn't wish to name.

"Do you not see," he began quietly, "that *if* you do stumble into the killer, you put yourself in mortal danger?"

"Particularly if they, unlike you, believe I have abilities beyond the explicable, you mean?"

"Yes," Gideon said dryly, "especially then."

A painting on the wall behind him seemed to fascinate her. She focused on the spot, and Gideon expected some sharp retort.

Instead, she strode toward him, as close as she'd been to Ballinger moments ago.

"I appreciate that you are concerned for my welfare."

Gideon's tie seemed to tighten at his throat.

"And I promise you." She gripped his sleeve for the briefest moment and then let go. "I do not have a death wish."

Her voice had dropped low, and he found himself bending toward her.

"But I failed to warn a lady before she died. I feel guilt for that, and only finding her killer will relieve it."

A little ripple of shock rattled through him because he had to fight the urge to give in to her. But then logic and reason saved him.

"I understand guilt, Ellie." The nickname spilled out, and only after he heard himself say it did he realize how thoroughly she still had him in her thrall. "Electra," he corrected. "But as to finding Lady Becknell's killer, that is *my* job. Not yours."

"I know," she said a bit too brightly. "There's no room for ladies in the police force at all. You probably think I should be content with finding myself a husband—"

"I didn't say that." Indeed, the very notion irritated him. "What I am saying is that I will find Lady Becknell's killer, and you must step back from this investigation."

After a long sigh, she nodded. "Very well."

Gideon didn't trust it. Her capitulation had come too easily. "And you'll stop meddling?"

"I won't hamper your efforts in any way."

It *sounded* accommodating, but he still didn't trust it.

"Should I ring for tea?"

"No, I'm sorry, but I must be on my way." He genuinely regretted turning her down. Tea and conversation with her was something he'd missed. "Time is running out before the inquest, and there are a few others I must speak to."

"Then I hope they're fruitful conversations."

Gideon couldn't read her the way she could read him. He'd never been able to, but as he took his leave, he had a terrible feeling he'd lost and she'd won.

After she'd walked him to the Redmaynes' front door and he'd donned his hat and collected his gloves, his mind felt a bit less befuddled, and he remembered something he needed from her, beyond her vow to stop meddling.

"The locket. May I have it?"

"Oh." She blinked, then frowned. "Lady Becknell seemed to want me to have it."

"I understand, but it will be helpful with the questioning I mean to conduct today."

She reached into her pocket. "You'll return it to me?"

He nodded. He believed Electra's claim that Lady Becknell had slipped it into her pocket. As it seemed to have been one of the lady's last acts, he couldn't see a reason to gainsay it.

At his agreement, she reached for his hand and deposited the locket in his palm.

After striding from the Redmaynes' house, he made his way

down the pavement to hail a cab. Once inside the hired hansom, Gideon leaned his head back against the carriage's wall, holding tight to the locket Electra had passed to him. Her fingers had brushed his palm. He hated that he'd noticed and that he was still thinking about it now.

The case. That's where he needed all of his focus, all of his control.

He'd yet to speak to the one person who might potentially have the most insight into Helen Becknell's personal entanglements, as well as her family history: her sister, Beatrice Linwood.

As the vehicle carried him toward Mayfair, he did his best to keep his mind on the case—the facts he'd learned, the witnesses and suspects he'd questioned. But too much of his attention remained on the fact that he'd touched Electra, that she'd touched him. He'd vowed long ago to put any feelings for her beyond friendship to rest. He reminded himself of that now. Forcefully.

London's busy thoroughfares gave way to white-washed townhouses as they approached Hanover Square, and something teased at his mind, as insistent as someone tapping on his shoulder.

He looked down and realized he still held Lady Becknell's locket in his hand and was mindlessly stroking his thumb across the burnished, rounded top.

Why had the viscountess been so determined to slip the thing into Electra's pocket?

Electra felt oddly bereft without the locket in her skirt pocket, though even after days in her possession, it had revealed nothing else, no matter how many times she touched it.

She continued pacing awhile, even after Gideon's departure. Rattled by that brief moment when she'd touched Gideon. And unsettled by Lord Ballinger too. The nobleman had a draining energy, as if sharing space with the man required a great deal of her, though Gideon had put most of the questions to him.

She'd felt such a thing only once before, when she'd touched a lady at one of her sittings who'd been almost crazed with fresh grief over her daughter's death. Both that lady and Lord Ballinger were like open conduits, their feelings so raw and powerful that they overtaxed Electra's abilities.

Crossing her arms, she recalled the odd energy between herself and Gideon too. For a moment, she thought he might relent. She'd seen something shift in his gaze, but then he'd lived up to her every expectation by being maddening and resolutely determined to refuse any help she could offer.

But it wouldn't stop her.

She went up to the room Cordelia had designated as hers, even after Electra had decided to carve out a bit of independence and secure her room at the boarding house.

In truth, she preferred residing with Cordelia.

The narrow boarding house room was too quiet, giving her too much time to think about the past.

In the Redmayne household, there were always servants bustling about, even if Cordelia was away or Kit wasn't visiting.

Up in her room, she went straight to her writing desk in the corner and withdrew her journal. For nearly half an hour, she documented all she'd seen, sensed, and experienced at Becknell House, at Lucan Fox's townhouse, and during today's visit with Lord Ballinger.

Only when her hand began to cramp did she sit back and read over her notes.

Though she could not be absolutely certain, she suspected

Gideon would have headed straight back to Becknell House and was likely there even now.

Which meant she couldn't go back to Mayfair today, though she intended to at the first opportunity.

Beatrice Linwood would know more about the matter of a lost child. And Electra was determined to find some reasonable way to lay her hand, if even for a moment, on Lord Philip Becknell.

When she'd done so with Martin Ballinger, she'd been swamped with feelings of loss and grief, and she'd observed the argument he'd had with Lady Becknell through his eyes. He'd begged her to leave her husband, promised her his protection, and offered her a home. When she'd refused him, he'd been devastated and returned to his home to down in an entire decanter of whiskey.

Electra's every sense was that Lady Becknell's death was a shock to Martin Ballinger. Whoever Helen Becknell had cried out to as she fell, Electra felt certain it was not Ballinger.

But who was it? Glancing at the lines in her journal, Lucan Fox's name caught her eye. Had he gone to Becknell House that night after everyone else departed?

Two quick raps on her bedchamber door brought Electra to her feet.

"Visitor for you, Miss Poole," Annie, one of the Redmaynes' housemaids called.

Electra opened the door. "I'm not expecting anyone. Who is it, Annie?"

"Miss Dobbs?" she offered in a questioning tone. "Said you'd know her and would wish to speak with her."

"I do know who she is. Thank you."

"She's in the parlor, miss. Should I bring tea?"

"I'll ring for tea if she stays awhile." Electra smoothed out the skirt of her dress and hurried down the stairs, curious why the Becknell housemaid would come to her. Curious too about how the girl managed to get away from her duties.

Electra stepped into the parlor to find Grace pacing as she'd done earlier. She twisted her hands together, mumbling something Electra couldn't make out.

"Grace?"

"Oh, miss." She rushed to Electra, tears welling in her eyes. "Please tell me what I should do."

"Tell me what's upset you, and I'll help if I'm able to." Electra gestured toward two chairs. "Shall we sit?"

Grace nodded, though even as she made her way to the damask-covered chair, her movements were jerky, betraying her anxious distress.

"It's Jacob, miss," she said once she'd settled onto the gilded chair and pulled a handkerchief from her pocket. "He's left without a word."

"Jacob Finch? The footman?"

Grace shook her head. "He's the master's valet." Tears began to spill down Grace's cheeks.

"Was he an admirer of yours?" Electra reached for her, only with the intention of offering comfort, not to seek anything. But the minute she touched the girl's overheated skin, a shiver raced down her spine.

Grace Dobbs was terrified.

The young maid made a half laugh, half choking sound. "No, he never fancied me that way. Especially after he found out—" She stopped mid-sentence, her eyes going wide. Then she looked down at where Electra had touched her. "Could you tell when you touched me?"

"I could only sense that you're frightened. Do you want to tell me why? And what it has to do with Jacob Finch."

For several minutes, Grace sniffed back tears and twisted

her handkerchief into a tangle. "I don't owe him no loyalty anymore, do I?"

"Mr. Finch?" Electra had sensed that the young man felt guilt, but nothing about why.

"No." The girl swiped at her tears. "Philip. Lord Becknell."

"I don't understand, Grace." Though Electra recalled Lord Ballinger's claim about Grace and Lord Becknell, she'd doubted the truth of it. But maybe the nobleman had been correct.

"I thought he loved me. He said as much once." She cried in earnest, bowing her head.

Electra rose from her chair and went and knelt beside Grace, stroking her back as she wept.

"I was a fool." Her breathing remained ragged, but the tears had stopped. "How could I think he'd love the likes of me?"

"He sounds rather awful." Electra recalled Philip Becknell's face from that moment during her sitting with Lady Becknell. She'd sensed a kind of magnetism, or that Helen saw him in such a way. But if he'd taken advantage of his housemaid, he was a blackguard. Plain and simple.

"I wish he were." Grace twisted her mouth ruefully. "Would make it easier."

Electra straightened and returned to her chair, turning toward Grace. "May I ask what this has to do with Jacob Finch?"

"He lied for Philip." She tsked at herself. "For Lord Becknell. He often did."

"You mean about going to Oxfordshire?"

Grace pressed her lips together and nodded. "Some other lady was with his lordship all weekend. Jacob always told me that the master had a bevy of them. I didn't want to believe him."

"Was Lord Becknell in London last weekend, Grace?"

"Very likely." She shrugged. "I don't know for sure, but when Jacob ran off..."

Electra still didn't understand Jacob Finch's motivation for leaving his post. "Did Jacob know something about Lord Becknell's involvement in Lady Becknell's death?"

The girl's eyes widened. "Now, he never told me that, miss. I swear it." She gnawed at her lip. "But if Jacob told anyone that the master was in town last Sunday, wouldn't the Inspector think Philip'd done it?"

"Inspector Pierce would seek evidence. Suspicion alone wouldn't be enough. Where was Lord Becknell on Sunday?"

"I don't know. I swear it. I went to my aunt's house after you left that evening. And Jacob only told me they were never at any hunting party." Grace stared at Electra intently. "You'll tell the inspector, won't you?"

"Or we could summon him and you could tell him yourself."

"No, miss." The maid shook her head firmly. "I should go back to the house, shouldn't I?"

"Are you afraid of returning? If so, you could stay here. Or at my boarding house with me." Electra wanted to protect the girl if she could.

"I mean to speak to Mrs. Evans about giving me a character. I won't go like Jacob did."

"I can speak to Lady Redmayne and perhaps we can find you a new post."

"Oh, thank you, miss." Grace pressed her hands together palm to palm. "Thank you. I must get out. Can't watch him marry some other lady. Swan about as if he's some perfect gentleman. I can't."

"I understand."

Grace glanced at the long clock and her eyes widened. "Lord help me, I've been gone a long while. I must go, miss."

Electra stood as Grace rose from her chair. "Do you have any idea where Mr. Finch may have gone?"

"He said he had a sister, a nurse who worked at the Whitechapel Hospital. Margaret, he called her, but that's all I know about his family." Grace started toward the drawing room door.

"Just one more question, Grace."

She turned a look over her shoulder. "Yes, miss?"

"Did Lady Becknell ever mention having a son?"

Grace looked utterly confused by the question. "No, miss, not to me. They had no children, but I suspect she wanted a son. Lord Becknell did. Needed an heir and all."

"Thank you, Grace." Electra followed her to the door. "I can have one of the footmen fetch you a hansom."

"I can find my own." Grace bobbed a quick curtsy and was off toward the foyer.

Electra followed and waited until Mrs. Hurst, the Redmayne's housekeeper, returned her cloak and gloves.

"Remember, Grace, you have a place to go. Come back here if you feel unsafe." Electra had sensed fear from Grace Dobbs from the first moment she'd met her on Sunday night.

She hoped Grace could get a reference from Mrs. Evans and find a new post as soon as possible.

Chapter Nine

Beatrice Linwood wore her grief with a kind of stoic dignity Gideon had often seen in ladies of her class. But there were a few noticeable cracks in her decorum —a tremor now and then, red-rimmed eyes, shaking hands as she lifted her teacup to take the first sip.

Gideon guessed her to be in her mid or later forties. She wore an elegant mourning gown, jet earrings, and a bracelet with a rounded glass circle at its center containing a lock of hair. When the light hit it, he noted that the hair was reddish-brown, much like the curl of hair in the locket resting in his waistcoat pocket.

"Thank you for taking the time to speak with me, Miss Linwood," he began, then took a sip of tea.

Instinct told him that Helen Becknell's spinster sister would require a soft touch, and that if he rushed this conversation, he'd get far less from her than if he took his time, wielded his best manners, and played the proper gentleman.

"Of course, Inspector. I must thank you for looking into this matter so diligently." She held her shoulders back like a lady schooled in the ways of poise and propriety. "Though I know you may not wish to tell me, I do wonder what you've found thus far."

"As you say, there is a great deal I am not at liberty to share, but it is early days. But rest assured, ma'am, I will discover the truth of your sister's death."

The second the word "death" left his lips, Miss Linwood flattened her mouth and tears welled in her eyes. "Forgive me, Inspector."

"There's nothing at all to forgive. I hope you'll accept my condolences for your loss."

She nodded and slipped a black-edged handkerchief from the sleeve of her gown to dot at her eyes.

He sipped more tea. It was far too weak for his taste, but he mirrored Miss Linwood's movements, hoping to put her at ease.

"May I ask you a few questions?"

"Of course." She sat her teacup aside and folded her hands primly in her lap.

"I understand you were away from home on Sunday evening. Might you tell me where you were?"

"Ah, yes. I was visiting Mrs. Dunstan. I met her via the charity Mrs. Ellsworth organizes. She's a retired schoolteacher and has no family to visit on Sundays. So I've made a habit of calling in to see her."

Gideon had pulled out his notepad and took his time noting the details she offered. "What is Mrs. Dunstan's given name and her address?"

"Agnes. And she lives in Islington. Number Five Compton Terrace." She smiled softly as if remembering the lady. "Such a dear soul."

"A bit of a journey via carriage. Did you visit her overnight?"

"No, not at all. I left her home at about nine in the evening, and then I called in on Lady Ashcombe, who'd fallen ill. I did stay with Rosalind overnight as she seemed so poorly."

"Does she not have servants to tend to her?"

She blinked and looked a bit taken aback. "Of course, but would you rather be cared for in an illness by servants or a friend, Inspector?"

During the rare times he was ill, Gideon tended to grit his teeth and never wished to impose on anyone to care for him, certainly not a friend. Since the death of Erasmus Poole, he had few he called friends, aside from a few fellow officers.

For the briefest moment, he imagined Electra fussing over him, tending him with poultices and possets, and almost chuckled. Then he looked up into Beatrice Linwood's grief-stricken eyes and felt chagrined for losing focus.

"What time did you return to Becknell House?"

"Later on Monday morning." Her voice had gone taut. "I could not comprehend why there were so many carriages out front." She sniffed. "Mrs. Evans met me at the door, tried to steer me past..." With a little shake of her head, she seemed to collect herself and lifted her chin, squaring her shoulders. "She is the one who told me about Helen. We thought it must have been some terrible accident, but it seems you've found facts to contradict that." She tipped her head and studied him.

"We're treating the death as suspicious until the coroner's inquest, ma'am. Ultimately, the inquest's jury will decide." Strict accuracy was the safest course until he knew more about the goings-on in the Becknell household.

"I've debated whether to attend the inquest, but I suppose I must. I owe it to Helen to face this dreadful thing that's happened."

Gideon offered a noncommittal nod. "If foul play is found, do you have any notion who might have wished her ladyship ill?"

"If an intruder has been ruled out, Inspector, then I truly can't say. Helen was beloved. She had many friends. An indulgent husband. A passel of admirers."

"Admirers?"

"Oh, I mean only that she was admired by many. By men for her beauty and charm, by other ladies for her kindness and loyal friendship."

Gideon had bent to note anything she might reveal, but he raised his head at that glowing description. "She sounds like an extraordinary lady." It was common for family members to see their lost loved one in an idealized manner. He understood that, but it did him little good when digging for the truth.

"Indeed, Inspector." She lifted her teacup with trembling hands and sipped more tea.

"So she never fell out of favor with anyone? Not ever?"

Beatrice Linwood's dark eyes seemed to cool a bit at the implication in his question. "I acknowledge she was not perfect, Inspector. Of course, there were disagreements."

"Between the two of you?"

She flashed a strained smile. "We were sisters living together under the same roof. Our natures were quite different, even in childhood. So, yes, we clashed at times."

Gideon smiled, trying for affability. "The usual sibling bickering."

"Regrettably, yes. Though in the past few years, we'd overcome our differences. We'd realized there is no use raking over old coals."

"Some of what I've discovered indicates that Lady Becknell was quite distressed on Sunday, and perhaps in the last days of her life." Gideon knitted his brow. "Did you notice her emotional state that night or in the days prior to Sunday?"

Miss Linwood clasped her hands together and stared at the carpet, hesitating. "Helen possessed, as her doctor once told me, a fragile disposition. Nervousness, ennui, melancholia. She tipped from one to the other, and there were even moments of... hysteria." She looked miserable to have made that admission.

Women were confined to asylums for less than the list of conditions Miss Linwood had mentioned.

Gideon jotted down her descriptions, noting how different it was to the paragon she'd described a moment ago.

"It sounds as if she struggled a great deal."

"Yes." She nodded. "That is a kindly way to put it. But she did her best to remedy all of it, though sometimes those efforts went astray."

"Astray?"

Miss Linwood gestured told a folded newspaper on the table. "I read that she consulted a spiritualist." She tsked. "Utter nonsense. Such people could so easily take advantage of Helen. Heaven knows what that charlatan told her."

His hackles rose protectively at the mention of Electra, and at the characterization. Though he did not believe in other-worldly powers, he could not see her as a trickster. Willful. Determined. Reckless, maybe. But whatever she did in the *sittings* she conducted, he suspected her goal was to help others. That had always been her way.

"Would you call your sister a gullible woman then?"

"I do not wish to speak ill of my sister, Inspector. But, yes, at times, she was easily misled." She bent to lift the teapot from a tray on the table between them. "More tea, Inspector?"

"By all means." While she poured, Gideon asked, "Do you have a brother, Miss Linwood?"

Porcelain scratched porcelain as she started at the question, then continued topping up her cup and his as if he hadn't spoken.

Only when she'd taken up her teacup again did she offer, "No, it was just Helen and I."

Gideon ignored his teacup and slid two fingers into his waistcoat pocket, pulling the gold locket out. "Do you recognize this, Miss Linwood?" He held the chain, letting the pendant swing gently, its burnished face glinting in the gaslight.

Beatrice Linwood paled, then seemed to clench her jaw. "Where did you get that?" She forced the words past tensed lips, then stuck out her hand as if demanding he hand the locket over.

He did not. "I collected it during the course of my investigation."

"I would like you to return it to me." She reached her hand out a bit farther.

"That won't be possible, I'm afraid." Gideon tucked it back into his pocket. "But I take it you do recognize the locket."

"Of course, I do. It's mine. A very personal memento." When he'd tucked the locket away, she finally lowered her hand. "How did you come by it, Inspector?"

"I'm afraid I can't disclose that at this time, ma'am."

Miss Linwood worked her jaw, seeming to fight for the composure she'd presented for most of their conversation.

"It contains a lock of hair," Gideon continued. He lifted a finger to indicate her wrist. "Very similar to the lock there in your bracelet."

She cupped her palm over the lock of hair enclosed in a circle of rounded glass at the center of the bracelet's gold band, blocking his view of its contents, or perhaps drawing some comfort from the bit of jewelry.

"Yes, because the hair belongs to the same person." Swallowing hard, she added, "Our mother. Helen and I both had a few keepsakes commissioned after we lost her."

According to Electra, the locket belonged to Helen Becknell. He would have understood if Miss Linwood wished to have the locket returned as a family memento, but why claim it as hers?

Gideon allowed a moment of silence, during which he heard servants conversing loud enough for it to carry into the parlor, though he could not make out their words.

"To your knowledge, Miss Linwood, did your sister ever bear a child?"

"No," she replied as if confused by the question. "She and Philip... Well, it was a source of great sorrow to Helen that she had not yet borne the viscountcy's heir."

She and Gideon locked gazes, and he could detect nothing in her expression. Indeed, she'd returned to the utter poise with which they'd started the conversation.

"Did she often type her letters?"

The change of topic evoked a minor response, the slightest arch of one auburn brow.

"She did." A flicker of a smile lifted her lips. "I could never quite understand her fascination with the contraption. But I assure you the clicking and clacking of its keys could be heard from her chamber almost every day." Her head dropped a fraction at that. "I suppose I shall never hear that sound again."

Gideon dutifully noted her answer, giving her time to compose herself again.

"And who is Edward, Miss Linwood?"

"Edward?" She tipped her head and tensed her brow as if contemplating the question. "I'm not sure I know an Edward of Helen's acquaintance, but she knew so many people. Charity connections, other nobles who were friends of Lord Becknell. I didn't always know all their names." With a slight lift of her slim shoulders, she added, "I'm sorry I can't be more help in that regard."

"You've been most open and helpful, ma'am, and it's much

appreciated." Gideon glanced down at his notes as if he was reading from them. "Just a few more questions if I may."

Beatrice Linwood's slight inclination of her chin was downright regal. "Go on, Inspector."

"Do you know what her ladyship consumed on Sunday evening? Did you dine together?"

"I don't know. And, no, we did not. I was gone by then, on my way to visit Mrs. Dunstan."

"The staff mentioned a sleeping tonic Lady Becknell was known to take. Are you aware of whether she took it on Sunday evening?"

Miss Linwood nodded. "I can only assume she did. It was her habit."

"The housemaid indicated she sometimes took too much."

Her brow pinched together in a frown. "Unfortunately, she sometimes combined it with a glass of port, or she would forget she'd taken a dose and take some again."

"Did that not concern you?"

"It certainly did, and we warned her to take care with the tonic, but Helen did as she pleased."

"We?" Gideon leaned toward her an inch. "Who is we?"

"Lord Becknell and I. And I suspect Mrs. Evans might have too. I believe she was responsible for refilling the tonic at the chemist's. She mentioned that Helen reordered quite frequently."

"More of late than in the past?" he asked.

"Not that I'm aware of."

"Mrs. Evans shared such information with you?"

"She did." There was a flare of pride in her eyes. "You see, in many respects, I manage the household."

Gideon tried not to show his surprise at that admission. "Not her ladyship?"

"It is a...cooperative effort." Dipping her head, she seemed to fight for control of her emotions. "*Was* a cooperative effort." When she looked at him again, her eyes were glassy, tears welling.

He supposed, if Lady Becknell's nervous condition was as severe as her sister claimed, it made sense that her ladyship would need assistance.

"Is that why you came to live with the Becknells, Miss Linwood? To assist with the household."

"Precisely." A smile softened her features. "Siblings help each other, don't they? As the elder sister, I could never deny Helen anything."

Gideon didn't know how siblings behaved, or even if he had any. His mother died when he was seven, and his father had run off long before that. The closest to anything like a sibling he'd ever known was Electra, and his feelings for her were far too complicated to ever think of her in that regard. Though it might have been easier if he had.

As he got lost in his own thoughts, Miss Linwood shifted on her chair, the crinkle of crinoline drawing him from his wool-gathering.

"Do you have any further questions to put to me, Inspector?" She glanced at the mantel clock as if she might have an appointment or some task to get to.

"Not at this time, ma'am."

"Then I'll have Grace see you out." She lifted a polished silver bell from the table beside her and rang it.

But it wasn't Grace who responded to the bell. Mrs. Evans entered the room, looking somewhat harried.

"Please see the Inspector out, Mrs. Evans."

"Yes, madam." Mrs. Evans crossed her hands in front of her while Gideon stood. He offered Beatrice Linwood a nod, then strode out of the drawing room.

Mrs. Evans led him toward the townhouse's front hall at an

oddly quick clip, as if she had better things to be doing and wanted rid of him.

"What poisons do you keep on hand, Mrs. Evans?"

The older woman jerked to a stop and stared at him. "Poisons, Inspector?"

"For vermin. In the kitchens. Many houses use them, do they not?"

Several minutes passed, and Gideon could almost see the moment when the housekeeper understood—or at least suspected—why he was inquiring. "We keep a clean kitchen, Inspector, but do purchase the occasional rodent powder," she finally said. "A note would have been made in my household ledger whenever we purchase it." She pressed a hand to the waist of the white apron pinned to her dress. "Was her ladyship—"

"I cannot say more at this time, Mrs. Evans."

"Would you like to come down and check the ledger?"

Gideon gave a quick dip of his chin. "I would be much obliged."

As they changed course and headed toward the servants' stairs to take them to the kitchen, he asked, "You put through all orders to the chemist yourself?"

"For anything related to the household or kitchen, yes, sir." The lady's voice had taken on a shaky quality.

"What about for Lady Becknell's sleeping tonic?"

Mrs. Evans flicked a glance over her shoulder. "Lady Becknell saw to that herself in most cases, sir."

"I was given to understand you did."

"Oh, I tried, but Lady Becknell insisted she'd type off her own notes to the chemist, and he would send whatever was required via post."

Gideon noted that in his mind. There'd been a law a few

years back that required stricter controls on poisons, a recording of who purchased them and when. He'd check her claim.

"What chemist did she send to?"

"We used Hatchers Chemists, sir."

Inside her narrow office, Mrs. Evans pulled a blue-spined ledger off a shelf and laid it open on her desk. She flipped her finger down one page, then another.

"We last ordered the vermin powder in October." Lifting her gaze to him, she added, "That is quite common as the few that come in do so when the weather turns cold."

"May I see where you keep the poison?"

Her eyes widened. "You suspect someone took poison from within the household?"

"I'm collecting facts, Mrs. Evans, for the inquest tomorrow."

Turning to a cabinet built into the wall behind her, she extracted a key from a collection of them on a brass ring hooked to the waist of her skirt. "I have the only key here, Inspector," she said quietly. Then she unlocked the cabinet.

It contained various cleaning agents, chemicals, and somewhere there must have been camphor, for the scent was sharp.

"The camphor?"

"We use it to keep the moths from the closets," she explained.

"May I?" Gideon asked, already extending his hand toward a bottle labeled "Rat Poison."

"Of course, though I usually only handle it with gloves." She quickly opened a desk drawer and handed him a pair of white cloth gloves such as a footman might wear when polishing silver or serving at table.

Gideon slipped them on as well as he could—they were small. Then he lifted the glass bottle from its shelf. On the label, below the powder's name, was a single word: strychnine. His heartbeat sped in his chest as he noted that the bottle was a little over half full.

"Half has been used in a month's time?"

"Yes, sir. We usually place some down in the cellar in October and sometimes pour more if necessary."

"And no one else has access to your keys?"

The lady froze, opening her mouth as if to speak, and yet no words emerged. Finally, she said, "Others do borrow them on occasion."

"Who?"

Gideon could see the fear in the lady's eyes. She understood how consequential her answer might be.

"Her ladyship, his lordship, Miss Linwood, Mr. Paxton, Mr. Finch, and, once in a very great while, Grace Dobbs."

The keys could hardly be called secure when most of the household had ready access to them.

Lifting the collection of keys on a brass ring, she added, "You see, there are many keys on the ring, and I simply unclip the ring and lend it to whoever requires one of the keys. But they're always returned promptly."

"Who borrowed them most recently?"

Mrs. Evans lifted a hand to tug at the starched collar of her black gown. "Lady Becknell, sir."

"When?"

"On Sunday morning, Inspector. She said she wished to go up to the attic. Didn't say why."

"But she didn't access this cabinet?"

"Not that I'm aware of."

Mr. Paxton strode through Mrs. Evan's open office door, then noticed Gideon's presence.

"Forgive me for interrupting."

"It's quite alright, Mr. Paxton." Mrs. Evans seemed grateful for the interruption.

"I'll be taking this, Mrs. Evans." Gideon lifted the rat poison bottle, then peeled off one glove, wrapped it around the bottle, and slipped it into his coat pocket.

Mr. Paxton's white brows lifted several inches up his forehead. Mrs. Evans' only response was a grim nod.

"Thank you both." Gideon strode past Paxton, who still hovered near the door.

"Still no sign of her?" Mrs. Evans whispered, though not quietly enough.

"Nor him, I'm afraid," Mr. Paxton said gravely.

Gideon pivoted on his heel and returned to the office's doorway. "I couldn't help overhearing. Who were you referring to?"

The butler and housekeeper exchanged a long look.

"His lordship's valet left his post last evening without a word to anyone," Mr. Paxton said, his voice tinged with anger. "Most unprofessional. I thought better of Mr. Finch."

"And Grace Dobbs left the house in the middle of her duties a little more than an hour ago," Mrs. Evans added. "Exasperating girl."

If a murder hadn't occurred in the household but days ago, Gideon might have surmised the two had gone off together, but instinct told him this was something else.

"Send for me if either of them returns, will you?" Gideon asked.

"If you like, Inspector."

"I insist, Mr. Paxton."

Chapter Ten

The weather had turned bitingly cold by the time Gideon headed home at near seven in the evening. He'd returned to the station after meeting with Beatrice Linwood and had been presented with two crucial pieces of information: a telegram from Lord Ansley and a report from a constable inquiring into matters related to the Becknell murder.

Ansley's message was brief. To wit, Lord Becknell had not attended his hunting party in Oxfordshire, which meant the viscount's whereabouts on the evening of his wife's death were unknown.

Constable Thacker's report had been equally intriguing. Lady Ingram, a Mayfair neighbor of the Becknells, returned to her home at nine on Sunday evening and noticed a man exiting Becknell House. She described the gentleman as youthful, blond, and "devilishly handsome."

Lucan Fox, Gideon surmised. If so, the painter had lied about his whereabouts on the night of Lady Becknell's death too. The duchess paramour he'd named had never confirmed or denied his alibi, having made herself unavailable each time a constable called.

Gideon would bet a guinea that Lucan Fox left the marks on her ladyship's neck, and she in turn had scratched the artist's face.

He'd sent word to Dr. Tate, in case he wished to add Fox or Lady Ingraham to the inquest witness list. Gideon needed to locate Becknell's valet, Jacob Finch, to refute Becknell's alibi, but Constable Clegg had not yet turned up any fruitful leads regarding the young man's whereabouts.

Gideon planned to seek out Fox and Becknell before tomorrow's inquest at eleven, but as the hansom rolled into Camden Town, he lifted his hand to rap on the wall.

Why not call on Fox tonight? And Becknell?

Yet before he knocked on the lacquered wood, he spotted a figure on the pavement in front of his house as they turned onto Murray Street. A black-haired, dark-cloaked figure, who turned as his carriage approached.

His first thought was to wonder how Electra had found him. He'd only purchased the house two months ago after years of saving. But what he felt was more dangerous—a flicker of pleasure that she'd sought him out. When she'd cut ties after her father's death, his darkest thoughts told him she no longer wished to associate with a thief's son who her father had found collecting detritus choked up by the Thames.

When he alighted from the carriage, she drew close. "I have information that you must know before the inquest."

"Then come inside and get warm." Gideon unlocked the front door and glanced back at Electra. "I should warn you—"

"Oh, heavens me," Mrs. Perkins exclaimed from the far end of the hall. "Didn't know when to expect you. Never do, do I? I was just on my way out."

His three-day-per-week housekeeper bustled forward, then noticed Electra at his side. The older woman gasped. Electra flinched.

"Mrs. Perkins?" Electra's voice emerged soft, almost awestruck.

Mrs. Perkins opened her arms, and Electra hesitated only a moment before stepping into them. The two—the housekeeper who'd been with the Pooles since before the death of Electra's mother and the girl she'd treasured, having no children of her own—wrapped each other in a long hug.

Tears welled in Mrs. Perkins's eyes and Gideon's throat tightened with unexpected emotion.

"Dear Miss Poole." Mrs. Perkins chuckled. "How good it is to see you." She smiled at Electra with the unique warmth the lady had always exuded.

He and Electra had both been grateful for her care and wisdom, especially as her father had descended into dark, unreachable grief for months.

Then, when he'd died, leaving Electra without a farthing —the man's gambling habit had been his one tragic fault— she'd had no choice but to sell the home they'd all lived in to settle his debts and let the servants who'd served the family go.

Mrs. Perkins cupped Electra's cheek. "I told him we'd see you again." She turned a beaming smile Gideon's way. "And now she's your very first visitor."

Gideon groaned inwardly but gave the woman a smile. A moment later, his mantel clock chimed the seven o'clock hour.

"Oh, do forgive me, but I must be on my way." She gathered her hat and coat from the stand near the door, then turned to Electra. "I hope I'll see much more of you."

"I'd like that." Electra smiled.

Something in Gideon's chest flared to life, and he pushed down the yearning he'd fought for years.

After Mrs. Perkins had gone, he took Electra's cloak and hung it on a peg next to his coat. She stepped into his parlor and went to warm herself by the low-burning fire Mrs. Perkins had laid.

"You might have mentioned." Electra glanced back.

"I should have."

"And I should have kept in touch with her."

"Well, now you can." The notion of her coming to visit again was far too appealing.

When she turned, a shimmer had returned to her eyes. "I'm glad you were able to give her work."

"Oh, she's flush with it now. She splits her time between me and another bachelor a few roads over, and she lives with her niece and her husband to help tend their children."

"I worried about her," she said as she glanced around, taking in his sparsely furnished parlor.

He resisted the urge to ask *And me? Did you worry about me?* Instead, he crossed his arms, embarrassed by his meager decor. Most days, the house was simply the place he returned to in order to eat, sleep, wash, and leave again the next morning.

"Grace Dobbs came to see me," she said quietly, flicking her gaze up to meet his.

"So that's where she went."

"What do you mean?"

"Shall we sit?" Gideon gestured to his mismatched chairs. Electra took the one nearest the fire, then tugged off her gloves.

"I had reason to return to Becknell House," he told her.

"To speak to the sister?"

Gideon lifted a brow. "Yes." He reminded himself that it was a natural conclusion, since Miss Linwood was the person closest to her ladyship he'd yet to speak to, not some preternatural knowledge on Electra's part.

"And?"

"While I was there, I spoke to the housekeeper and butler

again too. They said the valet, Finch, had hied off last evening, and Grace Dobbs left her post midday."

Electra lifted finger and traced it across her brow. "I thought she'd gotten permission, but it seems she had not. She came to Russell Square in quite a state."

"How so?" Gideon leaned forward, arms braced on his knees, hands clasped.

"She said that Jacob Finch had lied for Lord Becknell and that the viscount never went to any hunting party."

"No, he was not in Oxfordshire the night Lady Becknell died," Gideon added.

"You knew?"

"The nobleman he'd claimed to be visiting confirmed it." Gideon imagined what might make a young man leave his post. "Perhaps Finch thinks, or knows, Becknell murdered his wife."

"Mmm." Electra chafed her hands together. "Grace didn't say as much, but his departure seemed to frighten her."

"Frighten her?" Gideon scrubbed a hand across his jaw. "Then she must know something too."

"Or fear the truth." Electra pulled her bottom lip between her teeth—a tell that she was pondering whether to confess something.

"What?" Gideon waited. She'd come to him, so there was no reason to hesitate. Unless she didn't trust him anymore. That thought disturbed him so much, he felt it bone-deep. He never wanted to do anything to forfeit her trust.

"Grace was not just Lord Becknell's housemaid." A blush crept up from the high neck of Electra's gown to wash over her cheeks. She shot him a look as if to emphasize the unspoken fact. "Lord Ballinger was correct."

Some devilish part of him couldn't help asking, "You mean she confirmed that they were lovers?"

The blush deepened. "Yes."

For all her boldness and determination, Electra had always been rather prim about such matters. Apparently, she still was, which intrigued him more than it should have.

"In that case, it's likely Miss Dobbs does know more. Or might have seen something that she didn't recognize the significance of at the time."

Electra smoothed her skirts. "I think that's why she's frightened. So much so that she intends to leave her post too, though she said she'd seek a character from Mrs. Evans first."

Gideon didn't think the girl's odds were good, considering how dismayed the housekeeper had been that Grace abandoned her duties without leave.

When they fell into silence, both of them seeming to ponder the tangle of the Becknells and their circle, Gideon couldn't help studying Electra as she stared at the low-burning fire.

"I could make tea," he offered, a bit too late to be a truly good host.

"I should get back."

"Are you staying with the Redmaynes?"

"Cordelia insisted, and she's hard to gainsay."

Gideon licked his lips and tried—and failed—not to smile. "Very like another lady I know."

She narrowed her eyes at him.

When she stood, he did too. Anxiousness overtook him, a desire to entice her to stay so that they might talk as they once did. Not about a murder case, but about books and history and Shakespeare.

Then another thought struck. An urge that went against every practical and reasonable principle he believed in.

"May I ask you, Electra, when you met with Lady Becknell, how did she present the locket to you?"

Her brows pulled taut as she put on her gloves. "What do you mean?"

"Did she indicate where she'd gotten it or who it might belong to?"

"It was hers." She blinked as if the answer was obvious. "A prized possession, containing the hair of a boy she loved very much. She said it was her brother, and I..." After a moment's hesitation, she fixed him with one of her fierce gazes. He knew them well. "During the sitting, I saw a child's grave, felt her grief for that child. After what Ballinger said, I think it must have been her son."

Gideon forced himself not to critique or question what she'd *seen*, presumably from Lady Becknell's mind. Instead, he reached into his pocket and pulled out the locket by its chain.

He caught up the gleaming pendant, then pressed the latch with his thumb to spring the top open.

Ballinger said Helen believed her child was alive. Was the curl of hair from a child Helen Becknell had once borne, or from their deceased mother, as Beatrice Linwood claimed?

He lifted his gaze to Electra's. There was a question in her eyes.

"What are you thinking?" she whispered.

What he was thinking was only half formed, but something gnawed at him. Gideon used the edge of his finger to slide the hair out of the locket.

Electra made a little sound of dismay.

Gideon inhaled sharply.

He tipped the locket so that she could see the engraved words on the pendant's inner hollow.

Edward J. Linwood
b. 1864

"There was an unfinished letter in her typewriter..." Gideon swallowed, realizing he was pulling her deeper into the case with such revelations, and that he should not do so. He said no more, carefully returned the lock of hair to the locket, and snapped it shut.

"Yes?" Electra prompted.

"Do you think...?" He clenched his jaw against the question he truly wanted to ask. "Did you *sense* that this brother, who may, in truth, have been her son, was still alive?"

Electra's inky lashes swept down, then she lifted her head. "You're asking me about my abilities?"

Gideon knew he was straying into fanciful territory, but he nodded.

She crossed her arms. For a moment, he thought she'd seen the doubt in his eyes and would refuse to tell him anything. Then she began pacing across the only fine thing he'd bought for the house, a pretty blue patterned rug he'd found in a shop on Portobello Road.

He could almost hear her mind whirring.

Finally, she turned to him. "Thinking about it now, and considering what Ballinger said, I suspect her entire intent that night might have been to have me answer that very question."

Gideon felt the tug of excitement that always came when the pieces of a case began to fall into place, or at least seemed as if they might fit together. "The question of whether this Edward was alive?"

"Yes, but she mostly wondered if others were deceiving her. She referred to him as her brother, but her feelings for him were strong, as one might expect of a mother." Electra swallowed and stilled. "She asked if I could reach her deceased mother too."

That, he understood, was what most mediums were sought for—their ability to communicate with the dead.

"Did you?" he asked, tentative and half regretting even implying he might believe in such matters.

"No." Electra shook her head in that firm way of hers. "I don't...wish to speak to the dead."

A tremor seemed to rush through her, then a sharpening of her jaw as if she might be clenching her teeth.

"I tried once and felt as if I was being...submerged. Like that time the wave surprised us in Cornwall and knocked the breath out of me. I don't like the prospect of who might come through, or of losing control. " Her confession was uttered quietly, and he was gratified she'd trust him with it. Admitting any sort of fear or anxiety was not something Electra Poole did often.

Gideon wondered if she was thinking of her own mother, who'd been hospitalized with a lingering illness shortly before Erasmus Poole took him in. The topic she steadfastly refused to broach with Gideon. It was only one of the ways Electra, who he knew so well in some ways, seemed unknowable, as if she was a lady full of secrets.

She lifted a gloved hand to her throat. "I couldn't discern anything about this brother, or son, one way or another. That frustrated her. And she again mentioned a fear of someone deceiving her. A she and a he, but the image I saw was a man. Could it have been this son? Could she have found him?"

He thought again of the unfinished letter, but it proved nothing about Edward Linwood. In grief or loss, it wasn't uncommon to write to a loved one as if they were still present, at least in spirit.

In the midst of an inscrutable case, he sometimes spoke aloud—in the privacy of his office—to Erasmus Poole, as if the man might appear and guide him as he'd done so well in life. And over the past three years, he'd written letters to Electra, not knowing if they'd ever reach her, certain she would never reply.

"We know Lord Becknell *was* deceiving her," Electra stated.

"Obviously, if he was tupping the housemaid." Gideon lifted a hand when the blush flared up her cheeks again. "Forgive me."

She ignored the gesture and went on as if he hadn't made her blush again. "And Lucan Fox does not seem like a man who'd worry for a second about deceiving a lady."

Gideon quirked a brow. "I'm glad you see that and hope you'll steer clear of the man."

She let out a huff that was half laughter, half scoff. "I'm offended that you'd even imagine a man like Lucan Fox could disarm me."

"You are a fearsome creature. Forgive me for forgetting." Gideon chuckled, then Electra did, and it was lovely for all of thirty seconds.

Then she seemed to realize she'd let her defenses slip, and he could all but see the moment she donned her armor once again.

"Well," she said, suddenly ill at ease, "I only came to tell you about Grace's visit and her...entanglement with Lord Becknell."

"And I thank you for it." Even if he would still prefer her nowhere near this investigation. "I intend to speak to him prior to the inquest tomorrow."

She stilled and studied him. He wondered if she was trying to read his thoughts as she claimed to do with others. "Do you know who did this to her, Gideon?"

He ran a hand through his hair, hating that he couldn't answer in the affirmative. "No. Thus far, I've uncovered lies, encountered prevarication, and have a list of suspects in mind. But I do wish I had more."

The disappointment in her eyes hit him like a physical blow. "They picked an optimal time when no one but Helen was known to be at home."

"Lucan Fox was seen exiting the house around nine in the evening." Gideon winced the moment the words were out.

Yet the way Electra's eyes widened as she stepped toward him, her breath quickening with excitement, almost made his slip worth it. "Then it was him. But can you prove he pushed her?"

Of course, she didn't know about the postmortem results. No one did, barring the surgeon who performed the exam, the coroner, Gideon, and whoever had put strychnine in something Lady Helen Becknell ate or drank shortly before her death.

He let out a ragged sigh. "You'll hear this at the inquest tomorrow, though I must ask you to tell no one—even the Redmaynes—before then."

"You have my word." She leaned in, clearly on tenterhooks, all but holding her breath for whatever revelation he might offer.

"Helen Becknell's fall down the stairs did not kill her."

Electra frowned, lines forming below a loose black curl on her forehead.

"She was poisoned shortly before her death. The particular kind of toxin causes a seizure in its victims, which might explain the fall."

"Poisoned?"

Gideon nodded grimly.

"Someone was there," she said immediately, not a shred of doubt in her tone. "She reached out for someone, begged them to help her."

"Who?" Gideon asked, then gritted his teeth. She hadn't been there. She shouldn't *know* any of this.

A STRANGE MIX of relief and uncertainty made Electra pause before answering Gideon's question.

The firelight that lit his sharp jaw and perpetually furrowed brow had turned his eyes to amber. In those eyes she'd once known so well, she saw regret, even as he inquired.

Maybe he regretted sharing anything about the case. Or perhaps he wished he hadn't asked what she'd seen beyond the five senses he trusted.

Moving back to the chair she'd occupied earlier, Electra sat, trying to recall all she'd seen, hoping for some new insight or detail to stand out. The irony didn't escape her that just this morning, she'd told Kit and Cordelia that she wouldn't tell Gideon Pierce any of this.

"I saw no face," she told him quietly. "Just felt Helen's desperation. She reached out, arms straight, almost as if she was grabbing for someone, maybe as she lost her balance. She beseeched them, whoever was there with her, before she fell."

Gideon sat too, hunching forward, toward her. "You see from her perspective?"

"Yes. Her memories, essentially."

"Do you...experience this constantly? With each person you pass on the street or sit next to on an omnibus?"

He was questioning her in the same tone he'd used with Lucan Fox, the tone he likely used with all witnesses and suspects. Cool, unemotional. But his tone didn't match what she saw in his eyes—curiosity and concern.

"No, not constantly." Electra ran her finger along the two buttons at the edge of her sleeve. "When I was younger, things came to me unexpectedly. The emotions of others, for the most part."

Gideon shifted, as if uncomfortable with that revelation. She couldn't blame him. Most people wished to keep parts of themselves hidden, or wanted to protect their true feelings, whether out of a wish for privacy, or shame, or fear. She knew

Gideon wanted his entire history hidden, at least up until the day her father found him.

"I tried to ignore it, or explain it to myself rationally. Then it stopped for a very long while. Or perhaps I refused to notice. After Father died, I began to notice again." Electra closed her eyes because mentioning her father always brought a rush of grief, followed by the sharpness of anger.

"I miss him a great deal," Gideon said in a raw tone.

Electra opened her eyes, frustrated to feel tears well up. "I know you must. He meant a great deal to you."

"And to you."

"Yes," she said. It was all she could manage. How had they gotten here? To talking about a man who'd once meant the world to both of them, but whose moments of coldness could also cut one to the marrow.

"Forgive me," Gideon murmured. "I can see it's difficult."

Electra pressed her lips together. Part of her wanted to tell him everything. He thought her reaction was because she still grieved her father's loss, but Gideon had no knowledge of her mother's madness. Her condition and her deterioration in the loathsome place her father sent her to was a secret he took to the grave.

But Electra knew. She'd visited the asylum after her father's death, demanded her mother's records, confronted her so-called doctor.

"I'm sorry I can't be more help," she told him. "If anything else comes through about that night, I'll tell you."

He scrubbed a hand across his stubbled jaw. "My goal was to keep you out of this, and I seem to have failed miserably."

"I failed too, Gideon. I failed to tell Helen Becknell I foresaw her death. And I was at her home the night she died, so you can't keep me out of it." Electra stood because the feelings the conversation had evoked, in this cozy, warm parlor of his half-furnished house, were too much. Not his feelings. She still guarded herself from those. Her own feelings troubled her.

With Gideon, it was too easy to slip into openness, to find that the conversation turned to the man they'd both seen as a father.

"I should go," she told him as she collected her cloak. "I will see you at the inquest." The fastening of her cloak got caught in a fold near her neck, and Gideon stood and approached as if to reach out and fix it.

Electra reached up and did the deed herself before he could.

"At least allow me to hail a hansom for you." He was already heading toward the hallway.

Electra watched as he slipped into his long black overcoat that strained across the shoulders that seemed to have broadened in the years they'd been estranged. Then he headed out into the cold.

While he sought a cab, Electra took a turn around his parlor. The walls were bare, the furnishings minimal, and there wasn't a single piece of bric-a-brac to reveal anything about Gideon. Only on the mantel did she spot something.

Before she strode over, she told herself it was likely some keepsake from her father or perhaps a medal of commendation for Gideon's police work over the years. But as she drew closer, her throat tightened as she recognized the object.

A cockle shell. *The* cockle shell she'd found and presented to him on a trip to Cornwall. Just as she reached out to touch the keepsake, Gideon returned to the parlor. She swung to face him.

"Cab's outside waiting for you."

"Thank you," Electra said a bit breathlessly and then strode past him, clambering up into the vehicle before he could help her.

She hadn't avoided Gideon Pierce for three years out of

disdain. Being near him still made her feel too much. Once, she'd imagined he might feel something for her beyond the bond they'd built as children, making her wish for the sort of future she could never have. She would never be a wife. No man would be allowed to control her life or decide her fate, as her father had decided her mother's.

So, after this case was solved, she sensed that she'd need to put distance between them again.

Chapter Eleven

The inquest was set to commence at eleven in the morning.

Unfortunately, Gideon had been waylaid at Vine Street, attending to other cases. He'd also received a report from the chemist Tate engaged, detailing the findings of tests conducted on her ladyship's sleeping tonic. No strychnine was found in the tonic bottle or other medicinal bottles collected from Lady Becknell's bedroom drawer.

It bolstered the theory that someone put poison in her food or something she drank shortly before her death.

Gideon hadn't had the chance to seek Lord Philip Becknell at home, but he was determined to intercept the man before he faced the coroner.

Now, fighting the gusts of a bracing breeze, Gideon strode down the row of carriages queuing in front of the St. Mark Workhouse, where the proceedings were to be held, looking for the fanciest carriage.

Halfway down the line, he spotted one that stood out from the rest, its lacquer gleaming, its team a matching pair of bay horses.

Luckily for him, the line of vehicles was temporarily stalled as passengers disembarked from those farther up the line.

Gideon leaned to peek inside the carriage, spotted Becknell, twisted the latch on the carriage door, and climbed inside without aid of the folded step.

"What in God's—" Becknell pressed his lips together and shot Gideon a chilly look when he recognized him. "Inspector, what's the meaning of this?"

"Think of it as a courtesy, my lord." In fact, it was more of a gift that the viscount didn't deserve.

"In what regard?"

"You were less than truthful when we spoke yesterday, my lord."

Becknell sat up a bit straighter, pulling back his broad shoulders. "That is a bold accusation, Inspector."

"Yet I am not the one making the claim." Gideon patted his coat pocket, though the statement, witnessed and attested by a local magistrate in Oxfordshire, was back in his files at Vine Street. "Lord Ansley, your supposed host in Oxfordshire, never saw hide nor hair of you at his hunting party."

Becknell's only response was to tighten his jaw as a bit of ruddiness colored his complexion.

"Another source indicated you were, in fact, in London. At a hotel with a lady who was not your wife."

The viscount reached up to slip two fingers behind his neckcloth as if the garment's hold was suddenly suffocating.

"The coroner has been informed and will ask you to account for your whereabouts. Since the proceedings are public, these details will likely appear in the papers. I thought you should be forewarned." Gideon touched the brim of his hat and inclined his head, then turned, opened the carriage door, and stepped down to the pavement.

Before shutting the door behind him, he peeked his head in

once more. "I trust you will tell the truth under oath, my lord, and I shall be eager to hear it."

With that, he left the viscount fuming and rushed toward the workhouse's entrance. Inside the board room, Lady Becknell's shrouded body had been laid out on gurney in a side room, and many had already claimed seats in the main area, where spectators could observe the proceedings.

Electra stood in a corner of the room speaking to the Becknell's housekeeper, Mrs. Evans. Gideon noted that Sir Christopher and Cordelia Redmayne were seated in the second row. He assumed they'd escorted Electra and was pleased she had their very public support.

Gideon also noted the passel of journalists, which set his teeth on edge. He could already imagine the frenzied headlines when today's revelations came to light about the Becknells—poison, secret scandals, false alibis, a spiritualist, and now a missing valet.

Gideon took a seat in front of the Redmaynes and next to Constable Charlie Clegg.

"Still no word on Finch?" he murmured to the young officer.

"No, sir. Not as yet. But we'll find 'im."

Clegg was working to track the valet's family or friends who might know where he'd gone to ground.

At five to eleven, the twelve men of the jury took to their seats. A moment later, Tate strode to the table from which he'd question witnesses, a collection of documents under his arm. A single straight-backed chair was positioned in front of him.

On precisely the top of the hour, Tate began.

"Gentlemen of the jury, you have been impaneled to inquire into the cause and circumstances attending the death of Lady Helen Becknell, aged thirty-six years, lately of Hanover Square, whose body lies before us."

After Tate swore in each jury member, they were led by Constable Thacker to view the body of Helen Becknell.

Gideon shifted in his chair, glancing behind him and scanning the spectators for the three who intrigued him most—Lord Ballinger, Lucan Fox, and Lord Becknell. The artist looked bored as he swiped at his coat sleeve. Ballinger appeared to be struggling against strong emotions—his hands were balled into fists on his thighs. Becknell had locked his gaze on a spot on the wall opposite him, as if determined to ignore everything around him.

Soon, the men of the jury returned to their seats, and Tate provided the basic details of the case, including when and where Lady Becknell had been found.

Constable Clegg was the first witness sworn in, and he explained what he'd discovered when Grace Dobbs sent for him.

As Clegg testified, Gideon looked around him again. He realized Electra had taken up a spot over his left shoulder next to Lady Cordelia Redmayne.

When their eyes met, hers looked fretful, and she shook her head in the tiniest, controlled movement.

Gideon lifted a brow in question, and she reached out, placing a gloved hand on his shoulder. Electra leaned forward, her mouth close to his ear.

"Grace doesn't seem to be here," she whispered, then sat back in her chair.

Not ten minutes later, Tate called for the next witness—Grace Dobbs.

"Let us now hear from Miss Grace Dobbs," Tate intoned, "employed as a housemaid by Lord and Lady Becknell, who found her ladyship on the morning of Monday, eighteenth of November."

No one responded to the initial call, and Gideon's body tensed.

"Beg your pardon, Coroner," Mrs. Evans said from somewhere behind Gideon. "I'm the Becknell housekeeper, sir, and I must tell the court that Grace Dobbs left her post yesterday and cannot be located."

Tate frowned, then cast a look Gideon's way.

Gideon had nothing to offer the man.

"Does Miss Dobbs keep lodgings? Has someone sought her there?" Tate asked.

"No, sir," Mrs. Evans told him. "She resides at Becknell House."

Tate wasn't keen on any snags in his inquest proceedings. "Very well," he said, his voice gruff with irritation, "we shall proceed to the next witness. Dr. Frederick Farringdon, police surgeon for C Division."

THROUGHOUT THE POSTMORTEM surgeon's descriptions, the ladies seated around Electra alternately gasped, let out little bleats of horror, or pressed kerchiefs to their mouths. Cordelia wasn't immune either. She'd reached for Kit's hand and continued to clasp it tightly.

What happened to Lady Becknell was horrible, a reminder not only that those with wealth and status could be murdered in their own homes, but also that a woman, even one seemingly beloved and admired, might not be safe among those she trusted.

The revelation of the presence of poison, confirmed by a consulting chemist's tests, made one lady nearby slump as if she would have fainted dead away if she'd been on her feet.

As soon as Dr. Farringdon took the witness chair, Gideon

had stood and gone to stand on the opposite wall behind the coroner's table. A few others who'd not been able to claim seats were standing along the wall too.

She knew precisely why he'd positioned himself there. Indeed, his brown eyes were as focused as she'd ever seen them —scanning, watching, waiting for any reaction among those he considered potential suspects. As far as she knew, the finding of poison would be news to Becknell, Ballinger, and Lucan Fox, as well as any family and friends of Lady Becknell who were attending the inquest. Unless, of course, they'd been the one to poison her.

Without being obvious and glancing over her shoulder, she couldn't study the men Gideon was likely watching. She held her breath as the surgeon finished up, knowing the final revelation would be the most shocking of all.

"During the course of abdominal examination," Dr. Farringdon continued in monotone, "I confirmed the presence of a fetus in utero. The pregnancy was in the early stages— approximately ten to twelve weeks gestation."

"Good heavens," Cordelia whispered.

"Dear God," Kit murmured quietly at almost the same time.

A few journalists exited the room after that detail, no doubt rushing to get what they'd learned so far into the afternoon edition of whatever paper they wrote for.

The reactions and hushed conversation grew to such a din that the coroner called for quiet.

After the surgeon's concluding comments, Dr. Tate called Gideon to give testimony.

As Electra watched him settle himself onto the witness chair that seemed far too small for his tall frame and long legs, her own leg bounced, her boot heel tapping the floor. She forced herself to still the nervous movement, but it did nothing to tame the rattle of her heartbeat.

She felt a terrible sense of foreboding—much as she had before she'd stepped into Becknell House—that something dreadful had happened to Grace Dobbs.

Indeed, Grace had been the first face she'd seen at Becknell House. Even then, she'd sensed fear from the girl.

She'd offered for Grace to come and stay with her, but she'd been a fool not to ask the young woman if she had friends or family she might go to. Perhaps she was safe with one of them now.

Yet some dark, heavy thing in Electra's middle told her Grace was not safe. It wasn't a vision or even her sensing of an emotion. Just a disquiet that would not be quelled.

She wanted to speak to Gideon, to tell him that constables must begin searching for Grace now.

Mrs. Evans assumed Grace and Finch had absconded together, but Electra knew Grace had been keen to return to Becknell House to ask for a character. Domestic staff without a character reference would struggle mightily to find a new post.

Gideon's voice as he gave his testimony was deep and steady and oddly reassuring. He sounded thoroughly competent and in full control of the facts he'd discovered thus far in the investigation. She knew he'd sometimes worked hard for that sense of control he seemed to wield so easily now.

When he began recounting what he knew of the night prior to Lady Becknell's body being discovered, he did not so much as glance at Electra as he spoke her name. She understood. His every word, every inflection, was being observed, and any revelation of their history would only provide thrilling fodder for the police gazettes.

The weight of someone's gaze on her drew Electra's attention to the row of chairs behind her. Lucan Fox winked when he caught her eye.

Even in these sober proceedings, the man looked amused. A

cocky grin tipped his lips up at the edge, and he gave her a slow nod as if in greeting. Electra studied him too long, trying to put all her focus on sensing any kind of genuine emotion from the man, but he was still as opaque as the black crepe strewn about Becknell House.

"Lord Martin Ballinger visited Lady Becknell," Gideon testified, "at approximately half six in the evening."

"He looks as if he might not survive this," Cordelia murmured, her head turned toward where Lord Ballinger sat in the far corner of the assembled chairs.

Indeed, at mention of his name, the nobleman had noticeably paled.

"Also," Gideon was saying, "a witness came forward to indicate that Lady Becknell had at least one other known visitor, who departed around nine in the evening."

A charged energy swept around the overpacked room. Electra glanced at Lucan Fox. The man didn't appear to feel an ounce of concern about his visit to Helen Becknell being revealed. Indeed, he grinned the minute Gideon spoke his name to the coroner.

"Lord Becknell..." Gideon began, "did claim to be in Oxfordshire, but he was not. That discrepancy is now part of the ongoing investigation into this matter."

"Was he known to be at Becknell House?" Tate inquired.

"No, Coroner. There is no evidence he returned to his home on Sunday evening, and I was present on Monday morning and can confirm Lord Becknell was not present at that time."

The spectators quieted, as if trying to catch every word, waiting for more revelations. Journalists' pencils scratched quickly across paper.

"Thank you, Inspector," Dr. Tate called out. "Now, we shall hear from Miss Electra Poole, who visited with Lady Becknell on the night of her death."

Cordelia reached out and gave Electra's arm an encouraging squeeze. Both she and Kit were fretful about that her appearance here might result in a notoriety that would paint her in an unfavorable light. Kit had reminded her, much as Gideon likely would have done, to stick to factual testimony.

She took the seat Gideon had vacated, swore an oath to give truthful testimony, and then recounted, at the coroner's prompting, how she'd come to visit Becknell House and when she departed.

Dr. Tate took care *not* to ask details about the sitting with Lady Becknell, but he seemed determined to get at her physical state at that hour in the evening.

"Did her ladyship show any signs of illness?"

"No, she did not."

"Any indication of a seizure or bodily discomfort?" Dr. Tate pressed.

"No, sir. None."

"She appeared in good health, Miss Poole?"

"She was pale, looked a little fatigued, and was quite nervous."

Tate narrowed one bespectacled eye at her. "What *physical* signs indicated the nervousness you mention?"

"The tone of her voice and tensing of her jaw, sir. And she spoke of...fear."

"Fear of what, Miss Poole?"

Electra sensed Gideon out of the corner of her eye, leaning forward in the chair he'd reclaimed in the front row, watching her.

"That someone was deceiving her."

A ripple of murmurs rushed across the room.

"Did she name this potential deceiver?" Tate asked.

"No, sir, she did not. Only her worry that several people were deceiving her." Electra was tempted to say more, to mention the child's grave she'd seen, but she suspected Tate would not ask her about the sitting itself or why Lady Becknell had summoned her.

The man seemed to wish to keep any hint of sensationalism from the proceedings.

"Tell us Lady Becknell's state when you departed at half past six."

"She was animated. A visitor had come. And she bid me to return to speak to her at some future date." Electra tightened her gloved hands in her lap, knowing her vision would not be taken by the court as factual.

"Thank you, Miss Poole, you are excused, unless the jury requires anything further."

Electra tensed and studied the faces of the men of the jury. They scraped their gazes over her in return, and from one in the front with a long, hangdog sort of face, she felt a pulse of undeniable disdain.

None of them raised their hand to question her further, and she had never been happier to be able to stand up from a chair and walk away. But she couldn't simply go and sit in her spectator seat again.

She cast one glance at Cordelia and then wended her way through the packed room toward the exit.

Out on the pavement, the chilly air bit at her cheeks, but it was welcome after the crush of the workhouse meeting room. Yet even on the street, a few people had gathered, whether journalists or those curious about the case. As soon as she had broken away from the crush, a tall reddish-brown-haired woman wearing mourning black approached.

"Miss Poole, is it?"

Electra nodded.

"Beatrice Linwood." She took Electra in with an assessing

gaze. "I wonder if you would call on me at Becknell House at your earliest convenience."

"My condolences to you, Miss Linwood."

The lady responded with a tight half-smile. "Thank you. Even after hearing such shocking horrors this morning about what she suffered, part of me expects I'll return to Becknell House and Helen and I will take our usual afternoon tea together." Miss Linwood's eyes welled with tears, and she lifted a handkerchief edged in black to her mouth. "Forgive me."

"No, please don't apologize."

"I could not endure more of the testimony. I know my sister was a lady with secrets, but is it not terrible that they should be revealed when she cannot defend herself?"

"Yes, it is terrible." Standing in front of the grieving sister, Electra felt her own guilt well up. If she'd told Lady Becknell of her vision that night, Miss Linwood would still be having tea with her sister today.

"Will you call on me, Miss Poole?" she handed over one of her calling cards.

It was a polite and no doubt habitual gesture, though she had to know Electra would recall her address.

Electra took the card and detected a ripple of unease when she touched it.

"It may seem odd that I should request a call while the house is in mourning, but I admired your forthright manner when testifying, and you spoke to Helen on that terrible night." A little shudder seemed to rattle through her. "Will you call on me?"

"Yes, of course. Name the day, Miss Linwood." She could hardly refuse the lady's request.

"Shall we say tomorrow afternoon?"

Electra dipped her head. "I will see you then."

Miss Linwood reached out and laid a hand on Electra's arm,

her fingers grazing the bare skin between the wrist of Electra's suit and the cuff of her gloves. "Thank you, Miss Poole."

The lady's hold was brief, but in those few moments, Electra stiffened as she found herself pulled into a vision.

She saw Helen Becknell kneeling on the floor of an elegant bedchamber, weeping in long wailing sobs, her body tense as her sister held her. As if through Beatrice Linwood's perspective, she sensed Miss Linwood stroking her sister's hair, murmuring, "All will be well."

When the images faded, Electra stood alone.

Miss Linwood had taken her leave and walked toward the line of coaches queuing in front of the workhouse. A coachman ushered her into an elegant carriage, then directed its team of matching horses out into the flow of traffic.

Shaken by the momentary vision, Electra remained still, catching her breath.

When she'd collected herself, she scanned the street for a hansom, and a face caught her eye. A young man stood under the awning of a tobacconist's shop. His collar, turned up against the cold, covered part of his face. But he wore no hat, and Electra recognized his prominent brow and reddish hair.

She immediately strode toward him, then stumbled back when a carriage wheeled past. The cabbie shouted at her, and she looked both ways, then rushed across the street. Pedestrians passed the spot where she'd spotted Mr. Finch, but he was gone.

But even the single glimpse of him gave Electra hope. If he was alive and well and walking the streets of London, then there was a chance Grace Dobbs was too.

Now she just had to find the young woman.

Jacob Finch might very well know where to find her, and the only thread Electra had would hopefully lead her to the elusive young man.

Chapter Twelve

As Gideon watched Lord Philip Becknell give testimony, he finally understood a bit of the man's power. Becknell displayed a list of admirable qualities —graciousness, charm, even self-deprecation. He expressed grief, dismay, and utter confusion, and he apologized for his "misstatement" regarding his whereabouts on the Sunday prior to his wife's death.

"It is a delicate matter, Coroner, and I was discreet for the sake of my own health. You see, I'd just returned from a trip to Bristol and realized I'd come down with a frightful cold. I decided to check-in at The Imperial Hotel rather than return home and endanger the health of my wife and others in my household."

Gideon couldn't yet prove the viscount's claim was balderdash, but he'd wager his very life that it was utterly and entirely balderdash.

"Were you at your Hanover Square address at any point on Sunday evening or the early hours of Monday, my lord?"

"I was not, Dr. Tate."

"Thank you, Lord Becknell. Unless the jury has any questions—"

A slim, grim-faced juryman raised his hand.

Tate tipped his head the man's way.

"Might I inquire, Mr. Coroner, whether his lordship was aware of the visits of Lord Ballinger and Mr. Fox prior to Sunday evening?"

Tate narrowed his focus on Becknell. "You may answer the question put to you, Lord Becknell."

For a moment, the dark-haired, broad-framed nobleman merely clenched his jaw, then his brow furrowed slightly, as if the topic pained him. "I was not, Coroner and Juryman. I'm very sorry to say I was not aware." Becknell pressed his lips together and looked up at the assembled jury from under his brow. "I should have protected her."

Gideon clenched the hand resting on his thigh. Becknell was a performer, of that he had no doubt, but as he swept his gaze around at the jury and assembled crowd, he realized the viscount was an effective one. Others did not seem to recognize his falsehood. Several of the jurymen's faces were full of sympathy.

"You may be excused, Lord Becknell."

The viscount stood to his impressive height, let out a deep sigh, and then returned to his seat among those observing the proceedings.

The coroner directed the jurymen back to the side room, where Lady Becknell's body remained for them to examine, if required.

No one who'd listened to the testimony given could have been surprised when the twelve men strode back into the crowded meeting room after little more than a quarter of an hour, resumed their seats, and waited for the coroner to announce their findings.

"Gentlemen and ladies." Tate spoke in an authoritative tone, and the room grew hushed. "The jury have returned their verdict in the matter of the late Lady Helen Becknell of Hanover Square. They find that the deceased came to her death on or about the 17th day of November from strychnine poisoning."

Tate lifted his head and glanced briefly at Gideon. "The jury, having returned a verdict of death by poison administered by a person or persons unknown, it is now the duty of the police to continue their inquiries."

Gideon dipped his head because many had turned their curious gazes his way.

Though he didn't need Tate or the jury or any member of the London public to remind him of the weight on his shoulders and the need to find Lady Becknell's killer.

As spectators and witnesses filed out, Gideon bided his time and waited for Lucan Fox to take his leave. The minute the young buck stood, a lady approached, engaging him in a seemingly lively conversation, as if she'd just encountered the man during a promenade rather than at a murder inquest.

"Excuse me, Mr. Fox," Gideon called as soon as the young man broke free of his admirer and began making his way out of the meeting room.

"Inspector, shouldn't you be straight onto continuing your inquiries?" The man seemed to be unable to say anything without making it sound like a quip.

"That's precisely what I'm doing, Mr. Fox." Gideon glanced around. Most had filed out of the room, leaving just a few who might overhear their exchange.

He stepped closer to the young man. "You lied when last we spoke."

A muscle jumped at the edge of Fox's sharp jaw.

"You visited Lady Becknell." Gideon was a few inches taller

than Fox and as he took one step closer, the difference became emphasized. "Was she alive when you left her?"

"Of course she was."

"Even after you attempted to throttle her?"

"How dare you?" Fox surged forward, stopping just short of coming toe to toe.

Gideon tamped down how satisfying it felt to finally get a response other than a smirk full of blithe arrogance. He wondered if Lucan Fox had snapped as quickly that night with Lady Becknell.

"Believe it or not, my goal is to eliminate you from my list of suspects." Right now, it was quite a list, and while he did not believe Fox killed the viscountess, he believed he'd put hands on her in violence. The man was no master criminal, but there was cunning behind his smiles.

"We argued. Satisfied?"

"Not at all. What did you argue about?"

"The bloody brat. What else?"

"The child she was carrying."

"It wasn't mine, and I tried to reason with the woman."

Gideon stared, unblinking, waiting.

Fox crossed his arms. "Why could it not be Becknell's? The long-awaited heir to the viscountcy. But she would press and press." The artist lifted a hand to push two fingers to his temple. "I lost my temper. We tussled." He had the audacity to shrug. "But I assure you the lady was alive and well when I left her."

Gideon gestured to the still-visible scratch on Fox's cheek. "When you put your hands on her throat, she did that?"

"I grasped her throat solely to get her off me. She would not stop clinging, beseeching."

For the first time in the case, he had an admission from a possible culprit that he mostly believed.

"Do you have any alibi for later in the evening?"

"I've already given you the name."

"She's declined to verify your claim."

The smirk was back. "A duchess refusing to admit to an illicit liaison? Shocking?" Fox leaned in again. "Ask one of her servants if you want the truth of where Her Grace goes," he whispered.

Straightening, he gripped the lapels of his frock coat. "Are we finished, Inspector?"

"For now, Mr. Fox."

As he had at his bohemian townhouse, Fox offered an elaborate bow that somehow felt like an insult, and then sauntered away.

Gideon immediately headed out of the meeting room, expecting to find Constables Clegg and Thacker waiting for him outside the workhouse. Locating Grace Dobbs was now a priority. The two were nowhere in sight, but another gentleman stood near the workhouse door, waiting for him.

"Inspector Pierce, may I have a word?" Sir Christopher Redmayne strode forward.

Gideon pivoted toward the baronet, noting that he was no longer accompanied by his wife. Or Electra, who'd slipped out before the inquest concluded.

"Electra wouldn't be pleased." Sir Christopher looked behind him, as if to confirm he wasn't being observed. "But Cordelia insisted I tell you."

"Tell me what?"

"She's set on finding Grace Dobbs. As such, she's gone to Whitechapel Hospital."

"To what purpose?" Gideon had walked out of the workhouse with a plan for seeking out Miss Dobbs, and he felt it all derailing because of Electra. Again.

"That's all I know." Sir Christopher's brow pinched over his hooded eyes. "We're concerned about her, Pierce, but she's rather difficult to stop when she's determined on a course."

"I'm well aware."

GASLIGHT FLICKERED AGAINST TILED WALLS, and the benches in the halls of Whitechapel Hospital teemed with people waiting to enter the casualty ward. Some were bent in pain, others had their eyes closed as if fatigue had overtaken them, their heads tipped back against the wall. A crying child drew Electra's notice because no one seemed to be tending to her, but soon a nurse approached and provided the little girl with a cup the child drank from eagerly.

As Electra cast her gaze across the wounded and ill, a young woman approached in a dark wool gown with a stained white apron pinned to the front. Below her white cap, a few blonde hairs had escaped and clung to face, which glistened with perspiration.

"Miss Poole?" she asked, her tone curt. "Matron said you wished to speak with me."

"Yes, thank you for taking a moment—"

"I've no more than five minutes. What can I do for you?" The shadows under her eyes suggested fatigue, and yet the young woman's gaze was sharp and assessing.

"I'm looking for your brother, Miss Finch."

Margaret Finch immediately dipped her head, then braced her work-worn hands on her hips. "I don't know where he is."

Electra couldn't think of a reason to reach for the young lady, yet she seemed to be brimming with emotions she fought to contain. She was one of those who seemed opaque, though her body was all but humming with tension.

"If this is about that murder, I've nothing to tell you.

Though I told him not to involve himself with the Becknells," she finally said, lifting her dark eyes to Electra's. "No good could come from it."

"Why did you think so?"

"Because he'd made a life with us. We didn't have much, but we loved him as our own. Still, he was determined to cast that all aside."

"I'm afraid I don't understand. Was he taken in by your family?" Electra tried to read the lady's emotions, but Margaret Finch refused to give anything away, other than her obvious irritation at Electra's questions and distress about her brother.

"Yes, my parents adopted him when he was a child." At that admission, a wistfulness came into the young woman's eyes, and then a slight blush, as if she was uncomfortable with having given such information away. "What do you want with my brother, Miss Poole?"

"I'm hoping he can lead me to someone. That he might help me locate her. A maid of the Becknell household. Miss Grace Dobbs."

Miss Finch frowned. "You don't know the truth about him, do you?"

"What truth?"

The nurse crossed her arms, her expression hardening. "That's not mine to tell, Miss Poole. Jacob must decide what he wishes you to know."

"I'd be happy to ask him, but first I must find him."

The young woman glanced at the clock high on the wall. "I've no notion where he is. He's always had secrets. I don't know who his friends are or where he goes on his half days. Since he took his post with them, he kept his secrets, even from me."

The young woman spoke and yet her meaning was maddeningly opaque.

Electra dug in her pocket for a calling card and offered it to Finch's sister. "If you do hear from him, would you tell him I'd like to speak to him?"

Arms crossed, Margaret Finch stared at the card, then finally reached out to take it.

"Thank y—"

Before Electra could get two words of gratitude out, the young nurse pivoted on her heel and walked away, her stride quick, as if she had work to do and Electra had delayed her.

Electra strode down the crowded corridor as if walking through a fog, not of industrial smoke or low-hanging clouds, but of emotions. Pain, worry, fear were thick in the air among those gathered, waiting for God knew how long, to finally get seen for their ailments.

When she reached the street, she drew in deep lungful of bracing November air.

"What did you discover?"

Electra whipped around to see Gideon leaning casually against a lamppost.

"I take it the inquest has concluded," she said.

"And the verdict surprised no one." Straightening, he reached down to resettle his cuffs as he approached. "Do you know where Grace Dobbs is?"

"No, but I am worried about her." Electra didn't like his curt tone, but she preferred it to his chastisement for involving herself in the investigation.

"Did you think she'd be at the hospital?"

"No, I came here to speak to Jacob Finch's sister."

"And?" He stepped closer, suddenly interested.

"She does not know where he is."

His shoulders sagged a bit at that. "I have constables searching for both of them. In fact, I must return to Vine Street to determine whether they've turned up anything."

She took a step closer, despite how much he looked as surly as a baited bear. "Shall we find a hansom and go together?"

He lifted a hand and pinched the bridge of his nose. "Why on earth would you need to come to Vine Street?"

"If you find Grace, she'll be much more likely to speak to me than to you. After all, she sought me out yesterday at Cordelia's."

He stared at her, working his jaw, debating. "Very well. We might as well share a cab," he finally conceded, "as I suspect you'd follow me anyway if I refused."

Hansoms had queued near the hospital entrance, and they approached one together. Electra climbed in first. Gideon settled beside her, so close their arms and thighs seamed together as the carriage jostled into motion.

"What's upset you?" she dared after a few moments of silence.

As she expected, he bristled at the question. The query alone highlighted his slip in control.

"Not having answers. Two missing servants. A killer on the loose. The way the press will whip up public fear after today's revelations."

"Goodness, is that all?"

His hands were balled into fists on his thighs. Electra quelled the urge to reach out and offer comfort.

At her quip, he glanced her way. "It's not an exhaustive list," he grumbled.

"No, I knew it couldn't be, since you forgot the bit about me interfering in your investigation *again*."

Out of the corner of her eye, the slightest twitch of his lips was there and gone again.

"I did not forget. I simply realize the futility of wasting my breath." He unclenched his hands at that.

Since he was allowing her to accompany him back to the

police station, she felt compelled to offer him something in return.

"Beatrice Linwood approached me outside the workhouse."

He shifted, pressing his shoulder into the carriage's wall so he could look at her. "To what purpose?"

"She's asked me to visit her at Becknell House tomorrow afternoon. I suspect her motive is much like Lord Ballinger's. To know what her sister said to me that night."

"Or to ask you to summon her from the great beyond."

Electra noted his mocking tone and stared straight ahead.

He settled back next to her and turned a glance her way. "Forgive me," he murmured.

"I'll consider it."

This time his flash of a smile lasted a bit longer.

When they arrived at Vine Street, Gideon waited for her to descend from the carriage before leading her inside. The desk sergeant eyed her with curiosity as she followed Gideon back to his office.

Midway down the hall, he called to a passing constable. "Any word on Finch or Grace Dobbs, Thacker?"

"We've a few leads, sir. Clegg is on them now. But there was someone else to see you."

"Who?"

Constable Thacker gestured back toward the public waiting room. "Said her name was Ashcombe. She didn't want to wait but left her calling card." The constable offered Gideon the card.

"Have Clegg brief you if he returns. I'll head to"—Gideon read from the calling card—"Eaton Square."

When the constable departed, Gideon turned back to her. "I must be off. And no, you cannot accompany me."

"Did you know I'm acquainted with Lady Rosalind

Ashcombe?" There was an extraordinarily slim chance that the fact would persuade him, but she couldn't resist trying.

"What a coincidence." He scrutinized her as if trying to decide if it was one of her less-than-believable fabrications.

"Not entirely. Apparently, she's the reason Lady Becknell contacted me. Lady Ashcombe was at my first sitting."

"And?"

"Her lady's maid spoke to Grace Dobbs about me, and Grace told Helen Becknell."

He stared at her, calculating. "Did you and Lady Ashcombe part on good terms?"

"Grace says she speaks of me often. I helped find something she'd lost."

He lifted his hand, gripped the back of his neck, then gestured back toward the station's entrance. "Shall we be off?"

Electra strode ahead of him and tried hard not to smile.

LADY ROSALIND ASHCOMBE'S reaction upon seeing Electra step into her drawing room next to him allayed all his concerns about allowing her to accompany him to the lady's grand stucco-fronted townhouse. Almost.

It was poor protocol, and detectives were under more scrutiny than ever with the establishment of the Criminal Investigation Department earlier in the year. But it was an undeniable fact that ladies, especially those of Lady Ashcombe's class, seemed more at ease speaking to a respectable young woman than a police officer.

"Oh my goodness, Miss Poole, how lovely it is to see you." The bejeweled wife of the Earl of Ashcombe took both Electra's gloved hands in hers as if they were bosom friends. "I'm so sorry you've been caught up in this tragedy, my dear. I read of your appearance at the inquest."

Only then did the countess acknowledge Gideon. "Is Miss Poole assisting your investigation, Inspector? That's quite clever of you. Her skills must be a very great help."

Gideon ground his teeth at the implication that he needed a lady psychic to solve this case. "I knew of your acquaintance with Miss Poole and thought her presence might put you at ease, my lady."

"Oh indeed." She smiled at Electra. "Very thoughtful of you, Inspector. Shall we sit?"

A tea service had already been set out on a low table, and Gideon willed himself to be patient as the ritual of pouring, adding honey or sugar or cream, and then distributing the dainty things was finished.

He took an obligatory sip, set the little porcelain teacup aside, and took out his pencil and notebook.

After clearing his throat, he broke into the polite chatter between Lady Ashcombe and Electra. "I understand you were a close friend of Lady Becknell's. How long had you known each other?"

"Oh." Lady Ashcombe sipped from her cup, then smiled. "About six years, I think. We both had an interest in a charity for the poor run by Mrs. Charlotte Ellsworth. Then, of course, we moved in similar circles."

"And the two of you were on good terms?"

The countess blinked and swept a hand up to run her fingers across the pearl pendant she wore. "Yes, very good terms. Helen confided in me and I in her."

Gideon wondered if Electra's presence would aid or hinder his next line of questioning. "Were there monetary entanglements between you?"

Lady Ashcombe stiffened, then squared her chin as if

summoning all her aristocratic hauteur. "That's a rather indelicate question, Inspector. And it can have no bearing on what befell my friend."

"But there were entanglements?"

Lady Ashcombe looked to Electra as if she might offer aid.

"He must ask such questions," she told the countess quietly.

Gideon bristled but tried not to give any indication of it to either lady.

The countess sighed, then lifted a hand to pat at her sable hair. "Lady Becknell loaned me a sum of money...on occasion. I was most appreciative. And it was a private transaction. Both agreed our husbands would not know of it."

Gideon frowned. "Lady Becknell had control of her own funds?" It was unusual, though he knew some families did make such legal provisions for daughters so that all of their money was not under a husband's control. Or generous husbands provided their wives with an allowance.

"She did. The Linwoods settled an amount on her, protected from Philip, and she invested that sum wisely."

Gideon noted the details and underlined them. Money could always be counted as a powerful motive.

"What can you tell me of their marriage?"

Lady Ashcombe looked suddenly frightened. Her teacup shook in her hand until she sat it upon a table beside her. "Now we come to the heart of the matter."

To Gideon's surprise, she turned to Electra and offered her a wary smile.

"If you held my hand, perhaps you'd know too, my dear."

Electra leaned a bit closer to the countess. "Know what, my lady?"

Lady Ashcombe licked her lips, then turned toward Gideon. "Helen was afraid of Philip. He got angry at times, and when he did..." She tightened her mouth, almost as if she wished to keep the rest in as long as she could. "He was violent. She denied it for a long while, but I saw the marks, and she couldn't deny those."

Electra laid a hand on the countess's arm for only a moment as if to offer comfort. Lady Ashcombe clasped Electra's hand where it lay on her arm and gave it a squeeze.

Then the countess raised her gaze to Gideon. "Will Lord Becknell be told that I've said these things?"

"No, my lady. But anything else you know may help me," he told her. His gut told him there was more. She was still tense, her breathing tight. Whatever she knew, the lady had not fully unburdened herself.

"Oh heavens," she suddenly said, tears welling in her eyes. "The rest is dreadful, but I don't know for certain it's true."

Gideon and Electra exchanged a look.

"If you tell the inspector, he can seek to verify the information." Electra used a soft voice.

Lady Ashcombe nodded and offered her the slightest of smiles, then reached for her hand. Electra clasped the countess's hand as she continued.

"First, I must say that Helen could be... Goodness, how shall I say it? Anxious. Fretful. I didn't know whether to fully believe all her claims."

"Claims?"

The countess let out a little scoffing sound. "She once told me that he gave her sedatives. Put them in her drinks so that she wouldn't know when he conducted liaisons."

Electra made a slight noise that the countess didn't seem to notice, but Gideon did.

"But it makes so little sense, since Helen herself took a sleeping tonic every night. No one made her do so. Indeed, I know she sometimes took it during the day to calm her nerves."

"There's something else," Electra said.

"Yes. I knew you'd know, Miss Poole." As she spoke, she glanced down at their linked hands. "Before her death, she and Philip were frequently at odds. She said he wanted to send her to an asylum."

Electra inhaled sharply.

"Helen was no madwoman. Emotional, yes, but also clever, kind, loyal." Lady Ashcombe nibbled her lip and then continued. "She told me that he never could send her away because she knew something about him that she would reveal in turn."

Gideon felt Electra's attention on him and glanced at her. She looked as disquieted as Lady Ashcombe.

When the countess hesitated, Electra urged softly, "You must tell him."

Lady Ashcombe inclined her head, then did as Electra bid her. "She told me that there'd been a housemaid, early in their marriage. Philip...carried on with her. On her half day, he would take the girl to a hotel off the Strand." The countess lifted frightened eyes to Gideon. "She was found dead in that hotel. Poisoned. Helen believed he'd done it."

At that, the lady's shoulders sagged and a tear slipped down her cheek. "From the day Helen told me that story, I would not return to Becknell House. I feared for her, and I feared him."

"Well done," Electra whispered to her, then released her hand.

"But, Miss Poole," the countess said, her voice shaky, "I've no proof. It is a dreadful accusation based only upon the claim of a very troubled friend."

Gideon closed his notebook and looked at each of them. "Miss Poole is right. I can check on her ladyship's claim. Do you know the maid's name or the hotel?"

"Mary at the Halcyon Hotel. That is all know, Inspector."

"That is enough," Gideon told her. "Thank you, my lady."

177

Chapter Thirteen

When Electra returned to the Redmaynes, Cordelia had not yet come back from her afternoon calls, and she paced the rug in the drawing room.

Gideon would be on his way to the hotel Lady Ashcombe mentioned. Though she knew she could take no formal role in the investigation, they'd worked in tandem in the last couple of days, and the fact that he was out, seeking information, while she was sitting idle in an elegant townhouse made her restless.

Lady Ashcombe had been even easier to read this afternoon than when they'd met at her very first sitting. Today, her emotions had been churning and powerful—fear, uncertainty, regret.

As soon as they touched, Electra had seen Helen Becknell. The sight of her through Lady Ashcombe's eyes had revived all of the Electra's guilt about failing the viscountess. And she'd sensed that Lady Ashcombe felt much the same, perhaps because she'd never shared the story about the death of Lord Becknell's lover until today.

If it was true, if it could somehow be proved that the young lady died from the same poison, then Gideon would have to face the challenge of charging a nobleman with murder.

Electra rubbed her hands together as a reckless impulse gnawed at her. She'd laid her hands on Lucan Fox and Lord Martin Ballinger, but she'd never even met Lord Philip Becknell.

At the inquest, he'd had the same magnetic presence as when she'd seen him in Lady Becknell's memories. Despite the circumstances, he'd seemed almost even-tempered as he gave his testimony. Even sympathetic. Though she found him loathsome, knowing how he'd taken advantage of Grace, she could see how he could charm others.

What she needed now was an opportunity to touch him, or perhaps some object he'd recently held. Even if she could be in the same room with him and had time to focus her abilities, she might be able to sense something.

But according to Grace, the house was admitting no visitors.

What reason might she devise to induce Lord Becknell to see her?

Even as she paced and considered her options, the thought of Gideon's reaction made her pause. After three years apart from him, it felt strange to have his admonitions rattling around in her mind again.

Yet she couldn't deny that it felt right somehow.

"Miss Poole?" Cordelia's housekeeper stood on the drawing room threshold. "A visitor to see you. A Miss Dobbs. Shall I send her to you here?"

"Yes, thank you, Mrs. Hurst." Relief rushed through her. It seemed Grace's absence from the inquest hadn't portended the worst after all.

"She's in quite a state, Miss Poole. Shall I bring tea up?"

"Yes, that would lovely." Electra approached the threshold,

a hand on the doorframe, watching in the hall for Grace's approach.

The sight of her made Electra's chest ache. She rushed forward to meet her.

"Grace, what's happened?"

The young woman's hair was in disarray, half unmoored from her pins, and she looked exhausted. From her tear-streaked cheeks and reddened eyes, Electra suspected she'd been crying for a while.

Rather than answer, Grace merely shook her head as if she couldn't find the words.

Electra guided her to a settee, then retrieved a throw blanket to wrap around the girl's shoulders. Then she sat beside her, a hand resting gently on her back while Grace wept, then sniffed and hiccupped, as if trying to stem her tears.

She twisted a sodden handkerchief in her hands, occasionally dabbing at her cheeks.

"I'm sorry for coming like this, Miss Poole."

"Do not apologize. I told you to do so if you had the need." Electra tipped her head, but Grace wouldn't meet her eyes. "Can you tell me what's caused you so much distress? I was quite worried when you did not attend the inquest."

"Couldn't face it, miss."

Electra dipped her head, not wishing to add to the girl's worries by telling her that the coroner might still compel her to appear or take action for her failure to do so.

"I went back to get a character from Mrs. Evans, but she refused. Said because I left, her only choice was to dismiss me."

"I'm sorry, Grace."

She sniffed, then clasped her hands together tightly. "Should have been the end of it, but I went to the park, had a good long cry, and then I went back."

Electra drew in a breath. "And?"

"Told her I needed to speak with his lordship. She didn't want to let me, but I insisted. Threatened to wait outside the door all night if I must."

"So you spoke to him?"

Grace nodded. "That was a mistake. He'd come back from the inquest. I could tell the moment I walked into his study that he was in foul state."

"Do you mean he was sad?" That was the impression he'd given from the witness chair.

"No, he was angry, miss. More than I'd ever seen him."

"Why?"

Grace shrugged. "Whatever happened at the inquest, I suspect."

There had been so many revelations—about the strangulation marks, the poison, the pregnancy, and Lady Becknell's late-night visitors. Electra supposed the information about her pregnancy could have been a shock, particularly if he had any doubt he had fathered the child.

"I'm afraid I made it worse." She breathed deep but raggedly, as if it took effort. "I asked him for funds. I wasn't in my right mind. I felt...he owed me something. For deceiving me. Saying he cared for me when he did not."

"I suspect he didn't take that well."

"No," she said quietly.

"I know it was my choice to carry on with him, and a bad one. But I thought, even if he'd only cared for me a little, he might help me. Without a character, I might never find another post."

"But he refused."

The girl shuddered as if recalling the encounter. Electra laid her hand atop Grace's clasped ones.

The breath seemed to catch in her lungs, and her heart raced. Fear filled her body until she trembled—Grace's fears.

Her reaction to Philip Becknell, whose noble features twisted in rage. He shouted, but Electra heard nothing.

"He raged at me."

At Grace's voice, the images faded. Electra let go of her hands and worked to steady the wild thud of her heart.

"Did he harm you?" Electra had not seen him lay his hands on Grace, but he'd stood close to her as he shouted at her.

Grace rubbed a hand along her upper arm. "He held tight to my arms. So tight I cried out, but he wouldn't let go." She tsked and shook her head again. "She warned me. Lady Becknell. Said he could be brutal, that he'd struck her and might do the same to me."

"Then she knew of the two of you?"

"Yes, miss. I don't know how. We were careful. Or I thought so. Sometimes, we met away from the house."

Electra stilled. "Where did you meet?"

"A hotel." Grace looked suddenly abashed. Color rushed into her cheeks.

"The Halcyon?"

Grace frowned. "No, miss. The Swan."

"May I ask you something that might upset you, Grace?"

She looked at Electra warily and inclined her head.

"Do you know of any other young ladies who Lord Becknell may have taken to hotels?"

"You mean the other maid?" Grace crossed her arms, rubbing gently at the spots where Electra suspected there were bruises from Becknell's rough handling.

"Do you know something about another housemaid?"

"Jenny."

Mary was the name Lady Ashcombe had given, but she could have been mistaken, or Lady Becknell may have hidden the girl's identity.

"What happened to Jenny?" Electra sensed Grace fear and resistance. It wasn't a story she wanted to tell.

"She was in the house when I got my post, but she'd only been there two years." She swallowed hard. "We never got on. I thought she had airs and believed herself above the rest of us."

Grace looked over. "She told me Lord Becknell fancied her. And the next week, she was gone."

"Gone where?"

Tears welled in Grace's eyes. "No one knew. She wasn't in her room. Her things were there, but she wasn't. And she never came back."

Electra patted Grace's back as tears slid down her cheeks.

"What if he'll do me in next?"

Gideon would stop him. If Becknell was a killer, Gideon would find the proof.

"Did none of Jenny's family ever inquire about her?"

"Mr. Paxton and Mrs. Evans would not have told me as much if they did."

"Can you tell me Jenny's surname and when she left?"

Grace sat up a bit straighter. "Jenny Wilson. And it must have been the autumn three years past."

Electra would send a note to Gideon. Perhaps the young woman's family had contacted the police, or, if the girl had simply left her post abruptly, she might be found.

"What shall I do, miss?" Grace asked softly. "What if he wishes to do me harm?"

"Did he threaten you?"

"Only told me that I mustn't speak of what passed between us." She settled back against the settee's cushions as if all she'd confessed had sapped her of her strength. "I think Jacob knew something, miss, and that's why he left his post."

Electra agreed. "If that's true, I hope he can be found."

Every bit of evidence that could be rallied against Becknell would be crucial.

And yet she still wanted to know, to see if she could, by speaking to the viscount. But now, after feeling the fear rippling off of Grace, she knew she couldn't go alone.

THE HALCYON HOTEL's lobby contained only a few guests when Gideon stepped inside and approached a desk clerk. The young man welcomed him with a smile that faded quickly when Gideon explained who he was and the purpose of his visit.

From the information constables had collected about the Becknells, he knew they'd been married for nearly two decades. The desk clerk didn't look too far beyond two decades old.

"Is there anyone currently on staff who would have worked for the Halcyon for fifteen or twenty years?"

The young dark-haired man turned his head. "Mr. Higgins?"

A balding, bespectacled gentleman with white wisps of hair and a gray beard appeared a few moments later from a doorway that Gideon suspected led to the hotel's office. He had sunspots on his head as if he often forgot to wear a hat, and though his beard was in need a trim, his suit was well cut and spotless.

"This is Inspector Pierce of the Metropolitan Police." The young man leaned toward the older one, cupping a hand near his mouth. "He's inquiring about a murder at the hotel years ago," he said quietly. "A girl named Mary."

The older man gave a grim nod. "Summer of '62," he said. "I remember it well. I'd been hired on a few months before. The press made a meal of it, and the owner at the time was livid."

"Is there someplace where we might discuss the matter more thoroughly?" Gideon suspected the current owners wouldn't be any keener to have the matter hashed out over the hotel's front desk.

"Come this way, Inspector," Mr. Higgins directed, welcoming Gideon behind the front desk and into the back office. The room was painted in the same gleaming white as the walls of the lobby, but it was cramped with multiple desks. Along one wall, he noted box files as well as what looked to be old ledger books.

He gestured toward the books. "Does the Halcyon keep its old guest registers?"

"Indeed, sir." The gentleman glanced over at the shelf. "You're looking for someone in particular that summer?"

Gideon didn't think Philip Becknell would be naive enough to use his own name when checking into a hotel for an assignation, but he had to check.

"Yes, could you find that particular register for me?"

Mr. Higgins pointed to a spare chair next to the nearest desk. Gideon sat down and extracted his notebook and pencil while the hotel man ran his finger over spines.

"Some of these run between years," he murmured. "Ah, here we are. This one covers the summer months of 1862."

He brought the large leather-bound ledger over to the desk and laid it on top, flipping through the pages. "August, it was. Late summer. What name should I look for?"

"Becknell," Gideon told him and then watched the man's eyes widen.

"That matter in the papers?" Mr. Higgins asked.

"I'd appreciate your discretion, Mr. Higgins."

"'Course, Inspector." Then he dropped his head, and ran a forefinger down the line entries, some written in a neat, tight script, others more messily penned. Then he flipped a page and frowned. "This page runs into September. Cannot find any notation for a Becknell, sir." He looked at Gideon over the top rim of his spectacles. "Do you know for certain he roomed here that summer?"

"I do not."

"Well, it seems he did not. At least not under that name."

Gideon nodded his understanding, then pointed to the chair behind the tidy desk he sat next to.

Mr. Higgins pulled it out and took a seat, folding his hands before him atop the desk blotter. "How else may I help you, Inspector?"

"Anything you recall from that period and particularly the day the young woman was found would be helpful, Mr. Higgins, and I'll follow up with the local police division for further details."

The hotel man said nothing, turning his gaze down as if summoning up the memories.

"Mary Keane was her name. A very pretty girl. Not yet twenty, I'd say."

"Would there still be records regarding what room she stayed in or who may have checked in with her?"

"Oh, no." Higgins frowned. "She never did check in, Inspector. That was why it became such a spectacle. Couldn't keep the reporters away when she was found right out in the lobby."

Gideon tipped his head. "The lobby?"

"Aye, sir. She came in and sat for nigh on an hour among the chairs set out for guests to converse or meet with others. I inquired, and she said she was waiting for someone, but they were late. It seemed odd that she'd linger so long, and I hadn't ever seen her check-in, but I told myself it could have been while I was off duty."

Higgins stared off at the wall ahead of him, his eyes flickering with emotion as if he was reliving the past. "When I left desk duty in the early evening, she was still waiting. Normally, we'd be expected to keep someone from loitering, but she was sweet and pretty. Didn't seem no harm to let her wait, so I told the next young man on duty to let her sit."

"What happened to her?" Gideon's pulse sped. How could anyone commit murder in the open view of a hotel lobby and its workers and then abscond?

"I saw none of this, you understand. This is what Collier told me. He was on duty after me." Higgins met Gideon's eyes. "She had a fit. Said he'd never seen anything like it. Face twisted up something fierce, arms stiff as rails, legs stiff as tree trunks." Higgins seemed to shudder. "Collier said the sound keening sound she made was so odd, he'd never forget it."

Gideon recalled what Tate said about the seizures Helen Becknell would have suffered from strychnine poisoning.

"Other guests tried to assist her. Collier says he tried to help her. Nothing could be done. Then she fell silent, eyes staring. Her heart had stopped."

Gideon could only imagine how terrifying it would have been to observe, let alone the suffering Miss Keane had endured.

"You say she was still waiting when you went off duty. Did anyone ever come to meet her?"

Higgins's mouth tightened in a grimace. "There's the rub, Inspector. Collier couldn't be sure. Once, when he looked over, she was talking to a gent, who stood beside her chair. Then a bit later, a lady sat down across from her. But neither of them seemed to have been guests of the hotel. Collier had never seen them before, and the police never could determine who they were."

"And you'd never seen Mary Keane before that day?"

"No, sir."

"Is Mr. Collier still employed at the Halcyon?" Gideon asked.

"No, Inspector. He was about a decade senior to me and is

retired now." Higgins's straight line of a mouth curved into an almost smile. "Rooms with his son and his wife. We take tea on a Sunday sometimes. You can find him in Warwick Court. Number Six."

Gideon wrote down the older man's the address and closed his notebook. "Thank you, Mr. Higgins. You've given me a place to start, and I'll be calling on Mr. Collier."

Gideon got to his feet, and Mr. Higgins did too.

"Will you solve it, Inspector? Even after the press made much of it and the police came to the hotel several times, none of them ever could solve it."

"I'll do my best."

Higgins made a little sound that was more dubious than hopeful.

Gideon understood. A case unsolved for sixteen years would have been relegated to a records room or file cabinet as new cases took precedence. He only hoped F Division, which would have handled a case in this part of the city in that year, would still have such files on hand. Or even better, a detective still in service who'd investigated the young woman's death.

Chapter Fourteen

Cordelia seemed to be taking Grace's presence in her Russell Square townhouse better than Electra expected her to.

When she returned from her calls, eager to tell Electra all that she'd heard from others in Lady Becknell's circle of charity friends, she found the staff whispering about the girl who'd shown up at the door disheveled and in tears.

Electra had allowed Grace to take a nap in her room, and that scandalized Mrs. Hurst even more.

"So she knows nothing about Becknell's involvement in his wife's death, but he may have harmed some previous maid?" Cordelia asked as they sat in the drawing room drinking tea.

"She only said the young lady departed suddenly," Electra clarified. She loved Cordelia, but she was well aware of her love for gossip, both collecting it and passing it along.

"But you said her belongings remained. Who would leave with nothing?"

"Someone too frightened to tarry." Electra suddenly wondered if Jacob Finch had taken his belongings when he'd left his post abruptly. She'd ask Grace when she awoke.

"What did you learn from your lady friends?"

Cordelia lifted a blonde brow, as if in challenge. "They could be your friends too if you'd ever accompany me when I make my calls."

"So you've said." Electra took a sip of tea to forestall any further discussion on the topic. Though her father had set aside funds to send her to a prestigious finishing school, they'd always lived modestly, and when he took to gambling after the death of her mother, even the simple comforts had become difficult to afford.

Her best dress was her oldest and a few years out of fashion. When she'd lived with Cordelia after her mother's death, Cordelia had insisted Electra supplement her wardrobe with visits to her own modiste. But even fine new clothes didn't make her feel as if she belonged among Cordelia's upper-crust set. Now, since they were the ladies who paid for her sittings, she was making more of an effort. Eventually, she knew she'd have to capitulate to making social calls with Cordelia.

Cordelia stared into the flickering flames of a newly laid fire. "The consensus is that Lord Becknell likely struck his wife, at least once. Mrs. Ellsworth and a few others recall a specific incident when she attended one of their gatherings and they observed fresh bruises."

"It seems if a man is willing to go so far as to strike his wife, he'd likely do it more than once."

"Yes." Cordelia's voice had tightened.

Electra sensed sadness and grief from her friend. "What are you remembering?"

Cordelia shot her a look. "Can you not read my thoughts?"

"Not at the moment," she told her softly. "Perhaps it's something you protect."

"You always read me so well." Her smile wasn't her usual

cheerful one. "My mother. I heard my parents arguing often. I didn't know any better. I thought that's what mamas and papas did."

Electra stood from the settee she was sitting on across from Cordelia and took up a spot beside her. "I'm so sorry, my friend."

"Did your parents row?"

Electra flinched at the question. "I suppose most couples do," she said, trying to give nothing away.

Cordelia scoffed. "Kit and I certainly do. But Kit would never harm me—" She caught herself, gave Electra a stark look, and added, "At least not by putting his hands on me in violence."

Electra suspected infidelity was at the heart of the break between her friends, but Cordelia had never divulged any details, as if, even regarding his own betrayal, she would not betray Kit.

"I heard noises when I was a child. Thuds, cries, the clatter of knick-knacks being dropped. I didn't think I should ask. Mama never spoke of it. Papa rarely spoke to me at all."

Electra reached for Cordelia's hand but tried to keep her abilities in check. Cordelia had never spoken much about her childhood, even when they were together in finishing school. It seemed wrong to attempt to see the memories her friend had safeguarded for so long.

"When I saw marks on her, she explained them away." Gripping Electra's hand tighter, Cordelia said, "The first time I knew was when I saw him reach for her in the drawing room. She edged away from him, closed her eyes, then put up a hand as if to fend off a blow."

Cordelia took up her teaspoon and stirred her tea. "I always thought Lord Becknell so charming. Striking in looks.

Commanding somehow. You'd think I would have seen that he is so much like my own father."

"We all keep things hidden." Electra had been keeping the secret of her mother's madness for much of her life. "And Lord Becknell seems a man who is adept at shaping the way others perceive him."

"Good heavens, if he's done this thing, I hope your inspector can prove it."

"He will." Electra's feelings for Gideon Pierce might be a complicated tangle, but one thing she never doubted was his tenacity. "I sent him a note via Eccles. I hope you don't mind."

Eccles was one of the Redmaynes' footmen.

"Of course. I suspect it was about our visitor." Cordelia cast a glance upward, where Grace was napping.

"He'll want to speak to her about something she revealed to me."

"Oh?" Cordelia's eyes suddenly sparkled with curiosity.

Electra smiled. "I don't want to stoke rumors or put Grace in harm's way."

Cordelia blinked and her expression shuttered. "I can be discreet when necessary."

Electra squeezed her hand. "I know you can, but this is all very delicate. However, I do wonder if Grace might stay here for a few days. She's frightened and will have to begin looking for a new post."

"I could help her find a post," Cordelia offered.

"Would you?"

"Yes, of course." Cordelia ran her finger along a line of beading on her skirt. "I know the girl is afraid, but do you think she's in danger?"

Electra hesitated to answer. Becknell had let her leave the house after laying hands on her. It seemed unlikely he'd search for her. But she also couldn't bear the idea of putting Cordelia or anyone in her household in danger.

Perhaps once Gideon spoke to Grace, she could give the girl funds to leave the city, if only for a while.

If Lord Becknell had been hiding his true nature for so many years, what might he do to keep his secrets hidden?

Bow Street bustled with activity, even before night fell.

Gideon almost felt a twinge of sympathy for the young desk sergeant, who already looked beleaguered as he approached.

"Detective Inspector Pierce, attached to Vine Street."

It still felt odd to identify himself with a specific division. Prior to the reorganization of the Detective Division, he'd worked out of Scotland Yard and investigated wherever he was needed. But he did have connections within C Division.

"Is Sergeant Jones or Detective Inspector Norris about?"

"The inspector is in his office. Straight back and left at the last office."

"Thank you." Gideon checked his tie and resettled his cuffs as he made his way down the hall.

He found Norris with his head bent, writing quickly, his hand skimming over the page in front of him. Gideon rapped lightly on the doorframe.

"Good God, Pierce. It's been an age." Norris stood and braced his hands on his hips.

He was a tall, wiry man with a long face, thinning brown hair, and sharp blue eyes. The perpetual lines between his brows made him look as if he was frowning, but Gideon knew him well enough to know those lines were furrows of concentration. There wasn't a moment when Norris did not seem on high alert.

"It has been too long." He approached and the two shook hands.

"Messy business you're in the midst of with that Mayfair murder." Brow peaked above his piercing eyes, he asked, "Is that tangled case why you're here?"

"It is tangled, but I'm working at each knot." Gideon gave his old friend a half-smile. "I'm here to see about an old case from the summer of 1862. A death at the Halcyon Hotel."

Norris's thin brows bounced up, then he nodded. "Records that old would be in the basement storage. I can take you down."

"I can find my way."

Norris waved a hand, dismissing the assertion. "Gives me a reason to get out of that bloody chair."

They headed toward the station's main stairwell and wound their way down to the below-ground level. Norris pushed open the door to a room that smelled of dust, old paper, and damp. A gaslight sconce lit the front half of the room's rows of tall shelves, but cast the rest in shadows.

Norris went immediately to a middle row of ledgers, boxes, and case files. "What month did you say?"

"I didn't. It would be August of '62. The case of Mary Keane."

Norris bent to scan the labels on several boxes, went down the row and then around the shelves to the next row. He pulled out a ledger, handing it back to Gideon. "The case files should be there." He laid his hand on a box. "And any evidence collected will be in this box."

"I'll take both to review."

"Certainly." Norris collected the box. "You're welcome to use the table in my office to go through these."

They climbed the stairs and returned to Norris's office to find a constable waiting for him, shifting from one foot to another as if he had some urgent information to impart.

Gideon took the box out of the inspector's hands and proceeded into his office while Norris went off with the constable.

At the table Norris had indicated, he sat and opened the ledger, flipping through until he found the reports connected to the Keane case.

The police surgeon's report detailed similar findings to those in the Becknell case. The muscular rigor, the grimace in death as if the tendons of the face had seized. And Higgins's description bore that out too.

A sketch of the young woman was completed by one of the officers who responded to the Halcyon. Unfortunately, there were no sketches of the man or lady who'd been seen with Mary Keane before her death. Accounts by several employees, including one Oliver Collier, attested that the two strangers were unknown to the hotel's employees.

Finally, Gideon found a description of the two. The man was described as being tall, with a solid build and light brown hair. The height and physique matched Becknell, though the hair color did not. The lady was reported to be elegantly dressed, and she wore a hat with a veil, making it hard to detect anything beyond upswept hair.

Gideon skimmed the other reports of the hotel employee witnesses. One described her as having hair that was not blonde but rather a shade on the darker side. Another said she was hard to see through her dark veil, but "her hair seemed to have a red tint."

Gideon tapped his finger against that quote and thought of Helen Becknell.

Finally, he came to a chemist's report and his pulse kicked up at the finding that chemical tests conducted on Mary Keane's stomach contents revealed the presence of strychnine.

Taking his notebook out, Gideon began making notes.

When he flipped to another page in the ledger, he found a witness statement from a guest at the hotel. She had seen Miss Keane with the veiled lady and thought it was odd because they each had cups of tea, and she wondered how the lady could drink without lifting her veil.

Higgins hadn't mentioned anything about Mary Keane being served tea. He found Collier's account again and located a matching mention of both ladies partaking of the tea service that went around the lobby in the afternoon.

So where were the teacups?

Bless the officer who'd sketched the area where Mary Keane's body lay. On the table next to her chair, he'd sketched a teacup. But only one. A list of collected evidence did not list any teacups at all, yet the investigating officers may not have initially suspected poisoning. The evidence list was short, consisting of what seemed to be the contents of Miss Keane's pockets, which included an unsigned note and another item found clutched in Mary Keane's fist.

"A scrap of paper, the size and shape of a calling card, torn so that no full words are visible."

Gideon stood and removed the lid of the box, then sifted quickly through its clogged contents. Finally, he found an envelope marked with Miss Keane's name. Inside, he found what he sought. The note and the scrap of a calling card.

The note had been folded in half. His gut began to churn when he unfolded the half sheet of paper to find a message written in block letters.

MEET ME AT THE HALCYON. I MUST SEE YOU.

No SIGNATURE. No date. Just those nine words. Then he took up the scrap of what did indeed look like a calling card fragment. Its remaining edge was a calling card's size and rectangular in shape. The remnant was still slightly bent, its torn edge ragged, as if it had just been wrested from Miss Keane's fingers. He flipped it to find a few letters and numbers and drew in a sharp, quick breath.

Bec
16 H

Number Sixteen Hanover Square was where Becknell House sat. Gideon had never seen one of Philip Becknell's calling cards, but now he was determined to.

He took a moment to sketch out the bit of paper, carefully noting the letters and numbers in the exact manner they were arranged. Then he replaced the note and calling card piece in the envelope.

A moment later, Norris returned to his office. "Find what you were looking for?"

"For certain, I found some intriguing details."

"May I assist in any way?"

"Yes, might I ask you to keep these locked in your office? If my theory of this crime is correct, they'll be crucial evidence."

"You mean in the Becknell matter," Norris said with more certainty than query in his tone.

Gideon smiled. "I hesitate to get ahead of myself, but it's a possibility."

"Well, you know where to find me if you need anything else."

"Thank you, Norris."

As Gideon started out of his fellow detective's office, a

thought struck and he turned back. "Do you have anyone who's devilish good with research in those files downstairs?"

"Constable Coleman. The others think he's mad." Norris shrugged. "Says he enjoys the quiet."

"Would you have him look for anything else like the Keane case, from 1862 to now? Not just young ladies found in hotel lobbies, but anywhere in or near a hotel around the Strand?"

"You think your killer made a habit of it?"

"Two murders sixteen years apart does feel odd."

Norris offered him a grin that verged on sardonic. "Only if one assumes that killers always make sense."

Gideon laughed and nodded. "You have me there."

"But I agree," Norris added, crossing his arms. "If a man gets away with murder once, seems logical he'd see it as a solution to future problems too."

"My thought exactly."

CORDELIA INSISTED on a formal afternoon tea service when she was home, and Electra had gone up an hour ago to invite Grace to join them. But as soon as she opened the bedchamber door, she realized she was still sleeping.

Electra felt nothing but relief that the young woman felt safe enough at the Redmaynes' to finally rest. She decided to let Grace sleep while she and Cordelia took tea together in the drawing room.

They were on the cusp of finishing when a maid appeared on the threshold. Alice, who Electra guessed was about Grace's age, wore a blush that had turned her cheeks bright pink.

"It's Detective Inspector Pierce again, my lady." She shifted her gaze from Cordelia to Electra. "To see Miss Poole."

"Send him to the drawing room, Alice," Cordelia told her.

When the girl had gone, Cordelia turned a sly smile her way. "Ever since he interrupted the sitting on Monday evening, your handsome inspector has been the subject of much conversation among the staff. Or rather, among the *female* staff."

Electra had almost gotten past Cordelia's insistence on referring to him as hers, but the addition of *handsome*, which was undeniably true, made it worse.

By the time he strode into the room, Electra could feel her own cheeks heating as intensely as the young maid's had been.

He didn't miss it, of course. One dark brow lifted almost imperceptibly.

Cordelia stood and Electra followed suit.

"Inspector Pierce, welcome back. What can we do for you?" Cordelia asked, flicking her gaze between him and Electra.

"I sent him a message," Electra reminded her. "I suspect that's why he's here."

"Indeed," he said.

When neither of them said more, Cordelia narrowed her eyes. Electra shot her a look, and she emitted a little sigh.

"I suppose you two would prefer a bit of privacy. I'll take a wander in the garden."

"Thank you, my lady," Gideon said as she passed him and exited the room.

Electra approached, then strode around him to pull the pocket doors closed.

"What did you find at the Halcyon?"

When she looked up, his jaw was clenched in the way that indicated he had information or thoughts he had no wish to divulge.

"I understand if you cannot share certain details, but did you find anything useful?"

"Potentially. No proof solid enough that I could act on that alone, but tantalizing evidence nonetheless."

It was quite something how he could reveal nothing and yet stoke her eagerness to a fever pitch. *Tantalizing* was not a word Gideon Pierce would use lightly.

"When Grace comes down, I think you should hear her story."

He dipped his head. "Of course, though the fact that she did not appear for the inquest is troubling. She will eventually need to give a statement under oath if it's to prove useful in this case."

"I know. I think she could be persuaded. Right now, she's terrified."

"Of Becknell?"

"Yes, of what he's capable of. What she's been warned he's capable of, and he did put his hands on her today."

Gideon's gaze hardened. "He brutalized her?"

"He held her arms tight and wouldn't let her go."

"But she did get away."

"Yes, thank goodness." Electra recalled how shaken Grace had been when she showed up at Cordelia's door.

"Would you like some tea or finger sandwiches? Biscuits?" Electra strode over and piled a plate with a few items before he could answer. "Here." She suspected he'd been on the go from the moment he awoke and doubted he'd eaten a morsel since then.

He licked his lips and then took the offered plate, settling onto one of the armchairs.

"Will you tell me something, Electra?" His voice had dipped low.

The sound did odd things to her. Warmth kindled in her middle.

"Of course, Gideon."

"What did you see when you touched Lady Ashcombe?"

The question startled her. For some reason, she'd expected something personal or more intimate. But this was far better because it made her hope that some small part of him, however infinitesimal, might believe her.

"Precisely what she told you, though I could not hear Helen Becknell's words. If I'm touching someone, I can sometimes hear their thoughts, but when I see someone's memories, it is like seeing images through a cloud. They're sometimes murky and always silent."

He'd eaten two finger sandwiches while she spoke, then a lemon biscuit.

Before he could respond, they both turned at the sound of someone sliding the pocket doors open. Cordelia stood on the threshold, eyes wide.

"I went up to check on Grace."

Electra shot up from her chair. "She's gone, isn't she?"

"She'd arranged the pillows in the bed and pulled the coverlet over them, so it's impossible to know when she left."

"Can you ask your staff if any note was delivered to her?" Gideon asked. He'd gotten to his feet and stood at Electra's elbow.

"Of course." Cordelia swept away from the threshold.

She looked up at him. "What are you thinking? That someone lured her away?"

He pursed his lips. "Possibly." He turned to her with a sheen of concern in his eyes. "She mentioned an aunt. I'll contact her immediately. If she returns, send word to my address."

"I will, but there's something you need to know."

He lifted his chin as if intrigued. "What's that?"

"Grace told me there was another maid Becknell had a... dalliance with, in addition to Mary Keane. A young woman named Jenny Wilson. Three years ago—"

"In a hotel?"

"No, she disappeared from her room at Becknell House.

According to Grace, the girl left everything behind and vanished. But Grace did admit that she met Becknell at a hotel. The Swan, not the Halcyon."

His eyes shifted as he stared at the carpet, then lifted a hand to pinch the skin between his brows, as if attempting to sift the new details into some order.

The weight of his worry was palpable and hard to ignore. There were so many pieces to sort through in this case, and now she'd just added another. Electra had the impulse to reach for him, to comfort and encourage him. Once, she would have done so without hesitation.

"I'll look into it," he finally said.

"If I could help in any way—"

"No." The word came out sharply. "Matters are coming to a head," he added in an even tone. "You've already been dragged into this case in the papers. I'd like to know you're safe while I continue this investigation."

"A note was delivered to Grace, Inspector," Cordelia said as she stepped into the drawing room threshold. "My maid Alice took it up to her."

"Does Alice know who sent it?"

"She does not. From the young man's dress, she took him to be a footman." Cordelia's brows had pleated in concern. "I had Alice check and the note cannot be found in the bedchamber where she was resting. I'm sorry I can't help more." She lifted her gaze to Electra. "But I can reassure you on one score. I fully intend to keep my friend safe."

Gideon offered her a slow, respectful nod. "Thank you, my lady."

When he'd gone, Cordelia resumed her seat on the settee and rang the bell for the tea service to be cleared away. "I take it you don't plan to be guided by his concern for you," she said softly.

Electra saw no point in denying that she had a plan in mind. The pertinent question was whether Cordelia would assist her.

"What do you say to devising a way to *encounter* Lord Becknell?"

Cordelia immediately stood and went to an escritoire in the corner. "Kit will help," she said with utter confidence as she sat and took out a fresh sheet of paper.

Chapter Fifteen

Gideon had reached the point in the Becknell case when his mind and body, regardless of fatigue, refused to allow him more than a few hours of sleep. So, when he found himself awake before dawn, he washed and dressed and made his way to Vine Street.

After gathering a cup of scalding tea, he began to review his notes about the Becknell case as it now stood. He acknowledged the most obvious fact first, that three men had both the opportunity and a motive to end Helen Becknell's life. Two of them—Ballinger and Fox—could be placed at the scene of the crime by credible witnesses. And her husband was in town and may have returned to Becknell House, regardless of whether or not anyone in the house or the neighborhood saw him doing so.

Though Lord Martin Ballinger seemed to have genuine feelings for the viscountess, he also seemed tormented by the fact that she could never truly be his—not without scandal and ruined reputations. Lucan Fox was one of the most loathsome men Gideon had ever met. Indeed, the way he'd looked at Electra... He'd never had a more visceral yearning to pummel a man.

But Fox was a fop, a hedonistic ne'er-do-well, who seemed

too self-absorbed to bother murdering anyone. Yet if Helen Becknell's child was his, she could have made his life a good deal less blithely carefree, though that, again, would have embroiled her in scandal and social ruin too.

Those two factors provided a powerful motive for Philip Becknell. The man seemed to think very highly of himself and would undoubtedly want to avoid the whispers and ostracism that might result if he was embroiled in public revelations of his wife's liaisons.

Of course, there were multiple witnesses who could attest to Becknell's own paramours, but men, especially powerful noblemen, were expected to conduct themselves in such a manner.

But for a nobleman's wife to publicly cuckold her husband was another matter entirely, however inequitable such judgment might be.

Now, it seemed that Becknell might have been a killer long before his wife's death a few nights ago. Though he had only a scrap of paper and the second-hand accounts from Helen Becknell's friend. Grace Dobbs could confirm that he'd taken her to a hotel, if the young woman was ever found again. He was convinced the two young servants who'd now absconded— Grace and Jacob Finch—had witnessed, or had knowledge of, key events that might allow him to make an arrest. But the leads to Finch were almost non-existent, and Grace Dobbs seemed to possess an aptitude for avoidance and flight.

Yet what of the locket? The half-finished letter. They might mean nothing at all, at least in regard to how a noblewoman ingested poison and tumbled down the stairs.

Beatrice Linwood insisting the locket was hers struck him during his conversation with her, yet he now knew of its inscription and had yet to ask her to explain the markings about a child who apparently died within a day of its birth. Was it a brother, as Lady Becknell indicated to

Electra? Or her child, as Lord Ballinger claimed? If the locket did belong to Miss Linwood, why was Helen Becknell so seemingly determined to pass it into Electra's possession?

At the thought of Electra, his focus scattered, and he worked to rein it back to the case.

He had a gnawing sense that she would not cease her meddling in his investigation. He even understood her need to feel she'd made amends for failing to inform Lady Becknell of the premonition she'd had of her death. And, somehow, he'd now come to accept that she had foreseen something.

While he didn't have time to watch over Electra, especially on a day when he planned to question Philip Becknell again, he did have reason to arrange his call on Lord Becknell at a time when Electra might be at Becknell House too. She'd mentioned that Beatrice Linwood had invited her to tea.

Against protocol and his better judgment, he'd permitted her to accompany him when visiting Lady Ashcombe. It seemed like fair play for her to allow him to join her for afternoon tea with Miss Linwood.

But first he wanted to see if he could have a conversation with Mrs. Ellsworth, despite the early hour. Several of the women connected to Helen Becknell had mentioned her as an organizer of a charity many of them participated in, and if their claims were true, she could also provide a statement—under oath if this case went in the direction he expected it to—that she had seen marks of violence on Helen Becknell.

He stood, donned his hat, and headed out of the station, stopping only to inform the desk sergeant of his intended where-abouts—Mrs. Ellsworth's home in Cavendish Square and then Becknell House—so word could be got to him if Mr. Finch or Miss Dobbs were found, or any word came from the constable searching the files at Bow Street.

"THIS IS the quietest I've ever seen Hyde Park," Cordelia said as she peered for the umpteenth time out of her carriage window as they awaited the arrival of Kit and Lord Becknell, assuming that Kit's persuasion had been successful.

Electra vowed to herself that she'd return to the park at this precise hour once Helen Becknell's killer was caught. The peacefulness of the almost empty park was tantalizing. In the early morning light, a bit of mist hung over the Serpentine, and ducks and swans glided serenely across its surface.

"Perhaps Becknell turned him down," she said.

Cordelia made a little sound of protest. She trusted in her husband's charm, and Electra had to admit Kit possessed it in abundance. He was admired and well-liked by all of his colleagues and seemed capable of winning favor with even the staunchest curmudgeons in Parliament.

"You see!" Cordelia said at the sound of far-off hoofbeats, steady thuds on the sand of Rotten Row.

Electra craned to peer out. Two riders approached, and she recognized Kit's tousled brown hair and lean physique, and the larger, broader figure of Lord Becknell.

She lowered the veil of the ensemble Cordelia had loaned her and opened the carriage door. The Redmayne footman appeared and lowered the step, then handed her down.

Electra moved toward a copse of trees and waited. Through the black lace, she watched as the two men stopped their horses and dismounted.

Kit led Becknell to where she stood. "I believe you saw each other at the inquest, but may I introduce Miss Electra Poole."

Becknell wore dark glasses as if prepared for a sunny day, a dark suit, and black gloves. "This is quite irregular, Miss Poole, but I admit I did hope for an opportunity to speak with you privately."

"We thought this might suit," Kit said genially. "Early enough to have few observers, and away from Becknell House, where reporters and neighbors must surely be watching everyone who comes and goes."

"Quite." Becknell turned a tight-lipped gaze Kit's way. "Would you give us a few moments, Redmayne?"

"Of course." Kit gave Electra a single long look that said *I'm not going far.*

"Thank you," she told him, then he took the bridle of Becknell's horse and his own and approached the spot where Cordelia waited in their carriage.

Becknell gestured to a wrought-iron bench not far from the trees. "Shall we?"

Once they were seated—Becknell settled against the bench's back and Electra perched on the front edge—she turned toward him.

"Thank you for coming, my lord."

He side-eyed her from behind his dark glasses. She could see the shift of his eyes.

Then she saw red. A corona of it seemed to surround him, though she'd not noticed it when she watched him at the inquest. The color shifted from bright to muddy, shimmering in the air around him. Rage. Passion. The two emotions rippled off of him.

Electra swallowed and sought to focus her mind. "I suspect you want to know about what Lady Becknell and I discussed on Sunday evening," she said, her voice unaccountably low. It was as if she couldn't quite catch her breath.

"I confess myself curious," he said. His voice had pitched low too. "What did she want from you, Miss Poole?"

"To know if you were deceiving her." She'd decided on this

approach with Cordelia, and watched him—the colors around him fading now—for any reaction.

Though the movement was almost imperceptible, his mouth seemed to curve slightly. Then he shocked Electra by reaching up to remove his glasses as he shifted to turn his body toward hers.

"Miss Poole." He all but purred her name, and she felt a bit of the man's charismatic power, even if she was immune to it. "There were many secrets between Helen and I, I regret to say." He smiled, an incongruent flash that didn't match his words. "She had hers. I had mine. But I suspect that's not truly why she invited you to come that night, is it?"

"She asked about her brother."

He narrowed his eyes, and he cocked his head slightly. "Did she indeed?" He'd clenched his jaw and turned his gaze out to stare at the Serpentine. "And what did you tell her?"

"That I could not reach him."

"No, I imagine you could not," he gritted out, as if he struggled to loosen his jaw, even to speak.

"Were you there that night?" Electra reached out and touched the sleeve of his jacket, gripping his arm through the fabric.

Rather than pull away, he stared at her. "Miss Poole?" he whispered. "Are you quite all right?" He stunned her by laying his gloved hand over her bare one that still clasped his arm.

Her body juddered, and she saw him arguing with someone in what appeared to be a darkened hallway of Becknell House. A woman strode ahead of him, her back to him, and Electra noted her auburn hair pulled into a tight knot at her nape. Becknell's armed reached for her, wrenching her by the shoulder, and Beatrice Linwood looked back at him with fury in her eyes.

"Miss Poole." His voice had risen in volume, and it sharpened to an irritated edge as he pulled away from her. "What on earth is the matter with you?"

"I...felt a moment a dizziness."

His dark eyes narrowed, then his jaw softened and a bit of warmth lit his gaze—whether genuine or feigned. "And are you fully recovered now?"

"Yes. Forgive me."

"Take off the veil," he said in a commanding tone.

Electra looked around them. "I thought it better to remain disguised."

"I want to look into your eyes," he said, his voice low and calm again.

His composure was so at odds with the roiling anger she'd felt from him. It felt as if he'd shed it now, or concealed it somehow.

"I'll lift my veil if you'll remove a glove."

He barked out a laugh. "I see. You wish to clasp my hand and tell me my fortune, is that it?"

"Yes."

"Very well. Shall we shed our coverings together?" He was already gripping the fingers of his glove with his opposite hand.

Electra lifted the edge of her veil. He slipped his glove off and held his hand out to her, his eyes now locked on hers.

"What strange eyes you have, Miss Poole. Perhaps you are a seer of some kind after all."

Electra felt a flicker of that energy—passion, anger, and a relentless sort of determination. He was not a man used to be denied anything.

"Go on, Miss Poole," he urged, moving his hand an inch closer. "Take my hand. Read my palm. Do what you do. I have nothing to hide." One dark brow inched up at that.

But then, out of the corner of her eye, she noticed the tremble of his lower lip, a muscle ticking in his cheek. Then he stilled again. So calm and unbothered that she could almost convince herself she'd imagined those little indicators of his unease.

Yet she hadn't. For the merest moment, she'd seen beyond the facade, and realized now that it was an almost flawless one. He had a magnetism that made him seem compelling, even with everything she'd heard about him, and everything she suspected he'd done.

Electra slipped her palm against his and curled her fingers around his much larger hand.

"Did you kill your wife, my lord?" she whispered.

His dark brows bent. "Shouldn't you know that, Lady Seer?"

That moment arose again—the confrontation with his sister-in-law. She saw Miss Linwood shouting, but heard nothing. *What have you done?* The question hung in the air between Becknell and his sister-in-law, or perhaps he held the thought in his mind now. Electra couldn't be sure.

Try as she might, she could not see Helen Becknell. Until she did.

As if the image in Becknell's mind of the argument with Miss Linwood merged with the vision she'd seen when Lady Becknell embraced her, she saw the viscountess lying dead. But the view was from above, as if from someone standing at the top of the stairs.

Did Becknell stand at the top of the stairs and look down on his dead wife? Had he pushed her?

Becknell flinched and pulled his hand from her hold.

"Well, tell me, what is my fortune?" he said almost teasingly. "Tell me my fate."

Electra searched his dark eyes, but she couldn't detect a single emotion. They were as still and deep as an unmoving pool. As dark as spilled ink.

"To face the truth," she whispered.

The pleasant mask slipped a bit, his mouth tightening, eyes narrowing. Then he got to his feet.

"What was the point of this interlude, Miss Poole?" He sneered down at her. "To convince me of your spiritual prowess? I'm afraid you have failed to impress, young lady."

Electra stood. It fascinated her that even as his tone turned derisive, she did not feel the anger she had when they'd first sat down.

"I wanted to meet you, my lord."

At that, he transformed again, flicking an assessing look down the length of her body. "If only the circumstances were different. But as they are, I can only bid you adieu and hope you got what you came for."

With a sharp nod, he applied his glove again and stalked off toward where Kit still held the reins of his mount.

Electra lifted a hand to her throat, tracing her fingers over the outline of her mother's cross pendant underneath her high-necked blouse as she steadied her breathing.

"I think," she murmured to herself, "I very well might have."

Unfortunately, Gideon would not believe any of it.

THE ELLSWORTHS' Cavendish Square townhouse didn't quite compare to the Becknells' fully white-washed facade, but it was elegant enough to announce the wealth and respectability of its inhabitants just as effectively.

A wizened butler opened the door to him, and bid him to wait for Mrs. Ellsworth in the drawing room with scrupulous politeness, and not a single look of disdain when Gideon announced his title.

Mrs. Ellsworth entered the room only a few minutes later.

Gideon was immediately struck by her youth—close to his own thirty years, he'd guess—and beauty. She had a heart-shaped face, Cupid's bow lips, bright blue eyes, and her sable hair was swept up in an artful arrangement.

"Detective Inspector Pierce, I saw you at the inquest." She spoke in a light, lilting tone, and he detected a bit of a Welsh influence.

"I didn't realize you'd attended," he said.

"I felt compelled to, since Helen and I were quite close." She gestured to a chair on the opposite side of a low table between them. "Shall we sit?"

He waited until she'd situated herself on the settee before taking a seat.

"I have a feeling I know why you've come," she said immediately. "Rosalind, Lady Ashcombe, said she'd spoken to you." She looked at him expectantly. "You'll want me to confirm her account."

"Actually, I'd like you tell me of your relationship with Lady Becknell," he said as he positioned his notebook on his thigh.

A sad smile curved her mouth, almost wistful. "I've known Helen for almost a decade. She was a renowned London hostess when I married my husband, and she took me under her tutelage." Mrs. Ellsworth dipped her head, looking up at him under thick dark lashes. "I was a young wife to a widower, and some of the other ladies didn't take to me. But Helen did. She accepted and guided me."

"That was kind of her."

"And I never forgot that kindness. But eventually, I found my place in establishing a charitable organization. I was gratified Helen helped me promote it and drew her own friends in as well."

"In the decade you knew Lady Becknell, I presume you

observed her with Lord Becknell often. Can you tell me about them?"

She nodded. "Yes, we might as well come to the point. Helen and Philip had been together nearly a decade by the time I met her. As a newlywed, in the first days of love, I noticed how different they were to Henry and I."

"In what regard?"

Her light laugh seemed more nervous than mirthful. "We were still quite doting. Helen and Philip were more like allies, perhaps friends, than what I thought a marriage should be."

"Can you tell me more?" Gideon prompted.

"They had their own lives—interests, pursuits...paramours."

"Did Helen tell you that they both had paramours?"

Rather than answer, she gave a quick nod. "She said they were open with each other about their dalliances."

"Did you spend much time at Becknell House?"

"Early in our friendship, I did."

"Was her sister there at that time?"

"Yes, from the time I knew Helen, she was."

"And did you have occasion to observe their relationship?"

It was the first time her eyes seemed to shutter. "May I be forthright, Inspector?"

Gideon gave a half-smile. "I certainly hope you will be."

"I never got on with Miss Linwood. She is so expressionless. And she has no friends. Rarely goes into society. I found it most irksome. Could she never smile or make conversation? The lady withheld herself, as if her feelings were stoppered up in a bottle. How can anyone be so unceasingly controlled?"

As she spoke, Mrs. Ellsworth became more animated, her cheeks flushing and voice rising. "Goodness, forgive me."

Gideon tried not to smile, nor take offense that she'd all but described him. "You were being honest."

"Too honest."

What struck him as odd was that Mrs. Ellsworth's account was incongruous with the lady who'd been too overcome by emotion to speak to him the day after her sister's murder. Though perhaps the loss of her sibling had broken her usual reserve.

"How did Lady Becknell and Miss Linwood get on?"

"Oh, Helen, would not hear a cross word about her sister. They were confidantes. She said Beatrice was the only person she truly trusted." Mrs. Ellsworth inhaled and squared her narrow shoulders. "Until those last weeks."

Gideon lifted a brow. "How were those weeks different?"

"Helen was increasingly agitated. Very suspicious of everyone."

"Suspicious?" He cocked his head. "Did she divulge why?"

"She suspected her husband and sister were lying to her." She lifted her shoulders in a shrug. "I don't know what she thought they were deceiving her about. I asked her to explain, but she said it was something she couldn't reveal. A family secret."

Gideon's ears pricked up. "She said that? A family secret?"

"Yes, and I knew not to press. She never spoke ill of her sister or of Philip, though I knew he likely deserved it."

"Why did you know that?" he asked.

She bent her head so deeply, he could not read her expression. When she lifted her chin and faced him again, her cheeks had turned a bright pink.

"Because I knew Philip better than I should have," she said in a shuddery voice. "It was a mistake. A moment of exceedingly poor judgment."

Gideon felt the tips of his own ears burn in sympathetic embarrassment for the lady. As cold as he sometimes managed to be, he knew that matters of the heart were complicated and denying one's desires took a toll.

"In your experience of Philip Becknell, socially and otherwise, can you give me your opinion of him?" Gideon asked, keeping his voice flat.

"I suppose my opinion would match the general consensus. He is handsome, charming, compelling, and powerful."

Gideon nodded. "And did you see aspects of him that did not match the general consensus?"

She pressed her bow lips together. "You refer now to the marks on Helen that Lady Ashcombe spoke of."

"Yes, tell me about those."

"Rosalind refers to a specific incident, perhaps, but I saw marks on Helen many times throughout the years of our friendship. She explained them away as clumsiness, a tumble she took, scratching herself on a rose bush."

"Did you believe her?"

Mrs. Ellsworth's blue eyes darted away from his, and she stared toward the window on the far side of the room, though a curtain was drawn across it.

"Sadly, I did." She wrapped her arms around herself, chafing her arms, though the room was warm from a blazing fire in the hearth. "I believed her until I could not. Until he left marks on me."

"Would you tell me about that?" Gideon learned forward.

"Henry can never know. My husband."

"He will never hear it from me, Mrs. Ellsworth."

She stood up from the settee, and Gideon thought she might walk out and refuse to say more. But she crossed the room to a drinks cart and poured herself a bit of pale wine into a dainty etched glass.

"Sherry?" she said lightly. "I know you cannot as you are about your duty, but it felt impolite not to offer."

Gideon waited, expecting to resume her seat, but she didn't. She stood near the fireplace.

"As I said, our...liaison was brief. I sought to end it, regretting my mistake immediately. Philip became angry, insistent. On one occasion, he pinned me, squeezing my arms, holding me so tight I could not breathe." She sipped at her drink. "A servant happened by and he released me, but that incident terrified me. I never wanted anything more to do with him. And I told Helen I understood."

Gideon cocked his head. "How did she respond?"

Mrs. Ellsworth lifted her hand and gestured toward the settee she'd occupied. "We sat there and cried together. She never acknowledged anything openly, but her tears told me enough."

"So she never spoke openly about his propensity for violence?"

"Not to me, no. But I experienced it myself, so I know it to be true."

Gideon closed his notebook softly and settled it into his pocket along with his pencil.

"Thank you for being honest about difficult matters. I may need you to give a sworn statement regarding those matters."

Gideon stood and Mrs. Ellsworth stepped closer. "Did he do this thing to her?"

"If he did, I must prove it. And any testimony regarding his prior acts of violence may assist me in that endeavor."

Chapter Sixteen

Gideon left Mrs. Ellsworth's townhouse determined to return to Vine Street in order to make a case to Chief Douglas that Becknell should be taken into custody.

Becknell had means, ample motive, and a history of violence that several witnesses would attest to. The chief would balk at their inability to put Becknell in his house on the night of the murder, and their failure to detect the means by which her ladyship had been poisoned. But strychnine was at hand in the household, accessible to Lord Becknell, and since none of the servants were present, they might never know precisely how her ladyship had been persuaded to eat or drink something dosed with poison.

But he now had a handful of witnesses who'd described violent encounters with the man, and Gideon could not stomach the notion of leaving him free to perpetrate more.

If nothing else, he wanted a statement from the man while he was in the station and fully aware that he had been centered in Gideon's crosshairs.

He strode down the street, looking for an available cab, and then heard someone behind him call his name.

"Detective Inspector Pierce," the man repeated.

Gideon turned to find a uniformed constable approaching at a quick clip. "Message for you, sir."

The young man handed over a folded piece of paper, and Gideon nodded in thanks. As the young constable walked away, he unfolded the note. As he read the message written in Constable Clegg's neat, narrow hand, every muscle in Gideon's body drew increasingly more tense.

"Rot and damnation," he said under his breath, then shoved the note in his pocket and broke into a sprint to find a hansom farther down the street.

Once he found one, he all but jumped inside, quickly folding the doors over. Then he called Sir Christopher Redmayne's address up to the driver and prayed that a certain irrepressible, vexing woman was there and would stay put until he could speak to her.

All the way, he tapped his fingers atop his thigh and ground his teeth until his jaw ached.

When the Redmayne townhouse was in sight, he flipped up the half doors on the cab, ready to descend the moment it stopped. After paying the driver, he approached the door in long strides.

The young maid he'd encountered on Monday evening answered and immediately smiled. "Inspector, are you here for Miss Poole again?"

"I am indeed. Please tell me she's here."

"She is." The girl stepped back so that he could enter the foyer. "The drawing room."

"I know the way."

She bobbed a little curtsy to him, which was a first in his life. It was somehow both slightly amusing and a bit unsettling.

Gideon made his way to the drawing room and found her.

She sat at a small desk against the far wall, her head bent as she wrote.

"Electra."

She blinked when she looked up at him, then her eyes rounded. "I was just writing you a letter."

"Well, now you can tell me whatever it is you wished to say."

Gideon flipped back the edges of his long coat and braced his hands on his hips. Would she tell him the truth, he wondered, or prevaricate? Or omit. He was barely keeping the fierce stew of anger at her and fear for her under control.

"I spoke to Lord Becknell." She narrowed her blue-green eyes. "You knew that," she said. "It's why you're here, isn't it?"

Gideon tipped his head up and stared at the molded ceiling, fighting to tamp down his feelings. He didn't want to shout or chastise. Electra never reacted well to such high-handedness. She certainly hadn't ever been bent to her father's will when he attempted to discipline her.

"Why, Electra?"

She stood, her hands clasped before her almost primly. "He's your prime suspect, and I wanted to see for myself."

Gideon lifted a hand and ran it through his hair. "With your...powers?"

"Yes. I thought if I could touch him—"

"You touched him?"

"It's how I see best."

He said nothing, mostly because he'd decided silence was the best course since she never listened to him regardless.

She stepped closer, so close they were almost toe to toe.

"I know you're angry," she said quietly. "I understand that I've not obeyed—"

Gideon burst into laughter at the word. "That would imply that you've ever obeyed me in anything at any time."

It wasn't laughter of amusement so much as a release of all the anxiety he'd been wrestling with since Clegg's report that Lord Becknell had left his house with Sir Christopher Redmayne shortly after Clegg went to watch Becknell House and was seen speaking to Electra in Hyde Park.

"What did you learn from him?" he had to ask. Regardless of how much it terrified him to think of her having anything to do with the man he suspected had murdered his wife, as well as several other women.

"He was there the night Lady Becknell died."

Gideon froze, and a shiver skittered down his back. "You saw him kill her?"

"No." She shook her head, looking supremely disappointed. "I never saw him touch her at all. But I do believe he was there at the moment she fell down the stairs or immediately afterward."

"So you spoke to the man for nothing."

"I saw something else too."

"Go on then."

"He was arguing with his sister-in-law."

Gideon narrowed an eye. "She was there the night her sister was murdered?"

"I don't know. I can't say I was seeing the same moment. When I touched his hand—"

"Damnit, Electra."

She reached up a hand and laid it on his chest for the briefest moment, as if to calm him. When she pulled her hand away, Gideon glanced down at the spot where she'd touched him.

"I saw Miss Linwood looking at him as if she was angry. Then the images shifted, and I saw Lady Becknell lying at the bottom of the stairs, but from above, as if Becknell was looking down from the top of the stairs."

"As if he'd pushed her?"

"I never saw that, but possibly he did."

Gideon scrubbed a hand across his face. "I need to return to Vine Street. What can I do to convince you to stay here and far away from Becknell House?"

ELECTRA DISLIKED SEEING Gideon so hard-pressed. She could almost feel the tightness in his body as he stood just inside Cordelia's drawing room. He was like a pulled bow, ready to rush off at any moment. He must have had a dozen other things to do, but he was here, and she could sense his concern for her.

He looked as if he'd gotten no sleep, yet that ever-present determined flint still sparked in his eyes.

"I can stay here for a bit," she told him, wanting to give him something. "But have you forgotten that I am supposed to meet with Beatrice Linwood for tea?"

"No." He shook his head, emphasizing his refusal. "I want you far away from Becknell House."

Anticipation—that's what she felt rising off of him.

"Are you going to arrest him?" she asked quietly.

He bit his lip as he held her gaze. "That is my intention."

Electra turned away from him and began pacing the edge of the rectangular rug that occupied much of the drawing room floor.

"What if you waited?"

"Why the devil would I do that?"

"Because Beatrice Linwood might know something."

Gideon made a sound somewhere between a sigh and a growl. "That can be done later. Becknell is my priority."

"You've discovered evidence against him?" Electra suspected he wouldn't answer, and when he didn't, she tried a different approach. "What if Beatrice Linwood could give you more? I saw her arguing with him. Perhaps she knows he did it. If she admitted as much, it could be used to leverage him, could it not?"

"I'm not letting you walk into Becknell House until I speak to Chief Douglas."

"What if you came with me?" Electra warmed to the idea. "We could take tea with her together."

"Electra..."

"We do well as partners. Don't you think?"

He swallowed visibly at that, and something warm flickered in his amber-brown eyes.

"How is it that each time I have a perfectly good plan, you upend it?"

"Perhaps you might consider whether I'm enhancing it."

Reaching up, he pushed a thumb into the curve above his right eye. "Why are you so bloody determined to speak to Miss Linwood when I already have?"

"Because I might see more from that night."

The longcase clock chimed the top of the hour, and Gideon crossed his arms. "Electra, I need to go. Send a note to Miss Linwood and cancel your tea. If you still want to speak with her at day's end, do it then. With any luck, Becknell will be in custody by then."

What he said was reasonable, and if she didn't feel certain that Beatrice Linwood might strengthen his case against her brother-in-law, she would have simply nodded and let him be on his way. But she couldn't.

"Stay here, please" he said in a low voice, then he pivoted and began to walk away. To her shock, he stopped and turned back to her.

"Did you get one of Becknell's calling cards by chance?" he asked.

"No. Why do you ask?"

"I'd like to get a look at one of them. I'll be sure locate one when I go to Becknell House."

Electra was frustrated she couldn't go with him, not only to satisfy her hunch about what Beatrice Linwood might reveal but because she couldn't help him.

"May I ask one favor?"

"You may ask."

"If you do take Becknell into custody, will you let me know? I'll then go to see Miss Linwood."

His mouth curved in a smile, but then he scoffed as if exasperated. "You're the most determined woman I know." He doffed his hat. "Yes, I'll send word."

After he'd gone, Electra couldn't help but smile. She was determined, and she intended to keep her word to him and to Beatrice Linwood. She went to the desk to write a letter, letting Miss Linwood know she could not attend their planned tea, but would come later in the day, if that was convenient.

As she signed her name, Cordelia's housekeeper stepped into the room and handed her a folded piece of paper.

"Messenger brought it not a moment ago, Miss Poole."

Electra unfolded the piece of paper and was startled by the name at the bottom.

My sister says you asked for me. Meet me at Covent Garden as soon as you can if you still wish to speak to me. Jacob Finch

Electra shoved the note in her skirt pocket and rushed out into the entry hall to fetch her cloak. As she put on her gloves, Mrs. Hurst approached.

"Going out, Miss Poole?" she asked.

"Did Inspector Pierce tell you to keep watch over me?"

The housekeeper's kind brown eyes rounded a bit. "He did, miss."

"I'm only going out for a moment, but will you have a message sent for me to Becknell House?" Electra offered her the letter she'd written.

The older woman looked a bit hard put, as if she wasn't sure whether to refuse or help her.

"Of course, miss," she finally said, reaching for the letter but casting a concerned look Electra's way. "Inspector Pierce won't be best pleased."

"But he will be, Mrs. Hurst, because the young man who sent me the note the messenger brought is someone he's been trying to locate, and I can deliver him into the inspector's hands."

Electra opened the door and heard Mrs. Hurst working up to a sound of protest.

Turning back, she clasped one of her hands. "Worry not, Mrs. Hurst. All will be well."

Gideon's first act when he returned to Vine Street was to send a constable to Becknell House to fetch one of his lordship's calling cards so that he could compare it to the scrap found in Mary Keane's hand. He asked the constable to obtain one as surreptitiously as possible, but not to leave until he had one in hand.

Then he sat down to do what he and most of the other police officers he knew disliked most about their work. He wrote reports. Namely, he compiled a report for Chief Douglas, documenting every bit of information he'd gathered about Lord Becknell's proclivities. Evidence of his propensity for violence, particularly toward women. And noting what was obvious from the moment he realized Becknell had not been in Oxfordshire on Sunday night and early Monday. The man had been in London and may very well have been at his home.

Obviously, he couldn't mention anything that Electra had conveyed to him about what she'd *seen* in her visions. But as much as he didn't want to believe such flimflam, something about her certainty bolstered him. He trusted her, and he always had.

He wrote until his hand cramped, then stood, stretched, sat, and wrote some more. He knew that he needed to be as thorough now at the start of this process as possible. There could be no loose threads. There could be no mistakes if they were going to successfully prosecute a peer of the realm.

After nearly an hour, he set down his pen and started at the beginning, reviewing what he'd written while massaging the soreness in his hand. He wondered, not for the first time, why the police didn't have one of those new-fangled typewriting machines like he'd seen in Lady Becknell's bedchamber.

As he stood to get himself a fresh cup of tea, Constable Braithwaite came into his office and plunked down one of Lord Philip Becknell's calling cards. As soon as he took up the cream rectangle of thick pasteboard, his gut twisted.

He told himself Becknell may very well have changed the style of his calling card over the years. The one in Mary Keane's hand had been simple, not at all ornate.

But there was no denying the fact that the one he held in his hand did not match the scrap that had been found in Mary Keane's hand.

He opened his notebook and reviewed the sketch he'd made of the scrap of card. A rushing sounded in his ears, and he realized it was sound of his blood as his heart raced.

The paper was ragged at the very edge where the name would have continued. And he realized that what he'd noted down of the visible letters—Bec—could very well have been Bea.

Beatrice Linwood, whose hair had a red tint, as one Halcyon employee had described the woman who'd taken tea with Mary Keane. Could she have been that woman?

Electra said she'd seen Becknell looking down on his wife's body, and then Becknell and Beatrice Linwood having a row.

Could they have conspired to kill Helen Becknell? And Mary Keane?

Flipping pages in his notebook, he checked back on what Beatrice Linwood said about the night of her sister's murder. She'd been visiting a friend, then spent a night with Lady Ashcombe. He should have inquired of Lady Ashcombe when he spoke to her, both regarding her supposed illness and Beatrice Linwood tending to her that evening.

Standing, he went out into the hall and found Braithwaite, bidding him to follow Gideon into his office.

"I want you to call on a Mrs. Agnes Dunstan of Number Five Compton Terrace in Islington." Gideon read the lady's direction from his notes. "Ask her when Miss Beatrice Linwood arrived to visit and departed on Sunday night."

Braithwaite had his own notebook out and wrote down the details Gideon provided. "Yes, sir."

"Leave word here with the desk sergeant regarding what you've found. I'll be making my own inquiries, but I'll stop in to see what you discovered."

Braithwaite nodded, then headed off to seek out Mrs. Dunstan.

Gideon retrieved his hat and went out to find a hansom. He'd speak to Lady Ashcombe himself. He wanted to look into the lady's eyes when he asked her to confirm Miss Linwood's alibi.

As he settled into the hansom and the cabbie turned the

vehicle out into the flow of traffic, he thought immediately of Electra. The last time he'd spoken to Lady Ashcombe, she'd been crucial to causing the countess to reveal Helen Becknell's story about Mary Keane.

He rapped on the cab wall, and the driver slid open the small door above his head.

"Can we change course to Russell Square first?"

"Aye, sir." The cabbie slid the door shut and soon they were heading to the Redmaynes' townhouse. Now he could only hope that Electra had—for once—done what he'd asked and remained at home.

The rest of the journey there, doubts crept in. What if she had gone off to meet with Beatrice Linwood regardless of his wishes?

When the Redmaynes' young housemaid, Alice, opened the door, there was no blush or smile for him. The girl's eyes widened.

"Is Miss Poole here?" he asked as his throat grew tight.

Alice gave an infinitesimal shake of her head. "No, Inspector."

Gideon's balled his hands and fought for control. "Where is she?"

The girl darted her gaze away from his.

"If she bid you not to tell me, I would ask you to consider that her recklessness may put her in danger. I cannot help her if I do not know where she is."

"Covent Garden, sir. A message came for her. Left not quarter of an hour ago."

"Thank you." Gideon called the words over his shoulder as he had already turned to scan the square for an available cab.

Once he found one, he tried—and failed—to unclench his jaw.

He reminded himself that Electra was clever and resourceful. She was the daughter of the best detective he'd ever known. And *if* she possessed some extraordinary sense beyond the ones he understood, then that could aid her too.

But who had sent her a message? Who had lured her to Covent Garden?

His first thought was of the smug debaucher, Lucan Fox. But why would he draw her out to Covent Garden when he had that garish, untidy townhouse in Soho?

As the carriage careened off Long Acre and turned down James Street, Gideon's pulse began to race. Alice said Electra had departed a quarter of an hour earlier.

If someone meant her harm, they would have had time to do it and then slip away into the throng of people and stalls.

He prayed he wasn't too late.

Chapter Seventeen

Electra walked among the fruit and flower stalls of the busy Covent Garden market and wondered if the note she had received might have been some sort of ruse.

When she'd arrived ten minutes ago, she'd had no notion where to find Jacob Finch. He had not mentioned any landmark or specific location where they should meet, and the market was so large that she could only assume his intention was to keep watch for her.

As she passed a few gentlemen walking on their own, she searched for Finch's singular features and reddish-brown hair.

Then she returned to the piazza, since the space was more open and she could watch others more easily. She scanned faces. And then she saw him. Much as when she spotted him outside of Helen Becknell's inquest, he remained still and watchful while others moved about him. He wore a long overcoat and the same well-worn top hat she'd seen him in on Wednesday.

As soon as their gazes met, he approached. But rather than walk straight up to her, he paused and nudged his chin to the right, indicating she should follow him.

Electra did and he led her to a spot near a pillar, where they were partially obscured from others' view.

"Hello, Mr. Finch," she said as he stood, darting looks around them as if fearful they were being observed.

"Miss Poole. Thank you for coming."

"Your note was intriguing, and as you know, I've been looking for you."

He locked his dark eyes on her. "Why have you?"

"I thought you might lead me to Grace Dobbs."

That shocked him, judging by the jerk of his shoulders and rounding of his eyes. "I know nothing about Grace. I thought... you found out something about me."

"Your sister said there was something you might tell me, but that it was your secret to tell."

He shook his head. "Nothing you need to know."

"You were adopted by the Finch family?"

His head came up sharply. "Who told you that?"

"Your sister said they took you in."

"They did. They were good me."

"She didn't like you working for the Becknells, why is that?"

He looked at her a long while, and she felt his anxiousness, his fear, his guilt.

"The first day I met you, Jacob, you were feeling guilty."

The young man was emitting such a spiral of emotions that she considered how best to urge him to unburden himself. And it was apparent that he was struggling.

"Do you know something," she asked softly, "about what happened to Lady Becknell?" Electra took a chance and reached for him, resting her hand lightly on his arm. She'd removed her gloves in the carriage on the way over.

"If you do, you should tell me, and I will help you in any manner I am able to."

She moved her hand down to his hand and clasped it gently.

"You sought me out for a reason today."

I didn't want to do it.

The thought was his, but it was as clear in Electra's mind as if it was her own. Her body tensed as images arose—Helen Becknell holding Jacob's hands. Tears streamed down her face. She held up an object that shone gold—the locket. Lady Becknell reached up to touch his face, but Jacob pushed her away.

Electra drew in lung-filling breaths as the images faded.

"Miss Poole, you unwell?" Jacob clasped her hand and shifted their positions so that she could lean against the column for support.

"Is your true name Edward?" she asked him.

He dipped his head, then nodded. "Can you read the thoughts in my head?"

"No, not at all of them. But the locket with hair inside. It's your hair. But the baby, you, never died."

He swallowed hard and nodded. "She kept it all this time." Eyes almost beseeching, he said, "That's how I came to see she cared for me, even if she gave me away when she was young herself." A sheen of unshed tears glistened in his eyes. "I didn't think my father or mother ever gave me a second thought."

Electra imagined Helen Becknell would have been quite young and as yet unmarried to Philip Becknell. Perhaps, to avoid scandal, her family had insisted on taking the child from her.

"How were you able to find her?"

"No, miss, she found me. I don't rightly know how. She never said. Maybe she always knew where I was."

Electra thought back to that night she'd met Helen Becknell. "Was she afraid Lord Becknell was deceiving her?"

"They rowed a lot. But I know they loved each other once."

There was such earnestness in his voice that Electra knew it was what he believed, whether it was true for the Becknells or not.

"So, your mother found you and employed you in her home."

"Margaret told me not to take the post. Now I wish I never did."

"Why?"

"Look what's happened, miss."

"What *did* happen, Jacob?" Electra tipped her head to catch his gaze. "Do you know who murdered your mother?"

The young man recoiled, then pulled his hand from hers. "No, miss." His brow furrowed. "She's not my mother." He began to back a step away from her. "You're mistaken. I had nothing to do with Lady Becknell dying."

"Jacob, please." She reached for him, but he backstepped again.

"Electra." Gideon's voice echoed from across the piazza.

She glanced back to see him stalking toward her in long, ground-eating strides. Even from a distance, she could see the fearsome look on his face.

"Jacob..." Electra turned to reassure the young man, to keep him with her until Gideon could speak to him.

But Jacob Finch was gone. She looked around, then lifted onto her toes to see past two tall gentlemen blocking her view, but he'd slipped into the crowd.

"You've scared him away." She now wore her own scowl to match Gideon's. "Did you not see me speaking to Jacob Finch?"

Gideon scanned the stalls and people nearby. "I saw you speaking to someone. All I made out were dark clothes and a hat. Where is he?"

Electra planted her hands on her hips. "In the wind now that you startled him."

From Gideon, she felt the one emotion that she often did whenever she was near him in these past few days—relief.

"I'm all right," she told him, sensing he wished to know.

"You're certain?"

"Of course. I don't believe he meant me any harm. I think he wanted to confess something, but we never got that far." Electra sighed out a frustrated breath.

"Come with me," Gideon said, offering her his arm, elbow out, so she could hook her arm with his, "and you can tell me all about it in the cab."

"Are you taking me back to Cordelia's? Or perhaps you'd like to take me to Vine Street and put me in a cell," she said wryly.

"I could, if you prefer that." The merest hint of a smile flickered at the edge of his lips. "Or you could accompany me back to Lady Ashcombe's so I may put a few more questions to her."

"Oh." Electra crossed to him and slipped her arm in his. "Why didn't you say so?"

"So HE's the child Lady Becknell was convinced was still alive?" Gideon could understand why a mother might wish to seek out her child, but why employ him?

"I don't think so," Electra murmured beside him.

"But he admitted he's Edward, so the inscription refers to him?"

"Possibly."

"What aren't you telling me?"

"I'm not withholding," she said, bristling, "just attempting to work it out in my mind."

Gideon cast a glance at her. She was so close, he could feel her pressed against the entire left side of his body.

"If you tell me, we can work it out together," he said in a coaxing tone that sometimes—once in a great while—had worked on Electra.

"Though he admitted his name is Edward, he was appalled when I suggested Lady Becknell was his mother. He insisted she was not."

Gideon sifted the conversations he'd had in the past four days and an odd, tangential memory came to him.

"Do you remember when you dragged me to the British Museum?" he asked.

Electra shifted beside him. "I dragged you there many times."

"You did indeed, but do you recall the necklace you were fond of? The one you used to teach me the difference between cameo and intaglio."

"Yes, but why on earth are you thinking of that now?"

Out of the corner of his eye, Gideon could see her bent brows.

"I believe Beatrice Linwood may be like intaglio. Etched into the foundation of this entire case." He turned to Electra, as much as he could with their bodies in such close confines. "She told me the locket belonged to her. What if it does? What if Edward, Jacob, is *her* son, not Helen Becknell's?"

For a moment, Electra stared mutely out her side of the hansom.

"But why would that be reason to murder her own sister?" She tipped a look his way. "That is your hypothesis, isn't it? Despite all you've learned about Lord Becknell."

"I've not discounted Becknell. Did you not say you saw them together?"

"You believe me?" One of her black brows winged so high, it nearly disappeared into the line of her hair.

A lump rose in his throat, and he swallowed against it.

"I do." He couldn't stop himself from adding, "I don't understand such abilities. Indeed, I harbor enormous doubts. I cannot deny that. But I believe *you*, Electra."

"Thank you." She reached a gloved hand out and covered his where it lay on his thigh, but only for the moment.

A moment that threatened to unravel him, but he forced his mind back to the case.

"Why are we going to visit Lady Ashcombe?" she asked when they'd both fallen quiet.

"To discover whether Beatrice Linwood lied about where she was on Sunday evening."

"My dear Miss Poole, how good it is to see you again so soon." Lady Ashcombe sounded as pleased to see Electra as the first time they visited. "And you've brought your detective inspector with you this time too."

Gideon bit his tongue. He would allow the countess to characterize his presence as a mere addition to Electra's. As if they were making nothing more than a friendly social call together, especially if it put the noblewoman at ease.

Only when they were all seated—Electra on the settee next to him this time while Lady Ashcombe faced them in a gilt-edged chair—did Gideon notice something other than the warmth he'd seen before in Lady Ashcombe's eyes.

Today, unlike their first meeting two days ago, she looked hesitant.

"How have you been, Lady Ashcombe?" Electra asked in a low, gentle tone.

He appreciated her taking the lead because his instinct was to plow right into questioning Beatrice Linwood's alibi.

"I'm finally preparing to leave the city for our country

house. My husband is already there, but I wanted to remain for Helen's funeral."

"When will it be?" Electra asked.

"Next week. Have you not been invited, my dear? You may accompany me if you wish. With the press's fascination with the matter, I suspect there may be quite a crush."

"Thank you. I may do that." Electra offered a half-smile.

"Are you fully recovered from your illness?" Gideon asked.

Lady Ashcombe tilted her head. "Pardon?"

"When I first sought to speak with you, I was told that you were ill, and indeed that was why you did not call at Becknell House on Sunday evening as you often do." Gideon scrutinized her hesitation, the way her hand tightened around the fabric of her skirt. "Or was I mistaken, my lady?"

"You're not mistaken at all, Inspector. I was ill that night and did not make my usual trip. I knew that Helen would understand."

"Your staff said a note was sent, but no note was ever found."

Lady Ashcombe looked affronted. "Well, I certainly asked for a note to be sent. I was abed and could not oversee it myself."

"Did you convalesce alone?" Electra asked in that same warm, low, steady tone.

Lady Ashcombe turned her gaze away. "I was not on my own."

"Who attended you?" Gideon asked.

"A...friend called on me. Miss Linwood. I trust you have met her during the course of this investigation."

Gideon and Electra exchanged a look.

"She came to visit on Sunday night?"

"Yes." Lady Ashcombe pulled a handkerchief from the sleeve of her gown and dotted the skin above her lip. "She was here quite a long time. So long, in fact, that I suggested she could simply stay the night."

"That must have been a very great help to you," Electra said, somehow managing not to seem entirely incredulous.

"Oh, indeed." Lady Armstrong winced as if she'd just bitten into a lemon.

"You and Miss Linwood are close friends?" Gideon asked. "I've been told by others that Miss Linwood isn't terribly social and does not have many friends."

"No, that is true," the countess acknowledged succinctly.

"You are one of Lady Becknell's closest friends. Did that closeness extend to her sister?"

Lady Ashcombe tried for a smile that emerged as more of a grimace. "I wouldn't say it was the same degree of closeness. But...Beatrice was kind to call on me that evening."

"How did she know you were ill?" Electra asked softly.

Gideon barely resisted smiling. *Yes, how did she know?*

"Maybe," Electra posited, "she was the one who received the note you sent."

Ah, yes, the bloody non-existent note.

The countess smiled. "You're very clever, Miss Poole. That must have been it."

"Did she say where she'd been before?"

Lady Ashcombe shook her head. "No. She did not."

"And you're certain she slept here? If I were to ask your staff, they would confirm that?" Gideon leaned forward, elbows resting on his knees.

It felt as if he and Electra had been inching toward this moment, and now she was snared. That's precisely the look she gave both of them—a look of being caught in her lies.

"You should tell the truth, my lady," Electra bent forward too, hands together as if beseeching the noblewoman.

"At what cost?" the countess bit out. Her nostrils flared.

Gideon wondered if she was considering throwing them out of her house.

"Beatrice and I are not friends." Her blue eyes turned shrewd. "You've discovered something, I take it."

"I have."

She nodded at him. "Beatrice came to me on Monday evening. I was shocked. I'd only just heard the news of Helen hours before. If anything, I might have called on her to offer condolences." After dotting her forehead with her kerchief, she continued. "She said if I did not tell you the lie I just spoke to you, she would tell my husband of the funds Helen lent me over the years."

When she reached out to smooth the fabric of skirt, her hand shook. "Apparently, Helen had confided it to her at some point, which, I must admit, is quite disappointing."

"Did you have occasion to see the sisters together much?" Gideon asked.

"Very rarely. But when I did, I found them an odd pair. Everyone loved Helen, though she could be passionate and overwrought, she was amusing, lovely. Beatrice was the reverse. Cold, certainly not amusing. She's always unsettled me. More so, of course, after she threatened me."

Electra looked at him, then asked, "Would Helen have taken something her sister served her to eat or drink?"

Lady Ashcombe notched her chin up. "Yes, most definitely. Indeed, I know they had a ritual of taking tea together in the evenings. Helen added liquor to their tea. She said it was a tradition from when they'd sneak their father's brandy as girls."

Gideon would have constables look for the house's brandy decanter, but if Beatrice Linwood was clever, she would have disposed of any proof. *If* she was indeed the one who'd murdered her sister.

"Can you imagine any reason Miss Linwood might wish to harm her sister?"

"I suspect it was something to do with the child."

Gideon and Electra turned to each other again.

"The child that Helen believed was still alive?" Gideon wondered how much Lady Ashcombe knew of the story.

The countess nodded. "When she was a girl of seventeen, she was infatuated with one of the family's footmen and found herself with child. Her family was horrified. They'd already planned her match with Philip. His family lived on a neighboring estate."

"They'd known each other even then?" Electra asked.

"Yes, but with the child, it seemed all her opportunities for a good match were quashed. But the child died, or so she was told by her family. But she'd always wanted to believe that he had survived."

"We've been told she thought she found her child," Gideon told her.

"She did indeed, but Philip and Beatrice were quite insistent that he had died. And Helen was stunned to find that Philip knew the story. Apparently, Beatrice had told him. That seemed a great betrayal to Helen."

"And she felt that they were lying to her," Electra put in.

"She told me she sometimes felt as if she was losing her mind because she knew it was true. She had proof, she said."

"What proof?" Gideon wondered if Jacob Finch was her proof. If she'd believed he was her son.

"She said that she'd met the boy," Lady Ashcombe told them.

"Philip told her that any young man making such a claim was perpetrating some fraud."

"Could he have been living in her house?" Electra's voice

had taken on a breathless quality. As if she felt Lady Ashcombe was on the verge of a significant revelation.

"Oh, no. Philip would never allow that. Philip's greatest complaint was the fact that she could not produce his heir. Helen thought it was some kind of curse. She couldn't fathom why she could never give Philip a child."

"Of course, she wasn't cursed," Electra said pointedly.

They all fell into a solemn quiet for the mention of a child during Lady Becknell's inquest.

"You've been a great help, my lady." Gideon stood. "I would like to arrange for you to give a sworn statement regarding what you told us today."

"Will you be able to stop her?" Lady Ashcombe put to him.

"My goal is to solve this murder, my lady."

"Very well. I shall swear to all I've said."

After he and Electra took their leave, they stood on the pavement in front of the Ashcombe townhouse.

"Where are you off to now?" Electra asked as she pivoted to face him.

"I must return to Vine Street. Miss Linwood's alibi had two aspects, and I have a constable inquiring about the other." She was so close, Gideon had to tip his head to meet her gaze. "Then I plan to visit Miss Linwood."

Electra put on her gloves with intense concentration, then glanced up. "You do recall I was invited to call on her today."

"I do recall," he said.

"So may I accompany you?" Undeniable challenge shone in her eyes.

"You should not, but...if you're with me, I will at least know you're safe."

By the time they reached Vine Street, Braithwaite was out attending to another matter, but he'd left a message for Gideon with the desk sergeant.

He unfolded the note, read the message, and folded it again. "She has no alibi."

Electra's eyes sparked with interest.

"She claimed she was visiting a friend," he told her. "A Mrs. Dunstan in Islington. But the lady is eighty-five and has a shaky recall of facts. She cannot remember for certain whether Miss Linwood came last Sunday, but she insists Miss Linwood always came in the early afternoon. Mrs. Dunstan prefers an early teatime, and Miss Linwood always departs by three. So even if she did make her usual Sunday visit, it is not an alibi for the time of the murder."

"Well, that is interesting."

"Indeed."

"So now to Becknell House?" Electra all but bounced with excitement.

"Yes, but we must devise a plan," he said as they walked together out of the station to make the walk to Hanover Square.

"Should I speak to her alone?" Electra asked the question lightly, as if that might somehow convince him.

"I'd like to disarm her, and I think my presence could do that." Gideon knew Beatrice Linwood wasn't expecting him or that her alibi had collapsed.

"Do you think she'll confess? Do you think you can get her to?"

"That is my aim, of course."

"What if I spoke to her briefly," Electra asked, "while you waited outside the drawing room door? It would give me a chance to...touch her."

"And what is it you see when you touch someone?"

She hesitated and then glanced up at him. "It's not always the same. Sometimes I see a vision. Images. A memory. But I'm never certain whether it's a memory or a thought that person has in their mind of something that happened in the past."

"Is there a difference?"

She smiled but pursed her lips. "I suppose there is not. I'm as confused by it as you likely are, to be honest."

"But you wish to try with Beatrice Linwood?"

"I do. And I have a request."

"Which is?"

"Could I have the locket back?"

He reached into his pocket as he slowed his steps. "I retrieved it from my office earlier."

Raising his hand out, he offered the pendant. Electra opened her palm, and he dropped it into her hand.

"Thank you."

"I have one request too," he said as they picked up their pace again.

"Name it."

"Find a reason to obtain one of her calling cards."

Electra reached out, laying a hand on his arm to slow him. He stopped, and she locked her gaze on his as she slipped a hand into the pocket of her overcoat.

"I already have one. She gave it to me at the inquest."

Gideon took up the card and his heart thudded hard in his chest. It matched the scrap found in Mary Keane's hand. Perhaps Miss Linwood had tried to retrieve it, but Miss Keane's death grip wouldn't cooperate.

"What does it mean?" Electra asked, watching him closely as he examined the card.

"That we almost have her," he said, anticipation making his voice rough. "We must tread carefully at Becknell House."

Gideon suspected they could enlist the aid of Mrs. Evans or Mr. Paxton to allow him to stand just beyond the drawing room threshold without alerting Miss Linwood. They'd simply have to hope Lord Becknell was occupied in a manner that would allow them a few uninterrupted minutes with his sister-in-law.

Though Gideon's real hope was an ambitious one—that Beatrice Linwood would both confess and reveal the extent of Lord Becknell's involvement in his wife death.

Chapter Eighteen

Becknell House still stood apart, shrouded in mourning black with a ribbon on the door and draperies pulled tight.

Seeing it again, Electra felt a shadow of what she had just a few nights ago. Goodness, had it only been days since she'd sat across from Lady Becknell? It felt as if the viscountess and the tragedy of her death had been on her mind for much longer.

Gideon rapped, and Electra noticed a curtain twitching in the window of the townhouse next door. The murderer had not yet been apprehended. It made sense that neighbors would be watchful.

Soon Mrs. Evans answered and her eyes rounded slightly. "Inspector and Miss Poole."

"May we come in, Mrs. Evans?"

Her mouth tightened, but she gave a nod, then stepped back to admit them.

"We're not to allow any visitors, but I suspect you're here on a police matter, Inspector."

"I am indeed." Gideon kept his voice low. "I need to enlist your aid, Mrs. Evans."

The older woman frowned. "What may I do for you, sir?"

"Miss Poole was invited by Miss Linwood. I was not. While she speaks to Miss Linwood, I will be waiting outside the door to speak to her as well."

The housekeeper looked increasingly nervous the longer he spoke.

"I would ask you not to alert Miss Linwood or Lord Becknell of my presence here until I speak to Miss Linwood." He offered the housekeeper a warm smile—one of those rare, charming smiles that Electra had always found unsettlingly potent. "Do you understand?"

Mrs. Evans laid a hand on her middle as if the whole matter tested her nerves. "I understand, Inspector. And Lord Becknell is from home, so he need not know."

Gideon's flinched so slightly that Electra suspected that Mrs. Evans didn't notice, but she did.

"Where is he?"

"At his club, I believe, sir."

"Then we should be swift about this. Would you announce Miss Poole?"

"Of course." Mrs. Evans shifted her gaze to Electra. "You may wait in the drawing room, Miss Poole, while I tell Miss Linwood you're here." Looking back at Gideon, she said, "There's a wee alcove behind the staircase. When she comes down, you could wait there and the step toward the threshold when I close the door."

Gideon smiled again. "Excellent. Thank you."

He seemed to know he was asking a great deal of a servant who knew her loyalty should be to her employer, yet Electra had sensed from the first that the Becknells' staff were all aware of oddities in the household. That they might, in fact, know the cause of that oppressive sense of worry she'd felt the first night she'd walked into the house and that she still felt in the air now.

When Mrs. Evans began climbing the staircase, Gideon turned to Electra.

"Take care when you're with her. The admonition may be obvious, but do not eat or drink anything she offers you. And if you feel unsafe—"

"Gideon," she said, cutting him off as she laid a hand on his sleeve. "I'll bring you in as soon as I'm able. I will be all right."

"You'd better be, Electra."

"Go hide in the alcove."

He arched a brow at her commanding tone, then did as she bid him to.

Above her, she heard Mrs. Evans and Miss Linwood conversing in the upstairs hall and scurried into the drawing room.

As soon as she was alone awaiting Beatrice Linwood, her own nerves began to jangle. She'd never come face to face with a murderer, if the lady was indeed one.

She'd given her gloves to Mrs. Evans when she'd admitted them, and she chafed her hands together, hoping they would be an infallible conduit to whatever secrets Miss Linwood harbored about her sister's death.

"Miss Poole, you did come after all." Beatrice Linwood stepped into the room in her jet-black gown and gestured toward two chairs as Mrs. Evans slid the panel doors shut behind her.

Gideon was just outside those doors, or soon would be. There was no reason to fear.

Electra reached out to shake Miss Linwood's hand. She watched as the lady flicked her gaze down to her hand and then turned to settle into one of the chairs as if she hadn't noticed the gesture at all.

Once she was seated, she arranged her skirts about her, then looked at Electra with dark, unfathomable eyes, much like Jacob Finch's eyes. So unlike her sister's clear blue ones.

Electra sat in a chair nearby.

"You may wonder why I asked you here." Miss Linwood turned toward her as she spoke. "But you were with my sister in her final hours, and I know she must have been distressed to seek you out in the first place."

"She did indeed seem distressed."

Miss Linwood drew in a deep breath and then let out a long sigh, almost theatrically. "Would you tell me what worried my sister so?"

"She believed her child was still alive." Electra knew she was embellishing what Lady Becknell had actually said, but it was clear to her now, after speaking to Lord Ballinger and seeing the locket's inscription, that it was most likely the question which had been on her ladyship's heart that night.

Miss Linwood's body tensed, her shoulders seeming to compact as she drew her arms in. Her skin paled. "Forgive me, Miss Poole, that is a rather shocking assertion."

"Because her child did die?"

Miss Linwood flinched as the pocket doors parted and Mrs. Evans brought in a tea tray. She must have requested it prior to Electra entering the room.

Both of them waited while Mrs. Evans poured out, preparing Miss Linwood's tea and then casting a look Electra's way.

"Just tea, no milk or sugar," she told the housekeeper.

Though she had no fear that Mrs. Evans would have doctored the tea, Electra would follow Gideon's advice and had no intention of drinking any.

Once Mrs. Evans departed, Miss Linwood took a sip of her tea and seemed to have collected herself again.

"I take it," she began, her voice chilly, "that you have heard some vile rumors about my sister. The journalists will print anything."

"We needn't speak of it if the topic upsets you, Miss Linwood."

She flashed that stiff smile again. "Was there anything else my sister conveyed to you?"

"Well, she gave me a locket."

Miss Linwood clenched her jaw so tightly that Electra heard her teeth clack together.

"I believe Inspector Pierce has it in his possession now," she bit out.

"Actually, he returned it to me, Miss Linwood."

The lady snapped her gaze to Electra so quickly, her teacup rattled in its saucer.

"Where is it? It belongs to me." She set her teacup down and reached out her hand. "Would you be so good as to return it?"

Electra slipped a hand into her pocket and collected the chain in her palm. Then she lifted her hand out, fingers cupped, as Gideon had done to her not fifteen minutes ago.

Miss Linwood reached out, palm open.

Electra lifted a few fingers, letting the chain slip through, then made a move as if she'd dropped the rest, but instead, she reached out and clasped Miss Linwood's hand.

An image flashed in her mind. Through Miss Linwood's memory, she watched as Helen Becknell reached out, beseeching.

Miss Linwood yanked her hand back from Electra's, but she kept hold of the gold chain. Electra let it go and Miss Linwood made a sound of angry dismay to find the chain was bare.

"Where is my locket?"

"The one with your son's name etched inside?" Electra did

not know if it was true, but she trusted Gideon's hypothesis that it was, and she wanted to see the lady's reaction.

"Give me my locket now." Beatrice Linwood shot up from her chair.

"I don't have it, Miss Linwood." Electra stood too. "But I did see the inscription inside, and then I spoke to Jacob today."

"Liar. He would not have spoken to you."

"Yet he did." Electra inched back toward the door, a subtle movement.

Miss Linwood stood as if frozen in place. "What did he tell you?"

"That his mother found him after years he was abandoned by her. That he believed she had never cared for him. And he was frightened about what happened on Sunday night."

Beatrice Linwood narrowed her eyes until they were little more than slits. "He knows nothing of what happened, so that is very unlikely, Miss Poole."

"So he doesn't know that you poisoned his aunt?"

"How dare you." When Miss Linwood took a step toward her, Electra stepped farther back toward the door.

She was on the cusp of calling for Gideon when the doors slid open and he stepped into the room.

Beatrice Linwood lost color again, and her jaw slackened, even as her eyes hardened.

"What is the meaning of this?" she rasped.

"I'd like to join the conversation," he said smoothly, "and I'd ask that you answer Miss Poole's question. Does Edward know what you did to his aunt?"

To Electra's shock, Miss Linwood began to laugh. It began as a low chuckle, then became a discordant, higher-pitched cackle.

The sound chilled Electra to the bone. Once, in the throes

of anger at Electra's father's dismissive treatment, she'd let out a sound very like it.

"You have no idea what you're talking about," she said when she finally got a hold of herself.

"Then tell us, Miss Linwood." Gideon stepped forward until he was almost elbow to elbow with Electra. "Was Edward your son or your sister's?"

"Edward is mine!" Her voice rose to a fierce pitch. "Her child died. She never wished to believe it, but it was true." She lifted her shoulder. "She was jealous. Our child lived."

Gideon turned. Electra looked up at him. She could almost hear the cogs of his brain turning.

"Lord Becknell," he said quietly. "Is he...Edward's father?"

"Of course he is." She spoke almost proudly now. "I knew Philip was trapped in a longstanding marriage contract to Helen that our parents negotiated years before. He would have to marry her, so he persuaded me to let the child go, but I couldn't. Once I found Edward again, I wanted him near."

"Why did she think he was her son?" Electra asked, keeping her tone low, trying to think of a way to touch Beatrice Linwood again.

"We were with child at nearly the same time. Hers was hidden by keeping her at home. I hid mine by visiting family abroad." For a moment, she looked almost wistful.

"Why kill her?" Gideon asked.

Electra winced. She knew the question had to be asked, but she feared Miss Linwood would balk, gather her composure, and order them from Becknell House.

But she did not.

Her eyes lit with fury. Electra could feel it coming off of her in waves, a darker crimson than the anger surrounding Lord Becknell.

"She would have ruined him. His career. His reputation. Our family."

"Becknell?"

"She wanted to leave Philip. Thought that feckless painter would claim her child openly. The silly woman thought herself in love with him—a man who I suspect has never committed to anything in his life except his own pleasure."

"He is despicable," Gideon agreed.

Electra shot him a look. They weren't here to talk about Lucan Fox.

"So your sister died to protect Philip Becknell."

"Have you ever been in love, Inspector Pierce?"

Gideon stood motionless. Silent. Then he dragged in a sharp breath and said, "Yes, I have."

"Then you must understand," Miss Linwood said, as if certain of his agreement. "I would do anything to protect him. Both of them."

Gideon shifted. Electra looked down to see his fist clenched.

"Is that why Mary Keane died?"

Miss Linwood blinked slowly. "Goodness, you have been busy, Inspector."

"And Jenny Wilson?" Electra felt compelled to ask.

Before Miss Linwood could say more, footsteps sounded as someone entered the room.

"What the hell is this all about?"

Electra and Gideon swung around to see Lord Philip Becknell standing just beyond the threshold, his jaw clenched, shoulders squared, and eyes almost wild with fear and suspicion.

"They know, Philip," Miss Linwood said behind them.

Electra turned back to her. She couldn't bear to have the woman behind her if she could not keep an eye on her.

"Know what exactly, Beatrice?"

Miss Linwood settled hard into the chair she'd occupied a moment ago. "The truth. At least enough of it." She ran a hand along her neck, gripping her nape. "It's too much, even for me. Too many lies. Too many regrets."

"You wrote the letter..." Gideon murmured almost under his breath.

"I did, Inspector. We both used the typewriter at various times. Helen found the unfinished letter. She became angry, demanding. I held her while she wailed for her lost child. Then we took tea together."

"Say no more, Beatrice," Philip Becknell demanded, then approached the spot where she sat, resting a hand on her shoulder.

In any other situation, it might have seemed a gesture of comfort. To Electra, considering what she knew of Lord Becknell, it felt like a show of control. But though Becknell towered over Beatrice Linwood, Electra couldn't help but wonder at the balance of power between them. Who was the instigator? Were they equally as guilty of the crime?

"My sister-in-law is grieving the loss of her beloved sister," Lord Becknell intoned, his voice deep and imperious. "*We* are both suffering the loss of my beloved wife. How dare you come here and take advantage of Miss Linwood when she is so distraught?"

"What did you put in her tea?" Electra asked, knowing it might get them kicked out of Becknell House. Yet she saw something in Beatrice Linwood's expression—a resignation. The fury Electra felt from her earlier had dimmed.

"Inspector, please take Miss Poole and leave my house at once." Becknell's tone dropped to a near growl. "If you wish to speak to me, you may do so tomorrow. I can make arrangements for us to meet at my solicitor's office."

Gideon made no reply. Nor did he move an inch from

where he stood beside Electra. She sensed his resolve and felt bolstered by it.

"Miss Linwood?" Electra whispered.

"Enough!" Lord Becknell lifted his hand from his sister-in-law's shoulder and took up a spot in front of her, effectively blocking her from their view. "Unless you mean to take some action, Inspector, take yourself and this woman from my house."

"Honey." The word came in a whispery voice. "Helen preferred her drinks sweet to hide the bitterness of alcohol."

Becknell swung back to Miss Linwood so quickly, Electra thought he might strike her.

"Shut your mouth, woman. Do you want to hang?"

With a rustle of fabric, Beatrice Linwood got to her feet. She came into view, just past Becknell's shoulder. Her eyes fixed on him, almost adoringly, but for the tight, narrow set of her mouth. She lifted a hand and laid it gently against his cheek.

"Not without you beside me, my darling."

Becknell flinched away from her touch and marched toward the fireplace, tugging hard at the bell pull hanging beside it.

A moment later, the Becknells' butler, Mr. Paxton, entered the drawing room.

Lord Becknell pointed to Miss Linwood. "Take her to her room and call for Dr. Whitaker. She's taken leave of her senses."

When Mr. Paxton made no move to approach Miss Linwood, Lord Becknell strode over and gripped her upper arm, tugging her toward the drawing room threshold so swiftly, she stumbled and he wrapped an arm around her to keep her upright.

"No!" She shouted the word, wrenching back against his hold, though he was much stronger and she could get no purchase on the carpet as he pulled at her.

"Stop, Becknell." Gideon stomped toward the man, and Becknell swung out, his fist flying toward Gideon's face.

Gideon ducked the blow, then grabbed the viscount's arm, masterfully twisting it behind his back.

Becknell roared, whether from pain or frustration, Electra couldn't be sure, but Gideon did not release his hold.

"Let. Her. Go." Gideon spoke each word emphatically, pausing between each, his voice as low and lethal as she'd ever heard it. "Now." He punctuated his command by shifting Becknell's bent arm up his back an inch more.

The viscount let out a grunt of pain and loosened his hold, but he did not let Miss Linwood go.

Finally, Miss Linwood reached up to peel his fingers off her arm, scratching at his flesh and drawing blood.

When she broke free, she stumbled a few steps, then gripped a chair and pressed her hand to her chest as if to catch her breath.

Gideon had turned Becknell so that he faced Miss Linwood once more.

"It's over, Philip," she said as she straightened and turned a glare his way. "You have no sense of loyalty and never have. So why must I? Our son fears me now. He meets in secret with this woman"—Miss Linwood gestured dismissively toward Electra—"but will no longer speak to me."

Electra felt it again—that red, seething rage that shimmered around Becknell. In that moment, his mask slipped. His face twisted into a grimace, not unlike the look on Helen Becknell's face in Miss Linwood's memory as she fell down the stairs.

Then it was as if some force swept the viscount's expression clear. The muscles in his face softened. His eyes shone, but blankly. Not a window into his soul, but a wall, hiding the maelstrom inside him.

"She's mad," Becknell stated in a calm, steady voice. "I've feared it for a long while now. Her physician, Dr. Magnus Whitaker will attest to the same. He's seen her many times for a

Christy Carlyle

nervous condition and febrile delusions. Clearly, it has worsened, and I fear she must go where help can be had for her."

Miss Linwood did not look shocked by his words. In fact, a small, weary sigh escaped her, then she turned to Gideon.

"As you see, Inspector, his lordship has no notion of loyalty." She set her shoulders back and notched up her chin. "What must I do? Do you mean to take me into custody now? I am prepared to give you a full accounting."

Rather than answer, Gideon shot a look at Mr. Paxton, who still stood just over the room's threshold, his brow knitted. "Send for a constable, Mr. Paxton, and tell them to bring the police wagon."

At those words, Becknell twisted, struggling to pull Gideon off balance and get free of his hold. But the two men were matched for height, and though Becknell was bulkier, Gideon seemed to match him for strength too. The viscount could not break his hold.

"This is monstrous," Becknell snarled.

"Yes," Gideon said icily. "It is."

260

Chapter Nineteen

"May I tell you here, Inspector?" Beatrice Linwood's voice had softened once Philip Becknell was led from the room. She looked weary, yet still held herself ramrod straight.

Gideon could refuse her request. Perhaps she wished to avoid the embarrassment of being questioned at the station, but he didn't owe her that.

Still, he wanted her full confession now, and if giving it in her home would make her speak more freely, he'd allow it.

He gestured toward one of the constables who'd responded to Mr. Paxton's summons.

"We're going to take her statement here. Can you collect a pen, ink, and paper to record her confession?"

"Yes, sir." The young man immediately approached Mrs. Evans, who'd lingered in the hallway after one of the constables led Lord Becknell to his study, where he was to remain under guard until Gideon could question him.

"With Miss Poole present," Miss Linwood added once Constable Moore returned with writing supplies.

Gideon looked over at Electra, who wore an unreadable

expression. Though he knew she would very much wish to sit in to hear Miss Linwood explain what had motivated her to murder her own sister.

"Very well," he said, then gestured for Moore to close the sitting room doors and take up a spot at the writing desk in the corner of the room.

Miss Linwood sat in the same chair she'd previously occupied, arranging her skirts around her as if they were all simply sitting down for tea together.

Gideon sat on the settee across from her, and Electra sat beside him.

"Can you explain the matter of the locket?" Gideon asked.

Out of the corner of his eye, he saw Electra shoot a look his way. Of course, he wanted to get to the question of Lady Becknell's murder, but he suspected the child, the locket, and the inscription inside were all connected to that act.

"The locket is mine. The hair is my son's. Our son's. Philip's and mine." Miss Linwood notched up her chin the slightest bit as if proud of the proclamation.

"Was it not Helen's locket?" Electra asked. "She seemed to believe it was."

Miss Linwood closed her eyes and let out a weary sigh. "It was not. I'd worn it for many years, and then I'd put it away, trying to forget him. Telling myself he would have a good life without me. But Helen...overheard Philip and I discussing Edward a few weeks ago."

"Who is Jacob Finch?" Electra asked, then gave Gideon a look, as if to apologize for another question.

"Yes. The Finch family had taken him in."

"What did Lady Becknell overhear?" Gideon asked.

"It was after I'd brought Edward back. After he'd been working as Philip's valet. I said I was happy to have him with us. Philip reminded me that it must be kept secret, and that if

Helen or anyone began to suspect that he was more than simply Philip's valet, then he would have to go."

Miss Linwood shrugged, furrowing her brow. "From that, she spun some fantasy in her mind that I'd secreted her child away and that he was still alive. That Jacob was the son she'd lost. She even went rifling through the attic, seeking proof that her child had survived. She found my locket and that seemed to convince her that he had."

"And that her son had been named Edward?" Gideon still couldn't quite understand.

"Her son never had a name. He lived but hours. But in Helen's fevered imaginings, I'd taken her child, named him Edward, and then brought him into the house as Philip's valet."

"Did she confront Jacob?" Gideon suspected she had if she'd felt that strongly about the matter.

"If she did, he never admitted it to me. But she did speak of it to Philip and to me, and we both insisted she was wrong."

"You never told her the truth?" Electra asked.

"Of course not." She stared at each of them as if the very idea of telling the truth was ludicrous. "I love Philip and have protected him for decades. That's what I've always done."

"Is that why you killed Jenny Wilson?" Gideon asked.

Miss Linwood turned her head, as if suddenly fascinated with the light filtering in through the sash window curtains. "The girl was not discreet. She demanded money for her silence." Finally, she turned back to them. "Once they demand money, it never stops. Philip said something needed to be done about her."

"So Lord Becknell knew you killed the girl?" Gideon believed the viscount was complicit, but he still wasn't certain of the extent of the man's participation.

"He knew I'd solved the problem." A tight smile stretched

her mouth. "Philip never cared for details. He always left those to me."

"And Mary Keane?"

Beatrice Linwood drew in a sharp breath and pursed her lips. "She was another matter entirely."

"How so?" Gideon prompted.

"The fool man decided he was genuinely besotted with her. He was not discreet with Miss Keane." She leaned forward a bit in her chair. "Do you know, that was the first time Helen began seeking attention elsewhere because Philip made such a fool of himself."

"Did he know what you'd done to her?" Electra asked quietly.

"He knew she needed to go. He'd even tried breaking off their liaison, and yes, we discussed how to resolve the matter." Miss Linwood's expression changed when she looked Electra's way, as if she expected understanding from her. Her eyes turned beseeching. "You must understand, Miss Poole, I only wished to protect him. His reputation. Our family."

"Were there others?" Gideon asked.

"Other trollops who Philip wasted his time with? Oh, an entire brigade of them, Inspector Pierce. But no others who I had to deal with in such a manner."

"Except for your sister," Electra said, each word sharp.

"Why did you kill her?" Gideon asked.

Beatrice Linwood sat silent, staring down at her lap, then lifted her head and turned her gaze toward Gideon.

"She had become..." She stopped herself, looked down again, and finally said, "Uncontrollable."

Gideon looked straight into Miss Linwood's eyes and said nothing. He sensed she wanted to explain. Electra seemed to be holding her breath.

"She was enchanted with that wastrel painter. The poor woman had convinced herself he'd run away with her. That they'd create some idyllic life with their bastard child. With Lord Ballinger, at least she'd been circumspect. Sensible. Though heaven knows he was not. The man is pathetic. But with Mr. Fox, she behaved like a love-struck fool." Miss Linwood glanced at Electra and then looked back at Gideon. "And she wouldn't let the matter of her lost child rest. I feared she'd uncover the truth about Jacob and his parentage, and she was angry enough at Philip to reveal it. And if she'd run away, given birth to some blond by-blow, do you know what that would have done to Philip's reputation? To our family?"

She was breathless by the time she'd finished, having rushed out the last of her confession.

Neither of them replied to her rhetorical question. But Gideon considered how her evil impulse to take women's lives at Philip Becknell's suggestion, and with his knowledge, in some twisted desire to "protect" him would hopefully land the man in prison and would certainly stain the Becknell and Linwood names forever.

AN HOUR LATER, Beatrice Linwood and Lord Philip Becknell were both led to Vine Street holding cells after Miss Linwood's confession implicated Lord Becknell at almost every point.

Becknell had been less forthcoming during questioning in one of the narrow interrogation rooms at the station. The viscount denied any knowledge of Miss Linwood's crimes, even disclaiming any knowledge of what she'd done to his wife, despite his determination to silence her hours ago, as if he knew with absolute certainty what she might confess.

The viscount insisted that his answers would not alter upon further questioning and continually insisted on speaking with his solicitor. Gideon feared that Chief Douglas might allow the viscount to be released upon the promise to appear to face legal proceedings, but he intended to argue for holding Becknell until he, and Miss Linwood, could appear before a magistrate in a day or two.

If Becknell was released, Gideon was convinced the man would abscond. He certainly had the means to do so. The viscount could not be allowed to escape the consequences of contributing to three women's deaths. If a jury believed Miss Linwood, Becknell would be found guilty of inciting murder.

Becknell's power over her had been such that he could merely whisper of the need to remove an obstacle in his path, and she would act. He, clever snake that he was, apparently never played a direct part in the deed. Though he seemed to have a history of brutalizing women, he apparently stopped short at administering poison.

That was a task he left to his sister-in-law and lover. Though Gideon disdained the notion of applying the word *love* to any of what passed between the two, Beatrice Linwood seemed to view protecting the man she loved as her motive. Gideon would add jealousy, frustration, and rage. Ironically, the rage was mostly toward Philip Becknell for never giving her what she truly wanted from him—acknowledgment of their relationship, perhaps marriage in place of her sister—yet, until earlier this evening, it seemed she'd been exercising that rage on others, rather than the man who deserved it most.

As he headed back to his office, a clerk approached.

"Message for you, sir."

"Thank you, Eames." Gideon lifted the piece of paper and read, blinking because his eyes felt gritty.

He barely finished reading before he was striding toward the station's front doors. Out on the street, he stepped off the curb to stop a hansom that nearly careened into him.

Once inside, he struggled to unclench his teeth and still the rioting beat of his heart.

"An hour," he mumbled to himself. "I part from her for one hour..."

Ten minutes later, he passed payment up to the cabbie and all but leapt from the vehicle as it stopped outside of Whitechapel Hospital.

Rushing inside, he found himself struck by a wall of heat and the scent of dozens of people waiting to be seen for various ailments.

A young nurse caught his eye, and he beelined for her.

"Electra Poole," he said. "I need to see her."

The nurse looked as taken aback as if he'd just demanded to see the queen.

Then, from the corner of his eye, he saw her. Electra dashed toward him, her hair down and free of its pins, her eyes brimming with worry.

"Gideon—"

He closed the distance and pulled her into his arms. At first, she stiffened. Then she slipped her arms beneath his coat and wrapped them around his middle.

When he pulled back to get a better look at her, she immediately released him. Reluctantly, he dropped his arms to his sides too.

"I'm perfectly well," she told him. "I'm sorry if the note implied otherwise."

"If you're perfectly well, why are we here?"

"It's Grace," she said. "Come with me."

He followed her down a long corridor lined with benches

occupied by men, women, and children, then into an infirmary ward with a dozen beds.

Back in the corner, she pushed a white curtain aside, and he tensed at the sight of Grace Dobbs. The side of her face was covered in bright red abrasions, her lip was swollen, and a purple bruise ringed one eye. One arm was wound in bandages, and there was a swath of gauze wrapped around her head too.

"Inspector Pierce," the young maid said, then lifted her uninjured arm to sweep a hand across her disheveled hair that stuck out at the dressing's edge.

"She took a fall," Electra explained to him. "But it was not accidental."

She reached out and laid a hand gently on Grace's unbound arm. "Tell the inspector what you told me."

"It was Jacob, sir. I sought him out at a place he told me he went sometimes. A club here in Whitechapel. He seemed angry I'd found him, but he told me I could stay with him until I got a new post. As we were walking to his place, he asked me about that night when her ladyship was killed. He asked if I knew if anyone else was at the house that night. Then he suddenly pushed me. I swear he did."

"Right into the path of a passing carriage," Electra added with a look Gideon's way.

"Why would he do such a thing?"

"Tell him the rest," Electra urged.

"I think it was the question he asked. If I knew who was at home that night. Well, I admitted I did and that from the start, I thought it was Miss Linwood who'd done it. She *was* home that night. I knew it, but I never told anyone." Grace lifted tearful eyes to him.

"She was upstairs, wasn't she?" Electra inhaled sharply. "I saw two lit windows that night. One upstairs and one downstairs."

Grace dipped her head and gripped the edge of the blanket. "Yes, miss."

"And when you greeted me. You said, 'She's upstairs.' I thought you meant her ladyship."

"Her ladyship did tell me Miss Linwood had gone out, but I thought sure I heard her moving about upstairs." She lifted a fearful gaze to Gideon. "Will I go to jail? I was afraid, sir. Kept my distance from her, but after her ladyship was killed, I realized it must have been Lord Becknell or her who had done it."

"Did you witness the crime, Grace?"

The girl shook her head, then winced. "No, sir, I swear it. I left soon after Miss Poole, just as I told you."

"You won't go to jail," Electra whispered to her.

"Miss Poole is correct, but your statement that Miss Linwood was at home that night will be helpful."

"I'll do it, sir. I promise."

"Worry about getting better for now, Miss Dobbs. I'll send a constable to take your statement and do my very best to find Mr. Finch."

Electra joined him in the corridor after they left Grace's bedside. "Jacob was likely trying to protect his mother."

"Can a person inherit a twisted sense of how to protect someone they love?" Gideon bent his head and gripped the back of his neck. "We'll have to find him, charge him, and protect Miss Dobbs until he's found."

"This case seems never-ending," she said.

"It was tangled, but at least it's unraveling now."

"And quickly. You solved it in less than a week." She sounded impressed.

Gideon's chest swelled more than he should have allowed it to.

She lifted her blue-green gaze to his. "Of course, you did have a tiny bit of help."

He tried with all his might not to smile. God forbid he encourage her meddling.

But he couldn't hold it back. Whatever sleep this case had stolen from him, it had given him something back too—Electra Poole in his life once again.

Epilogue

Two weeks later

Electra cut into the apple pie Mrs. Perkins had prepared for the dinner Gideon invited her to at his house. The scents of cinnamon and the perfectly baked buttery crust made her mouth water.

She sensed Mrs. Perkins's gaze on her and looked up.

"I understand you went to Ireland, my dear, to visit your mother's kin." Mrs. Perkins had waited until Electra had offered to help her plate up the meal in Gideon's diminutive kitchen before speaking to her of anything to do with the past.

"I did indeed. I met both of my aunts and half a dozen cousins."

Mrs. Perkins smiled. "That must have been lovely."

"It was heartening, especially since my aunt is like Mother was."

Mrs. Perkin's slowed her movements as she dished up potatoes covered in butter and parsley. "I suspected that might the case." She glanced over at Electra. "That you'd gone to learn more about your mother's gift."

"Did you really think of it as a gift?" Electra felt the bitterness and anger welling up inside her. "My father certainly didn't."

"No, he didn't," she admitted quietly. "I told him once, you know, that I had an aunt who could predict things. When a caller was going to come. That my sister would be injured while riding her horse."

"And what did he say?"

"He looked at me with pity because he believed illness of the mind was the only explanation for such abilities."

Electra plated up the final portion of pie, then turned to Mrs. Perkins. "My father was mistaken."

"Yes, I believe he was," she said simply, then dusted off her hands and reached back to remove her apron. "And Inspector Pierce tells me that you have her gift too. Or something like it."

Electra swallowed and looked toward the kitchen doorway. Gideon was setting the table for the three of them to dine together. In the last couple of weeks, he'd kept her apprised of the progress in the Becknell case, including the apprehension of Jacob Finch, but there'd been no mention of her abilities, as if he wished to forget how she'd become entangled in the case in the first place.

"I fear Gideon will never understand, or even believe me."

"He may yet surprise you. He is a different man than your father was."

But Electra knew what an influence one man had on the other. "I think he has the same sense of logic, the same need for events to be explicable and rational."

Mrs. Perkins nodded. "Though he also feels a great deal for you and always has."

Electra couldn't deny that either. She wasn't exactly sure how to define what was between them, but she knew he cared for her. And that he trusted her.

When she'd returned from her trip to Ireland, she'd visited

the solicitor who handled the sale of her father's home and the settling of his debts. The man had presented her with a small stack of letters Gideon had sent to the old house.

In them, he'd expressed concern for her, a wish to see her, though he'd also acknowledged that she may need time away from any reminders of her father, including him. He understood her that well, at least. But he didn't know that after the death of her father, she'd finally felt free to acknowledge the powers she'd denied for so long.

Gideon knew she'd been odd—that she was oversensitive at times, secretive, and he'd only teased her a little about her propensity to wear gloves indoors at times.

But she'd never confessed more, and she'd never forget the look on his face that night he'd found her at Cordelia's. The disgust, the horror, at finding her leading a sitting.

Mrs. Perkins patted Electra's arm in a comforting gesture, then she lifted the platter that contained the carved roast and the large bowl full of potatoes and headed out to the dining table.

Electra scooped up the bowl of peas and the plate crowded with freshly baked rolls and followed her out. They left the plates of sliced pie to bring out later for their dessert.

Gideon grinned at the sight of them as he stood behind one of the three chairs circled around the table. Electra detected a bit of nervousness in the way he shifted his feet and clutched the chair's back with a fierce grip.

From the moment she'd arrived, he'd shot her looks as if he thought she might change her mind about the dinner and sneak out the back when no one was watching.

In truth, being gathered with the two of them brought back memories of her father's home and had put a little knot in her stomach when she'd first arrived. But her father was gone now, and Gideon and Mrs. Perkins were here, and she could admit to herself that she'd missed both of them.

"Shall we have a toast?" Gideon asked after they'd all taken a seat and he circled his fingers around the stem of his wine glass.

Mrs. Perkins nodded and smiled. "I think a toast is in order."

Electra reached for her goblet of water.

"To being together again," he said, smiling at Mrs. Perkins and then turning his gaze on Electra as he raised his glass in the air. "And to Mrs. Perkins for preparing this feast for us."

"To being together," Electra said, "and to Mrs. Perkins."

"To being together again." The housekeeper's cheeks pinked a bit as she raised her wine glass and then took a sip.

As they began tucking into the meal, Mrs. Perkins eyed both of them.

"Seems Electra was quite useful in your investigation," she said offhandedly to Gideon, focusing on cutting her slice of beef into smaller pieces. "Shall the two of you work together again in the future?"

"Perhaps," Electra said. The response had come out almost unbidden.

Despite how angry as she was at her father, and how much pain he'd caused with his rigid insistence on institutionalizing her mother, perhaps she had inherited something from him. The drive to uncover the truth in regard to Lady Becknell's murder had been personal because of her vision of the lady's death, but it had also felt instinctual. She'd quite relished the process of helping Gideon solve the case.

Now, as she looked at him with one brow arched in challenge, he surprised her.

Rather than entirely rejecting the prospect Mrs. Perkins had raised, there was a glint of interest in his eyes.

"Perhaps," he said, his lips titling in the whisper of a smile. Then ducked his head and took a sip of his wine.

Also by Christy Carlyle

Electra Poole Mysteries

A Grave Gift

A Deadly Invitation

About the Author

Fueled by Pacific Northwest coffee and inspired by multiple viewings of every British costume drama she can get her hands on, USA Today bestselling author Christy Carlyle writes sensual historical romance set in the Victorian era. She loves heroes who struggle against all odds and heroines who are ahead of their time. A former teacher with a degree in history, she finds there's nothing better than being able to combine her love of the past with a die-hard belief in happy endings.

Contact Christy at christy@christycarlyle.com or find out more at www.christycarlyle.com

www.ingramcontent.com/pod-product-compliance
Lightning Source LLC
Chambersburg PA
CBHW020407110726
47899CB00006B/1879